NORAH BENNETT

EVERNIGHT PUBLISHING ®

www.evernightpublishing.com

Copyright© 2017

Norah Bennett

Editor: Audrey Bobak

Cover Artist: Jay Aheer

ISBN: 978-1-77339-322-3

ALL RIGHTS RESERVED

NORAH BENNETT

DEDICATION

For Samy, the man of my dreams. We've spent thirty glorious years together, my darling. I can hardly believe it. It hasn't always been an easy journey, but we've been blessed to have one another. You, my sweetheart, have been and will always be, Everything I've Dreamed Of.

For Laura and Samantha, my beautiful girls who give me such joy every day of my life. I pray that you get everything you dream of. You deserve all the good life has to offer, my precious girls.

ACKNOWLEDGEMENTS

While many writers, write in solitude, I am fortunate to have two people in my life that help me keep the words and ideas flowing.

This book would not have been possible without the world's best plotting partner, editor, beta reader, and overall cheerleader— Laura B. Thank-you for putting up with my early morning calls, my late night calls, my ridiculously short, self-imposed deadlines, and the list goes on and on. I cannot tell you how much I enjoy sharing my stories with you. In fact, you are so good at your many roles that you are now hired for life!

Many, many thanks to Angela Bendyk, my fabulously talented personal assistant. I thank the heavens for you daily. Because of your many talents, I am free to write and write while you take care of all other aspects of my writing life. Thanks for putting up with my frantic texts, emails, calls, and smoke signals. You rock!

EVERYTHING I'VE DREAMED OF

Love in Lakes Crossing, 2

Norah Bennett

Copyright © 2017

Chapter One

Kate Willowbrook attempted to control her quivering body and racing heart as she balanced her small frame on top of the toilet seat. She curled her body into a tight ball as tears slid down her face. Kate prayed he wouldn't hear her, prayed he wouldn't see her, prayed she could wake up from this hellish nightmare. But God wasn't listening.

"Take it, bitch. You've been asking for this all year. Now you're gonna get it. Now you're gonna do what I tell you!"

The woman whimpered.

"P-please, please, st-stop," she begged.

Her pleading and crying seemed to fuel the man's rage. He slammed his fist into her with such force Kate heard the air whoosh out of the woman. Her body crashed to the floor with a sickening thud.

Kate squeezed her eyes shut and slapped a palm over her mouth, swallowing the screams that threatened to rise to the surface. She wished she could block out the sounds that followed—clothes tearing, the woman's pitiful moans, and the litany of curses coming from the man. When she heard the woman's piercing shriek, Kate's eyes flew open. Through the slit of the bathroom *stall door, Kate's eyes connected with agonized, sky-blue eyes—eyes she recognized.*

Kate watched the shock and recognition flood the woman's features followed by the minuscule shake of her head. Kate heard the man's heavy breathing and the revolting grunts he made with his every thrust. She dropped her eyes as her stomach heaved. She was going to be sick. She folded even deeper into herself—knees up and tucked into her chest, head down, eyes shut, hands covering her ears. She held still, never making a sound, never moving an inch—that is, until the gun went off.

Bang! Bang!

Kate jumped, and her hand holding the Styrofoam cup filled with hot Dunkin Donuts coffee jolted, spraying the steaming contents all over Kate's shirt, jeans, and the cream-colored interior of her Volkswagen Bug. Kate gasped as the hot liquid came in contact with her skin. Two more quick bangs filled her ears. Ignoring her burning skin, Kate's head popped up and her gaze darted about, assessing her surroundings as her heart leaped out of her chest and galloped away. Her chest heaved as her breathing became choppy.

Gunshots?

Kate jumped again. This time, it was a car horn. She peeked in her rearview mirror and noticed the annoyed driver behind her giving her the finger. She took a deep breath. With her whole body trembling, she slowly maneuvered her car to the side of the road and turned it off. Her gaze landed on an old car in a nearby strip mall with white smoke coming out of its tailpipe. It was backfiring.

Kate dropped her head to the steering wheel. What the hell just happened? How had she drifted off in the middle of traffic? The fucking nightmares had returned with a vengeance and kept her up last night, but she'd never had a daymare before. Is that what people called nightmares that came in the middle of the day? These certainly weren't daydreams.

Kate had gone almost three years without a nightmare, her longest stretch yet. She thought she was in the clear, through with the past for good. The past, however, was never far away. No matter how far she ran, she was easy prey in her dreams. If she let the past creep into the present, it would take her down as easily as a mountain lion took down a rabbit. No way was she letting that happen. She'd fought too hard for the life she created in Lakes Crossing, and she wasn't giving it up. Relinquishing control to cowardice, fear, and self-recrimination once again was not an option.

Wiping her face with the back of her hand, Kate closed her eyes and took slow, even breaths, recalling some of the imagery and meditation techniques she'd learned in yoga class. She visualized herself staring out into the beautiful Atlantic Ocean on a warm, sunny day. She felt the rays of the sun warm her skin and the soft, silky sand slide between her toes. The sounds of crashing waves and seagulls soaring and calling to one another started as a whisper and grew louder and clearer, filling the car with their soothing duet. Kate concentrated on her breathing—slow and steady—as she guided her galloping heart to a canter, then a trot, and finally to a walk.

It worked.

After a few minutes, the deafening sound of the gunshot and the memory of terrified sky-blue eyes that pleaded with her to stay quiet and stay in place, retreated to the recesses of her mind. It was over. She opened her eyes and scanned the vicinity. She was safe. She was in control. She was in the small town of Lakes Crossing, New Jersey, living a life she'd always dreamed of having, a life filled with peace and purpose.

Feeling more centered and in control, Kate started the ignition, pulled out from the shoulder, and drove home. It was time to put the past where it belonged and load up on caffeine and sugar. Kate grabbed a Boston Cream from the soggy Dunkin Donuts bag in her lap and took a huge bite, washing it down with the remaining coffee. Although the bookstore was closed for inventory, it was going to be a busy day. If she was lucky, she'd exhaust herself and fall into a dreamless sleep tonight.

Seven hours later, Kate completed the arduous task of taking stock of everything in the place and stopped for lunch before tackling the storeroom. Boxes of books and other items she sold in the bookstore were stacked high in the storeroom, waiting for her attention. In between phone calls from vendors and a constant flow of interruptions from deliverymen, Kate unpacked the week's deliveries and rearranged the display cases and bookshelves.

The day flew by, and by 6 PM, Kate was beyond wasted. She eyed the two remaining boxes, arched her back, rolled her shoulders, first one way and then the other, and sighed in utter exhaustion and pure bliss. Surveying her surroundings, she smiled. This—this was what she dreamed of since she could remember…Dreamscape! It was her baby now. Every table, chair, bookshelf, book, and bookmark was hers. Although it had cost her almost every penny to her name, Kate loved every square inch of it.

Kate ignored her body's protestations and reached for the box-cutter. Two more boxes, and then she'd go home and treat herself to a nice, hot bath accompanied by lavender-scented candles, Josh Groban, the world's largest glass of cheap Merlot, and perhaps one or two delectable pieces of dark chocolate. A deep, dreamless sleep would surely follow.

"Hell-low? Hell-low?" Shakespeare's high-pitched, nasally voice echoed through the silent bookstore.

"Hello?" A deep male voice answered.

Kate nearly jumped out of her skin. The hand holding the box-cutter jerked and the blade sliced into her left index finger.

"Ow! Shit!" Kate said and dropped the box-cutter. She winced and examined her injured finger as blood oozed from the wound and dripped onto the wood floor.

"Ow! Damn it, bird. Why the hell did you do that?" The deep, masculine voice now laced with incredulity and irritation said.

"Ow, ow," the cockatoo mimicked.

Kate grabbed a couple of napkins from a nearby table, wrapped her bleeding finger, and ran to the front of the bookstore. Had she forgotten to lock the front door after the last delivery? How could she be so stupid? She knew better. From the sound of it, Shakespeare lost control of his beak again and either nabbed himself a new customer or a new deliveryman. The seasoned ones knew better than to offer Shakes their finger as an afternoon snack.

"Sir, please don't touch the bird. I'm sorry he bit you, but…" Kate started her well-rehearsed speech as she sprinted into the sunroom at the front of the bookstore, preparing to deal with Shakes' newest victim and her man-eating bird. She stopped short, her mind blanking as she stared, open-mouthed, at the giant of a man towering in front of the bird's cage, shaking his head as he examined his injured finger.

Where in the hell did this mammoth of a man come from? He was ridiculously tall and powerfully built. Where did he find clothes to fit those broad shoulders and long legs? He resembled one of the firemen featured in the FDNY Fireman of the Month Calendar Kate kept above her desk in her bedroom. June or July? No, he resembled this month's delicious temptation minus the fireman gear. She'd been staring longingly at Mr. August for the last four weeks and tomorrow she would have to give him up for Mr. September, another piece of eye-candy.

Mr. August towered over Shakes' cage in a beautifully tailored charcoal suit, most likely preparing to snap her bird's neck with his big hands.

"Excuse me," the man said, holding up his injured finger. "Do you think I could get a Band-Aid? Jaws here did a number on my finger."

Hearing his amused, sexy baritone, Kate snapped out of her daydream, or at least she tried to. Her green eyes met his amused, warm brown ones as a lazy grin spread across his features.

Kate's breath caught.

Lord, that smile. Did he know that smile of his was a powerful secret weapon? Mr. August couldn't be described as classically handsome. He was ruggedly appealing with wavy blond hair, a slightly crooked nose, and a square jaw, which sported a delicious five o'clock shadow. But his smile, once unleashed, hypnotized and paralyzed, scrambling her every thought and rendering her speechless.

Kate couldn't stop gawking. It had been a long time since she reacted to any man in this manner. In fact, she couldn't recall feeling this intense attraction to anyone, not even Jeff. Mr. August was mouth-wateringly delicious, and she wanted a taste of that forbidden fruit. She licked her lower lip and caught it between her teeth, a nervous habit she couldn't get rid of. His eyes followed the movement of her tongue over her lips. His pupils dilated and darkened, resembling the chocolate molten lava cake she indulged in only yesterday.

Kate was surprised to see he was affected by her presence. She wasn't unattractive, but he was way out of her league in every way possible. She was an absolute mess in frayed jean shorts and an old Rolling Stones t-shirt. Her thick crimson hair fell to her shoulders and down her back in wild, disorganized waves she didn't bother to tame, and her curveless, five foot four frame was hardly noteworthy. But it was apparent by his smoldering gaze and sensual smile, this man saw something he liked. Maybe he needed glasses, or maybe he needed to get laid, and he thought she was an easy mark. One way or another, she was mortified at being caught devouring him. Heat crept up her neck and flooded her face. She was sure her face now matched the color of her hair. Perfect.

Kate dropped her eyes and stammered, "I-I'm sorry. Yes, of course, I'll get you a Band-Aid. I'll be right back." She scampered out of the room, almost tripping over her feet.

After grabbing the first-aid kit from the kitchen cabinet, Kate hurried to the front of the bookstore to find Mr. August holding his hands up in surrender and backing away from Shakes' cage as the cockatoo lunged, hissed, and flapped his wings at him.

"Psychotic bird," he grumbled under his breath.

"Please don't stick your finger in there again. There's a sign. See?" Kate smiled and pointed to the sign above Shakespeare's cage that warned, *I enjoy fingers as a daily treat—do NOT feed me!*

"Ahh. I missed that," he said with a sardonic smile. "Is this the way he treats all of your customers? Because I can't imagine you'll be in business for long if he does."

Despite herself, Kate giggled. The instant the

sound of her laughter hit her ears, she wanted to slap a hand over her mouth. She'd actually giggled. When was the last time she did that?

Kate shook her head. "No, he doesn't bite all of my customers. Just a select few he finds tasty."

Approaching Shakespeare's cage and using her sternest voice, Kate admonished, "Say sorry, Shakes."

"Sorry, Shakes," the cockatoo mimicked Kate's voice.

"I'm serious, Shakespeare. Say sorry or there'll be no more treats for you. Say sorry!"

Shakes shook his head and ruffled his white, silky feathers, eyeing Kate.

"Sorry. Sorry."

"Good, baby," Kate crooned as she reached into the pocket of her shorts and produced a cashew. "Here you go, baby. Now behave and control that beak better. You're going to get mommy in such trouble if you don't."

Hearing a deep, rumbling laughter coming from behind her, Kate straightened and saw she and Shakes were entertaining their guest. Mr. August had his eyes and that beautiful smile trained on her. Kate warmed under his appreciative gaze. It had been a long time since a man looked at her that way, and right then and there, an aching need started low in Kate's belly and spread through her entire body. Kate caught her breath and licked her lips as her heart started a new beat—a happy dance she hardly recognized. Dear God, she wanted him.

While most men either repelled Kate or made her feel nothing at all, with one smile, Mr. August did the impossible. He awakened parts of her she thought were permanently disabled. Since she walked away from Jeff three years ago, no man had warmed her bed or her heart, and she was resigned to the fact that she was broken.

While many women in their thirties were in some sort of relationship or at least enjoying a satisfying sex life, Kate had neither. Until the second her eyes connected with his, she didn't know she had unfulfilled needs, needs that were lying dormant, waiting for the right person to come along, awaken, and satisfy them.

Then there were the damn butterflies. What the hell was that about? Every time his eyes focused on her, hundreds of butterflies hatched and took flight in her belly. In the thirty-one years she'd been on this earth, no man made her blush, stutter, cause butterflies to hatch, or make her heart skip a beat. Not even as a silly, hormone-ruled teenager had a boy made every idiotic, romantic cliché come to life. If she heard violins playing, she'd have herself committed for a psychiatric evaluation. This was ridiculous.

Kate gave herself a mental slap. She had to get a grip. She wasn't herself today. She was sleep-deprived and starved. Her body was running amuck, demanding things it couldn't have and misbehaving right and left.

Kate let out a breath. "I'm sorry about Shakespeare. Most of the time he's harmless, but every once in a while, he picks on one of my male customers or deliverymen. I have no idea why. Here, let me see the damage."

Kate reached for the man's hand, but he moved quickly, capturing her left hand in his massive one. He brought her injured index finger, still wrapped in bloody napkins, up for his inspection.

Kate gasped.

On any other day and with any other man, that kind of unexpected move would have earned him a broken arm or a displaced shoulder at a minimum, but Kate's fight or flight instincts and self-defense training didn't kick in. Although she was tiny compared to him, she'd studied martial arts and self-defense for years and could have easily taken him down. Yet, her fine-honed, self-preservation meter never went off, and she made no move to protect herself.

Kate didn't feel threatened. That in itself freaked her out. Mr. August walked into her bookstore and her life ten minutes ago and yet, in his presence, she felt safe. Kate rarely, if ever, felt safe with people she knew, let alone strange man-giants with smoldering eyes and charming smiles.

"What happened? Did Jaws get you too?" he asked as he removed the napkins covering her wounded finger.

Kate shivered as the whisper of his breath brushed over her fingertips. She tried to pull her hand away, but his grip tightened around her hand.

"Easy now," he crooned, as his grip softened once more and his thumb caressed her palm in soothing circles. "I'm just taking a peek. I won't hurt you."

His eyes gentled on her, and it was her undoing. The velvety touch of his thumb and soft, cajoling tone made Kate's eyes sting with tears. The cut was deep, and it throbbed, but it wasn't responsible for the flood of emotion building with the speed and strength of a tsunami. Kate quickly broke eye contact.

"What'd you do to piss him off? This is much worse than my little nip."

Kate took a deep breath and cleared her throat.

"I'm afraid I did this all on my own," she said with a grimace, as she tried to pull her hand free once more. "I stupidly cut myself with a box-cutter. It's fine. Please, let's take care of your finger."

"I'm fine, but this looks pretty deep. Tell you what," he said, flashing a mischievous grin at her that revealed an adorable dimple in his cheek. "I'll play doctor first. You can be my patient, and then we can switch. Okay?"

Mr. August was pulling out all the stops. She was certain that on some level he sensed her confusion and anxiety. While he laughed and flirted with her, his eyes softened with understanding. It was sweet, but there was no way he knew the tangled mess she was.

Kate didn't make a habit of flirting with her customers, but he wasn't like her other customers, not by a long shot. What was the harm in playing a bit? She licked her lips again and bit her bottom lip. She hadn't flirted in…well, she'd never flirted.

"Okay," she said. "But I don't usually play with strangers. I'm Kate Willowbrook. You've already met Shakespeare. I'm Dreamscape's new owner."

Squeezing her hand, his face lit up as his smile extended across his face and right into his eyes. "It's a pleasure to meet you, Kate, although the jury is still out on Shakespeare. I'm Noah Reed."

Noah Reed.

Kate breathed in his name, and it repeated over and over again in her mind. She tested his name on her lips and found it rolled easily off her tongue and lips like she'd said it often and it was part of her daily vocabulary.

"Hello, Noah Reed," she whispered as a huge smile lit her features. "It's a pleasure to meet you as well."

"Now that we know one another, let's play. Have a seat and I'll put my advanced medical training to work," Noah said.

Noah's name sounded familiar, but Kate couldn't quite place it. She sat on the edge of the front desk, next to the first aid kit.

"Are you in the medical field?"

Chuckling, Noah opened the kit and took out what

he needed. "No, far from it. But I think I took First Aid when I was a kid. It's been a while, but I'm pretty sure I can remember how to clean and bandage a wound."

As Noah took care of her finger, Kate noticed he wasn't wearing a wedding band, and despite telling herself not to go there, she did. She couldn't help herself. The possibility he could be single and be hers was too tempting not to explore. She allowed herself a few moments to live in that fantastical scenario. Then she gave herself another mental slap. She was an idiot. Of course, he was taken, he had to be. He was attractive, polite, funny, and considerate. All of this she figured out in the short time he was in her presence, but she sensed there was much, much more to him.

Kate shook her head. There's no way a man like Noah Reed was unattached. If he was, there was either something seriously wrong with the women in this city or something seriously wrong with him that he hid well. One way or another, he was way out of her league. She was a small-town bookstore owner who already lived a lifetime and a half and who carried so much baggage, it was a miracle she walked upright.

Kate had no business setting her sights on this man or any man. She wasn't ready yet— not to trust and not to let go. Building a new life for herself wasn't easy, but she was proud of the progress she'd made. Kate was standing taller than she ever had and felt stronger and in control of her world. She'd come a long way to forgiving herself and discovering who she was without fear and guilt holding her down.

Bringing a man into the picture could set her back years. All the explaining, the compromising, and the trusting that came along with a relationship hurt her head and made her heart ache. She'd made some terrible mistakes in the past and paid for them dearly, losing years of her life. She took her licks and learned many valuable lessons along the way. Kate didn't feel sorry for herself. The last three years of her life had been remarkable. Thanks to Edith, she'd traveled all around the country, seeing places she'd only read about.

"It's time, Kate," Edith had said, her old eyes that were usually soft and gentle, now uncompromising and focused on Kate. "It's time to forgive yourself and start living once again. Stop hiding, girl. Start living, before it's too late. Open your heart. You're wasting the best years of your life hoping you'll wake up one morning and the past will be rewritten. Don't you know, God hasn't given man that ability yet? *Outlander* isn't real, honey. When I close my eyes for the last time, promise me you'll open yours and see the beauty of the world."

Kate kept almost all her promises to Edith. She'd put her big girl panties on and left the safety of Canton, Texas three years ago. She started living again and traveled the country until she stumbled upon Lakes Crossing and Dreamscape. Her heart, however, was a different story. She opened it to Shakes, and she opened it to Dreamscape. That was as far as she could get the door open. It had been enough…she thought. But now, was the door creaking open a bit more?

One thing Kate did know was that she was never going to settle again, never going to lose herself to a man again. She did that once, and that learning experience was more than enough. This time, when and if the right man came along, he would have to be something special, something she didn't think God had created yet.

Kate sighed and scrutinized the hands that were tending to her with such care. Noah handled her like she was made of crystal, like she was precious. For a big man with large hands, his touch was light, almost tender. Despite Kate's adamant thoughts about men and relationships, she reveled in his touch. She couldn't help herself. If she were a cat, she would rub herself against him and purr.

It occurred to Kate that it had been three years since anyone touched her beyond a handshake.

Three years!

Kate remembered reading that touch was the first sense to develop in infants, and its effects were far-reaching to a person's sense of well-being, emotional, and physical health. Now as she experienced it firsthand, she believed every word and allowed the sensation of Noah's touch to sink into her every fiber. She closed her eyes and breathed in and out, letting the darkness that dominated so much of her life float away. She allowed the light and warmth to seep in, if only for the short time as his skin touched hers.

Kate's eyes filled with tears. Noah couldn't have any idea that bandaging her finger, a small, seemingly insignificant act, meant the world to her. She felt it deep, down to her core. She'd been on her own for so long, she'd forgotten what it felt like to be cared for by anyone, let alone a man.

Noah made Kate ache. He made her want things she thought were unreachable. Kate's eyes were now open to a world of possibilities. Excitement and fear flooded her. This beautiful man was an unexpected gift, and she wasn't the kind of woman who received gifts, not even as a child. So she treasured each tidbit and each offering she was handed and knew its value.

Kindness, caring, gentleness—all rare, and all precious gifts in her world.

Chapter Two

"There you are. Good as new. Almost, anyway."

Kate startled from her thoughts. Her eyes briefly met Noah's amused ones before examining her bandaged finger. She couldn't stop the giggle that escaped her lips. Her finger was a massive, unbendable gauze sausage, three times its actual size. Noah had used an entire roll of gauze on the small cut. Whatever his day job was, he needed to keep it because his first aid skills were sorely lacking. What he lacked in skill, however, he made up for with charm and enthusiasm.

Kate laughed. "Uh, you did a nice job on this, Doctor Reed. You've certainly stopped the bleeding, and possibly all the blood circulation to this finger. Well done, man."

Noah shrugged and gave her a lopsided smile.

"I'm thorough if nothing else. Besides, I had no choice. Your kit is missing scissors. I was forced to use the entire roll of gauze."

Kate shook her head and smirked. "Yeah, I get it. I won't be calling you Dr. House any time soon."

She hopped down from the desk with a teasing smile on her face. He could definitely be called McDreamy though.

She held her hand out, palm up. "Now, it's your turn. Let me see the damage."

When Noah didn't place his hand in hers, she reached for it, but before she could touch him, he grabbed a Band-Aid and made quick work of covering his wound.

"It's not a big deal. No permanent damage done. Trust me, I've had much worse."

Kate sobered. Shakespeare had a powerful beak and could have done serious damage. She'd been the recipient of some pretty nasty bites in the past. Luckily Noah wasn't severely injured and had a good sense of humor or she'd be in big trouble.

"I'm sorry, Mr. Reed. Shakes is great with kids, but a bit unpredictable with adults. What can I do to make it up to you? Is there something specific you came in for?"

Noah smiled and shrugged. "Don't worry about it, and it's Reed."

"Sorry?" Kate furrowed her eyebrows.

"My mother's the only person who calls me Noah. My friends call me Reed."

Reed, not Noah? He didn't resemble a Reed. Kate let out a relieved breath and offered him a grateful smile.

"Glad you want to be friends even after my guard-bird greeted you so rudely. Is there something I can help you find?"

"Yes, actually."

Noah's eyes scanned the bookstore, and then they came back to rest on Kate. "It's my niece's birthday. Emma turned eight today, and she's a bit of a bookaholic. I think she's read just about everything written for her age. I have no idea what she has yet to devour."

Kate's eyes lit up. This she could do. She knew children's and young adult literature inside and out. It was her passion. "Hmm, that could be a challenge, but I can help you. I have a vast selection of children's books in all genres. What does she like to read?"

Noah's brows knit together in concentration as if she'd asked him to solve the mysteries of the Bermuda Triangle. He seemed stumped. It was comical.

Noah shrugged. "Uh, I have no idea what she likes to read."

He was so damn cute.

Kate tried a new tactic. "Okay, no need to panic.

What does she like in general? What fascinates her, excites her, makes her giggle? Does she like animals, scary stories, adventure?"

Noah's brows furrowed once more. Kate continued to smile and waited him out. A minute past before he threw up his hands and ran his hand through his wavy blond hair. Lord, that hair was gorgeous. Her hand itched to burrow deep within its thick strands.

Kate was struck by a feeling of déjà vu again. Something was so familiar about this man. Perhaps their paths had crossed, and she didn't remember? Lakes Crossing was a small lake community and even though she worked at the bookstore for the last year, she was quiet and kept to herself. Kate was certain, though, if she and Noah had met before, there was no way she would've forgotten him.

Noah shook his head. "I should know the answers to these questions, but I don't. Emma, for the most part, is a happy kid. She's eight, and she's a real girly girl. Everything makes her giggle, for the love of God. Normally, I support her reading habit by giving her access to my Amazon account and letting her have her way, but Deidra, my beloved sibling, frowns upon this arrangement."

Kate's smile widened. "Wait, are you talking about Emma and Deidra Lexington?"

Noah tilted his head to the side. "Yes, do you know them?"

"Of course. Dee is a friend, and Emma is Shakespeare's best bud and my Storytime helper. I couldn't run Storytime without her. She's a remarkable child."

Kate studied Noah's face carefully and saw the family resemblance. Both Deidra and Emma had the same luxurious, thick blonde hair. Although Emma's eyes were blue, she got her beguiling dimpled smile from her uncle. That smile could win her just about anything, and Kate frequently watched Emma put it to good use when she wanted her mother to buy her one more book.

"She's something, all right. If Dee would let me, I'd open an account for her here, but I know my sis would lose her mind if I did that. Em is a bit shy and self-conscious. She's happiest when she's lost in a book. I see nothing wrong with feeding her habit." Noah shrugged. "Dee says she needs to be more social, make more real friends, and not rely on the imaginary ones she finds in her books."

Noah's eyes softened, and his tone gentled when he spoke about his niece. Emma was special to him. There was no doubt he loved the child to pieces. Kate's heart melted even more. Emma Lexington was one lucky little girl. Kate had a feeling Noah would walk through fire for that child. Although Kate never experienced anything like that, she was happy Emma had such a kind, loving family and a fierce protector in Noah.

Emma was a sweet little girl. In Kate's eyes, she was a beautiful, sensitive child with a quick sense of humor and a big heart. Kate saw beyond Emma's significant cleft lip deformity she was born with and often forgot it was even there. At Dreamscape, Emma never acted shy. She was happy and confident, and strutted around like she owned the place. Even Shakespeare knew better than to misbehave in Emma's presence. Of course, Emma bought his cooperation with treats, but whatever, it worked.

"I met Em and Dee about four months ago when I reopened Dreamscape as a children's bookstore. Dee talked with me about Emma's shyness. While I understand her concern, I agree with you about reading, but I'm biased. Books are my passion."

Kate scanned the room and smiled. "In many ways, books saved me when I was a child. I learned at an early age that I could escape life by getting lost in a book. I could go anywhere, be anyone, do anything. There were no boundaries and no limits to my adventures. Long after I stopped reading and went to bed, I carried my stories into my dreams and escaped into wonderful worlds and had amazing journeys."

Kate sighed and peered up to find Noah studying her with a small smile and a contemplative expression on his face. Damn. Somehow the filter between her brain and mouth short-circuited in his presence. Kate had no idea why she revealed so much of herself to this man in such a short period. She never talked to anyone this freely, especially not to a man she didn't know. But she felt safe in his presence, and before she knew what she was doing, her guard dropped and her mouth opened.

Kate shook her head, and her cheeks burned as heat crept up her neck and face. "I'm sorry, Noah, I mean, Reed. Emma's not my child, and I shouldn't speak so freely. It's, well…she reminds me so much of myself and I…"

Kate squirmed and stumbled over her words under his assessing scrutiny. She was mortified. First, she told him about her childhood, now she called him by a name reserved for his mother. It was apparent the mental slaps she was doling out with regularity in his presence weren't doing the job. She needed duct tape.

Kate felt oddly off-balance under Noah's scrutiny. He wasn't looking at her, he was seeing her. He was seeing and hearing things she never shared with anyone. This had to stop. She had to regain some measure of control. She absently used both hands to gather her wild mane of hair off her shoulders and neck, lifting it off her nape. She was burning up.

Noah's gaze followed her every movement and the rise of her shirt. He focused on her breasts, which she inadvertently thrust toward him, then rested on the ribbon of exposed flesh between her shorts and t-shirt.

Kate felt the burn of Noah's stare on her and quickly dropped her hands, pulling her shirt down. She was embarrassed. He probably thought she was flirting with him on purpose, bringing her too-large breasts to his attention and exposing her belly to him with one innocent gesture.

Noah cleared his throat as his attention shifted back to her reddened face. "Please don't apologize. I'm happy Emma found a friend here who understands her. You two have much in common."

"Yeah, we do. You know"—Kate tilted her head and scrunched her forehead—"I've only known Emma for a few months, but when she's here, she's anything but shy or self-conscious. It's one of the reasons Dee brings her on Saturdays. Em's a drill sergeant, a force to be reckoned with."

"Really?" Noah said sounding incredulous. "My shy little wallflower is a drill sergeant? Are we talking about the same kid?"

Kate shrugged. "If you don't believe me, come by and see the little commander in action next Saturday morning around ten. Today, the bookstore was closed for inventory, but most Saturdays the show goes on as scheduled, and Emma shows up ready, willing, and able to whip us all into shape."

"Huh. This I've got to see. It's a date. I'll be here to see Emma in action, and I'll get to see you and my new friend Shakes again," Noah said, his eyes sparkling with mischief.

Date? Kate froze. She didn't ask him out, did she? What the hell did she do? She shifted from one foot to another as she licked her lips and chewed on her lower lip. What happened to regaining a measure of control?

Kate shook her head.

Uh-Uh. No date. No man. Only Dreamscape.

Why did the thought of seeing him again exhilarate and terrify her? Now what? She couldn't un-invite him. He was Dee's brother, Emma's uncle, and a gorgeous, mouth-watering temptation she had no business indulging in. Damn her inexperience.

Kate had no idea what to say. It was too late. She fixated on the glossy wood floor and gave a silent groan, wishing the floorboards would open and swallow her whole, putting her out of her misery. Noah would be back, and she'd have to spend more time in his presence feeling off balance and unhinged. But maybe he wouldn't show. People always said things they didn't mean. Why did that thought depress her? Did she want to see him again? Was she ready to travel down this road? Was she ready to go on this safari of discovery? What if she let go and joined in the hunt only to get mauled by a tiger? Kate was lost in her thoughts and confused.

Noah cleared his throat. He glanced at his watch and then back at Kate. "As much as I've enjoyed meeting you, Kate, and perhaps even Shakespeare, I've got to get going, or Dee's going to skin me for delaying dinner. Can you help me out and recommend some books Emma hasn't already inhaled? I was supposed to be at Dee's place an hour ago."

Kate found her equilibrium. She could do this. "Of course. For my regular customers, I keep an electronic file of their purchases, likes, and dislikes. Emma's wish list is rather impressive. You have plenty to choose from. But I'll let you in on a little secret. She's never read *The Boxcar Children* by Gertrude Chandler Warner. There are twelve books in the series, and I received the complete set last week. Emma has been trying to talk Deidra into buying them for her."

Noah grinned. "This is my lucky day."

Noah's eyes locked with Kate's and her pulse jumped. She felt her blood begin to simmer until she thought she would self-combust under his scorching scrutiny.

"Twelve books?" He paused, breaking eye contact and allowing Kate to catch her breath and lasso her out of control heart. "That'll make Dee nuts and will make Em squeal. Sold!"

"Great," Kate breathed out in a shaky voice she didn't recognize as her own. "I shelved the books in the Dreaming Room. I'll go get them for you."

Eager to get away, Kate practically ran to the Dreaming Room. There, she took in a deep breath and let it out slowly. She dropped her head against the wall and resisted the urge to bang it repeatedly. Why was life so damn complicated?

Noah was an unexpected pleasure, but a massive complication in her world. She didn't have the energy or the ability to deal with him. Men, on the whole, were a complete hot-zone for her. Every man who had played a role in her life had incinerated her. It was a wonder she wasn't a man-hater.

The man who provided half of Kate's gene pool was an abusive nightmare who God, she was certain, mistakenly created. Then there was Jeff. Jeff was Jeff. He wasn't a bad man, but at the end, he wasn't a good one either, not for her anyway. Finally, there was Jesse. Kate shivered and slammed the door shut on her current train of thought. No, that was done. She would not let thoughts of Jesse in. He was worse than a hot-zone. He was an explosive volcano erupting, spewing scalding lava.

Kate sighed and pushed away from the wall. She

couldn't continue hiding. She located the books and carried the set back to the front. She rang up the purchase and ran Noah's credit card through in silence. When she was done, she peeked up to find Noah studying her with a contemplative look on his face.

She may not have a lot of experience with men, but Kate knew he was attracted to her, as she was to him. She didn't fool herself into thinking a man like Noah would ever be interested in her for more than mere fun and flirtation. The thought of him using her for a brief period only to end things when he was through playing with her heart, was too much for her to consider.

Kate didn't doubt if Noah knew of her past, he would run so fast and so far, he'd be in a different country before he stopped and considered his actions. Noah came from a well-respected, upstanding family. They were the wealthiest, most established family in this small town. They were also known to be the kindest, most philanthropic people she could ever meet. The Reeds had deep ties to the community, and she couldn't find a soul that had one bad thing to say about them. Noah and his family were the definition of a life filled with beauty.

Kate came from an entirely different background, and they had nothing in common except for the air they breathed. Her life was a poorly written *Lifetime* movie. In fact, it had elements of every *Lifetime* movie ever written, all jumbled together, making it utterly unbelievable. Kate didn't have roots and didn't have a family. Instead, she had a past she worked hard to forget, a past that was the opposite of beauty in every way. That past, those demons, were not what a man like Noah and his family would ever want in their lives.

Kate sighed and handed Noah the books. "Here you go. I hope she enjoys them."

Noah smiled. "Thanks for your help."

Kate smiled back. "It was my pleasure. Again, I'm sorry about Shakespeare."

"Don't worry about it. Who knows maybe one day he and I will come to terms. I'll ask Emma for some tips. Soon he'll be eating out of my hand rather than trying to eat it."

Chuckling, Noah turned to Shakes. "Bye, Shakes."

"Bye. Bye," Shakes repeated.

Noah shook his head and made his way to the door.

"Oh, wait." Kate caught him before he made it to the door. "Can you give Emma something for me?"

"Sure." Noah sauntered back to her.

Kate opened the cabinet behind the front desk and removed a small, rectangular, midnight-blue box with gold stars and moons scattered throughout. She opened the box and took out a striking, handcrafted blue and gold bookmark with a beaded star strung on one end and a half-moon on the other. On one side in swirling calligraphy it read, *Go anywhere. Be anyone. Do anything.* On the other side, in the same beautiful script it said, *Read a book and dream*. She handed the bookmark to Noah and watched his face as he studied it with genuine fascination.

"Did you make this? It's fantastic."

Kate nodded and shrugged. "Thanks. It's a hobby. Please wish her a happy birthday for me and tell her I'll have a surprise for her next Saturday."

Noah focused on Kate's face. His mouth and eyes softened. "Kate, this is very special—just like you."

Kate took in a sharp, surprised breath. Noah didn't know her and couldn't know the impact of his words, the impact of one word...*special*. He would never know the gift he'd given her. Embarrassed and immensely pleased with Noah's praise, Kate nodded.

"Thank you," she said in a raspy voice filled with emotion. Clearing her throat, Kate began putting away the box containing the bookmarks and said, "Say hi to Dee for me."

Kate and Noah stood in silence for a few seconds. Kate felt the weight of his stare on her, cloaking her in its warmth. But she couldn't meet his eyes. She was emotionally wrung out.

"Goodnight, Kate," Noah said, not moving his body or his attention off her.

"Night, Noah," she whispered.

Kate stood rooted to her spot until she heard Noah turn and walk away. Only then did she lift her gaze and watch Noah open the front door and walk out into the warm August evening. This day started with a nightmare and ended with a dream. In the short time Kate spent in Noah's presence, her world was turned upside down. Noah made her want and dream of things she hadn't thought of since she was a young girl.

Meeting him was an unexpected pleasure that now left her feeling raw, vulnerable, and damn it— unhappy and unfulfilled. Before Noah walked into the bookstore, Kate thought she had it all—everything she'd always dreamed of. But one glance, one smile, one touch, and her carefully constructed, orderly world shattered. Kate didn't know whether she should thank him or ban him from her life. She needed to believe the life she worked so hard to build was enough. Kate needed the illusion of happiness to convince herself what she had was good, was enough or else she'd unravel.

By simply walking through Kate's front door, Noah rocked Kate's steady world. Damn him, but his caring, kind ways and that sexy smile of his reminded her of all the things she'd been missing for years—someone to share her life with, someone to make her smile and yes, someone to care about her stupid cut finger.

Chapter Three

Noah woke up to the sounds of New York City as it stretched and yawned, preparing for its inhabitants to come out and play. For most people, it was early, around 5:30 AM, but for him, waking up this late and this slowly was a luxury he didn't often enjoy. On most days Noah was up by 4:15 AM jogging and lifting weights, followed by a quick breakfast. By six he was in his office at Reed Technology Group, attempting to catch up with his brother, Luke, in London, for their daily meeting. His life was busy, regimented, and predictable. He liked it that way.

After a week of interrupted sleep, Noah made the decision to give up the fight he was waging with himself. It was time to see the source of his angst, Kate Willowbrook. He tried everything to push her out of his thoughts, but the petite beauty with waves of cinnamon hair, creamy skin, and big, forest-green eyes wouldn't leave him. She strolled through his dreams smiling that shy, mysterious smile of hers, keeping him up night after night, making him an absolute ass in the office.

Something about Kate intrigued him. Actually, everything about her intrigued him, and he had no idea why. In the social circles he ran in, he was surrounded by beautiful, sophisticated women, but he was immune to their charms. No one, not a single woman, was able to catch his attention and keep it since Kristin.

After he buried Kristin five years ago, he buried himself in work. He spent most of his time on the road, expanding the business throughout the U.S. and Europe, until he was forced to return to New York to stabilize the Manhattan office a year ago. Out of pure necessity, he started dating. On occasion, he needed a beautiful woman on his arm for business purposes, and he enjoyed the physical release. He wasn't looking for a long-term relationship. His dates knew the score, and those who wanted more found themselves out of his life with the door firmly shut behind them.

Kate, however, was different. She wasn't like any of the socialites he knew, and if he had to bet, she was nothing like Kristin either. That was a good thing on both accounts. Since the second Noah heard Kate's melodious voice and saw her exquisite. heart-shaped face, he was unable to get her out of his mind. Compared to his hulking size, she was positively tiny with delicate features that made her appear almost elfin. She brought out an unexpected gentleness in him that startled and irritated him. He was tangled in her web, unable to get free.

Then there were Kate's eyes. Jesus, those eyes were breathtaking, a rare gift that brought a man to his knees ready to do her bidding. They were so conflicted, haunted even. Her eyes reminded him of a trapped animal, fighting for release, but terrified of the outside world. Something about her screamed at him to tread lightly and treat her with care.

Noah recalled what Kate said about books.
Books saved me when I was a child.

Kate had given him a tiny peek into her world, but it was obvious she wasn't used to sharing herself with anyone. Each time their gazes met, she retreated, and every protective instinct in him came to life, ready to do battle and conquer her demons. He couldn't explain his reaction. He didn't know her, and she shouldn't mean anything to him, and yet for some odd reason, she did. He wasn't sure what she meant to him, but he was interested in finding out.

Fuck, he was in trouble. He had to reel himself in. Damsels in distress used to be his Achilles' heel, but

Kristin cured him of that affliction. One thing Noah was certain of, he had to get Kate out of his system and restore the balance and order in his life. If he continued to be a distracted ass in the office, his administrative assistant would quit, and he would lose an important client.

Noah had to force himself to get beyond this need to treat Kate with kid gloves, to protect her and fight off her demons. He would use the same formula he used with all women he found physically attractive. He'd take her out, take her to bed, and take her out of his life forever. It was time to start the process of extracting Kate Willowbrook from his head.

Stretching, Noah glanced at the bedside clock and decided he'd lain around long enough. He was overthinking this thing he felt for Kate. It was a physiological response. He was attracted to her. That was all. After all, he wasn't blind. She was stunning. By the way her eyes devoured him he could tell she found him as attractive as he found her. This shouldn't be that difficult. He had no time and no interest in further dissecting his feelings for Kate. He knew what he had to do.

Noah stood and headed for the shower. Today he was spending the morning with Emma at Dreamscape. Yesterday, he called his sister and volunteered to take Emma to the bookstore while Deidra ran errands. Dee was instantly on alert. His sister was no fool. She wanted to know why he was suddenly interested in children's bookstores, but when he barked at her to stop harassing him or he'd revoke his offer, she backed off. Afterward, he heard the hurt in her voice and knew he'd been an ass yet again.

Noah had changed since Kristin's death. He used to be even-tempered, always smiling and laughing. Now, he was surly most of the time. Dee wanted to see him happy. Hell, his entire family wanted the old Reed back. That man, however, was dead and buried right next to his wife. None of that was Dee's fault, and he owed her an apology.

As he parked his BMW in front of Dee's house, Noah tried to think of a way to apologize to his sister and make up for the shit he was always dishing out. She was his rock and put up with him no matter what he did, and he loved her for it. He got out of the car and walked to the front door. As his hand came up to ring the doorbell, the door flew open, and Emma's little body hit him. He scooped her up in his arms, held her, and covered her face with kisses as she squealed in delight.

Emma was small for her age due to severe feeding problems as a result of her cleft lip and palate deformity. It was not until the age of two, after her third surgery, that she was finally able to eat normally. Over the years, her appetite and feeding habits improved; however, she'd never quite caught up to others her age.

Noah cuddled the child close, loving the feel of her arms around his neck.

"Hello, beautiful. Where have you been all my life? I've been waiting for you forever."

"Uncle Reed, stop kissing me." Emma squirmed and tried to hide her face in his neck. "You're slobbering on me, and you just got here. You haven't been waiting forever."

"Beautiful, I'm hurt. Dogs slobber, I do not. You're going to pay for that comment." Burying his face in her neck, Noah blew a raspberry against her soft skin and thought he would go deaf from her little girl squeals.

"Okay, you two, enough," Deidra admonished. "You're going to be late if you don't get going. Emma, go brush your teeth and grab your red jacket. Hurry."

"Okay, Mommy."

Noah watched as Emma skipped to do as she was told. He loved that child as if she were his own. For a brief moment, he closed his eyes, and his heart ached as he remembered all that he'd lost. Damn Kristin for her selfish, reckless ways.

"Morning, Reed," Dee said with a soft smile.

"Morning, Dee."

Noah enfolded his sister in a big bear hug, kissing the top of her head and murmuring in her hair. "I'm sorry for being such a jerk. Forgive me?"

Hugging him back, she whispered, "Always, baby brother, always."

Twenty minutes later, Noah maneuvered his car into a tight spot a block from Dreamscape as he listened to the chattering of the excited little girl in his back seat. Her elation was infectious, and he couldn't help the smile that covered his face. The bookstore was packed for a Saturday morning. He knew why he was here, but what about Storytime inspired so many adults to leave their homes on a Saturday morning? Wouldn't they rather be sipping coffee and reading the paper in peace, while at home in their pajamas?

Dreamscape was located only a couple of miles from Dee's house. It took up the entire first floor of a large, two-story Victorian home located in the center of the small-town square. The house was painted a sunny yellow with white trim. It had a wrap-around porch adorned with white wicker rockers, inviting people to sit and enjoy a good book. While many of the old Victorians in town were restored to their former glory and were the homes of small businesses, Dreamscape had a unique charm and drew a lot of attention.

The minute Noah opened the front door for Emma, she released his hand and disappeared amongst the adults and kids filling the front sunroom, yelling over her shoulder, "I'm late. I've got to go set up. See you later Uncle Reed."

Noah wandered from room to room. The excited sounds of kids' laughter and teasing, the chatter of adults enjoying a cup of coffee, and the mouth-watering smell of baked goods infused his senses. The place was packed with bodies filling every nook and cranny. It appeared the entire town woke up for Storytime.

The sudden sound of wind chimes filled the room. Kids all around him froze in place, and all conversations halted. Like eager lemmings, everyone in the bookstore pushed and shoved their way down a narrow hall. Amused, Noah followed the sea of tiny humans and adults to the room designated as the Dreaming Room.

Like all the rooms in the house, this one had shiny hardwood floors, floor-to-ceiling built-in bookshelves, and overstuffed, comfortable seating with bright throw rugs and soft lighting. The furniture was pushed to the edges of the room and in their place were soft beanbag chairs of all colors, kid-sized rockers, and a variety of small, overstuffed, marshmallow-type chairs with different cartoon characters on them. At the front of the room was a large rocking chair next to an ornate bird stand.

Noah stood in the back of the room and watched in fascination as his shy, self-conscious niece took charge. In a confident, authoritative voice, Emma ordered the children to take a seat and be quiet so Miss Kate and Shakes could come out and start Storytime. He was surprised to see the kids, and even some parents, respond to Emma's edict and do as they were told. Emma even managed to referee an argument between two little girls who each staked their claim to the same chair.

In no time at all, the room was quiet, and Kate

came out with Shakes perched on her right forearm. Her beautiful smile lit up the room as she walked to the front and placed Shakespeare on his perch. A buzz of excitement filtered through the cramped space and every eye in the room focused on her.

"Good morning everyone," Kate said in a soft voice with a big, welcoming smile. "Shakes and I are pleased you could join us today. We are happy you took your seats quickly so we could get started. Shakes is also happy you remembered to whisper, so you don't scare him."

Turning to Shakes, she asked, "Are you ready to start Storytime?" Shakes vigorously nodded his head up and down, making the children giggle with delight.

"Say, 'good morning, friends,' Shakespeare."

"Good morning, friends," Shakes mimicked.

"Good baby. Now, are we going someplace fun today, Shakes?" Kate asked as she nodded her head. Immediately, Shakes nodded his head.

"Are we going shopping?" she asked as she shook her head side to side.

Shakes shook his head.

"Are we going to the doctor?" she asked as she shook her head.

Shakes shook his head.

"Are we going to the zoo?" Kate asked, this time nodding her head up and down.

Shakes nodded his head right along.

As Kate proceeded to tell her adoring fans a story about a bird named Shakespeare and his adventures at the zoo, Emma stood, stroked the bird's feathers, and fed him cashews.

Noah was awestruck by the petite beauty with the hypnotizing voice that had a room full of children and adults under her trance. Not only was she a master storyteller, but she was also enchanting. She sat regally on the rocker as if it was a throne, wearing jeans and a forest-colored silk shirt that matched her eyes. Her thick hair was swept in a high ponytail that flowed down her back, and her face was natural, without a hint of makeup.

Kate's eyes sparkled as she weaved her magic over her audience. Once the story came to a happy ending, she, along with Shakespeare and Emma, took a bow. Everyone snapped their fingers, rather than clapping. Smiling, Kate told the crowd next week Shakes was going somewhere extra special, and he would love it if they could go with him. Then she gave the bird to Emma. Emma walked out of the room, head held high with a huge grin as Shakes said, "Bye, Bye."

As the crowds dispersed, Noah made his way to the front of the room and waited until the person finished speaking to Kate before he approached her. He guessed she hadn't noticed him before by the way her pupils widened. A slow flush crept up her neck and across her cheeks. Then she started to ramble. He loved that blush and enjoyed seeing her flustered. She was ridiculously cute.

"Um, hi, Noah. It's nice to see you again. I'm sorry I didn't notice you earlier. It's a busy day. You must be searching for Emma. I can find her for you if you want. She's probably still playing with Shakes in the back room."

Kate's gaze bounced from person to person and object to object, scanning the entire room, but never landing on him. She'd called him Noah again and this time, and he didn't correct her. His father's name was also Noah, and he was called Reed since he could remember. Not even Kristen had called him by his given name. She tried it when they first dated, but he told her he preferred Reed. Coming from Kate, however, Noah found he liked the way his name sounded coming from her lips.

"Hi, Kate," he said with a warm smile. "You were great, as was Shakespeare."

Kate's face flushed even redder as she met his eyes. She licked, and then bit her lower lip. Noah considered reaching out and running his thumb across her lip, but thought better of it.

"Thank you. The kids are a lot of fun."

"You weren't reading from a book, though. Was that a story you made up?"

Kate nodded and smiled. "Yeah. It's a series of stories with Shakes being the main character. Sort of like *Curious George* except the series is called *Shakespeare Shakes Things Up*. Each week Shakes goes somewhere new and has an adventure."

Kate was beautiful and talented. She glowed with joy and excitement when she spoke about her stories. It was apparent she was in her element.

"What a great concept. Have you thought about publishing it?"

Kate stood straighter, and her smile widened. "It has crossed my mind, but right now my hands are full with Dreamscape, and I'm having fun with the kids. Emma is such a help. The show couldn't go on without her. Did you see her in action?"

Noah grinned. "Yes. You've worked your magic on her. She was transformed. I've never seen her so happy and sure of herself."

Kate shrugged and chuckled. "I didn't do anything. It's all Shakespeare. From the second he saw Emma, he kind of claimed her and one thing led to another."

Noah shook his head. "I don't think the magic you create is all about Shakes. You have an extraordinary place here. It's unique and nurtured with a great deal of love."

Noah scanned the room noting all the special touches—colorful woven rugs, low-level shelving, and corners filled with stuffed animals.

"One thing I can't figure out, though. How is it that this entire place smells like…" Noah inhaled and cocked his brow, "Sugar cookies and chocolate cupcakes? My stomach has been growling since I got here. Is there a bakery nearby that I didn't see? It smells like heaven."

Kate laughed and shook her head. "No. No bakery nearby. I'm a chronic baker. I bake muffins, cookies, and cupcakes for my customers. The place always smells this way. My customers get all the books they can read and all the treats they can eat. The dentist down the street and I have a special relationship."

"Hmm, you're full of surprises, aren't you?"

Kate's smile suddenly lost its shine. "Yup, I'm a mystery even Sherlock Holmes would find challenging."

Noah took a step toward Kate. "You know, I love a good mystery."

Kate took a step back. She wrapped her arms around herself and shook her head. Turning her head, she acknowledged the customers gathering on either side of her with a slight nod and a smile. Noah realized that people milled around waiting to speak with her. Although he didn't want to let her out of his sight, he had to let her take care of her business.

"Looks like I'm monopolizing your time. Do what you need to. I'll find Emma."

Kate's attention darted between the waiting customers and Noah. She bit her lip. "Uh, okay. I'm sorry, but Saturday mornings after Storytime are always busy."

She pointed to the back of the bookstore. "The

storeroom is that way. I'll be with you as soon as I can. I have something special for Emma, so please don't leave until I give it to her. Okay?"

For a few seconds, Noah was unable to answer as he tracked her tongue gliding over her lower lip and her teeth, abusing the soft flesh. It wasn't until she said his name again that he focused.

"Noah?"

"Sure, I'm in no hurry. We'll wait. Take your time."

Noah found the storeroom and watched from outside the room as Emma talked and sang to Shakespeare as if he was her best friend and understood every word she said. Although Emma tried to convince Shakes her Uncle Reed was a nice man, and he had to be sweet, it didn't work. As soon as Noah entered the room, the bird hissed at him and even threw a peanut toward his head.

For Emma, Shakes was docile. At one point the creature bent its neck and laid its beak submissively on Emma's cheek, closing its eyes in obvious delight as she stroked its feathers and cooed. Noah was convinced there was some trick to getting that bird to heel that he wasn't being told.

Forty-five minutes later, Kate found them. On a small plate she carried a massive chocolate cupcake with pink and purple frosting and sugary glitter sprinkled all over. A lit candle stood in the middle and tiny, edible butterflies circled the candle. As she walked into the storeroom, she sang "Happy Birthday."

"Happy birthday, Em. I know I'm a week late, but I made this early this morning just for you."

"I love it." Emma squealed, blew out the candle, and gave Kate a big hug. "It's too pretty to eat. Can I take it home to show Mommy?"

"Of course, but I hope you'll eat it later. There's a yummy surprise in the middle for you."

When Emma was done admiring her cupcake, Kate told her the bookstore was empty, and she could take Shakespeare to his cage in the sunroom. Emma jumped to do Kate's bidding, and Shakespeare followed Emma's "Step-up" command, leaving his perch and stepping onto her hand without resistance. Kate and Noah followed. Noah was surprised to see the Closed sign on the door.

"I thought you were open all day on Saturdays?"

Kate shook her head. "No, I usually close right after Storytime."

"Perfect," he said with a wide smile. "Why don't you join Emma and me for lunch?"

Kate's pupils dilated, and she opened and closed her mouth several times wordlessly before answering.

She straightened the edge of her shirt and fidgeted as she stepped from foot to foot. "Thank you. That's kind of you, but I can't. The place is a mess. It always takes me several hours to clean up after a busy Saturday."

Noah had no intention of giving up. He could tell he almost had her.

"Tell you what then, I have a couple of things I still need to do around town, and then I'm dropping Emma back at Dee's. Will you have dinner with me tonight instead?"

For a full minute, they stood in silence staring at each other. Kate's gorgeous eyes were wide, and her teeth worried her lower lip. Noah felt sorry for her bruised lower lip and a bit jealous it was getting all of Kate's attention.

"Kate? Will you have dinner with me tonight?
"Dinner?"

Kate appeared adorably confused with her brows

scrunched together, staring at him like he was speaking in Japanese.

He gave her an indulgent smile and persisted. "Yes. Your pick. We can go anywhere you like."

Kate studied him, and a host of emotions crossed her features. Her expressive eyes told of the internal argument she was having, a conversation that was probably about him, but one he wasn't invited to participate in.

"I…well…thank you, but no."

Noah frowned and cocked his head to the side. "No?"

"Sorry. No." Kate shook her head. "But thank you for asking me. That was kind of you."

That was it. Noah was sick of being told he was kind. Kind was the last thing he was being. Why did she keep saying that? If she only knew what his intentions were when he drove here, she wouldn't think he was so kind.

"I'm not asking you out of kindness. I'd like to get to know you better. Please have dinner with me."

When she began to shake her head, it occurred to him she might have a boyfriend. She wasn't wearing a wedding ring, but that didn't mean she wasn't in a relationship. Kate was sweet, funny, and gorgeous. Of course some lucky man had already claimed her. Disappointment flooded him, and the thought of another man having her in his arms, kissing those bruised lips, or watching her beautiful eyes change colors with her emotions disturbed him. For a man whose sole intention was to take her to bed and get her out of his head and life, that was certainly an odd reaction.

Fucking hell. Who was he kidding? He was screwed. He wanted this woman and not only for her sexy body and not only for a brief affair. He wanted to talk with her, get to know what caused the shadows that lurked in her eyes and see where this would lead them. He wanted her, and he couldn't have her because some other lucky bastard already had her.

"I'm sorry," he said, holding his hands up and taking a small step back. "Say no more. I assumed you weren't in a relationship, that you weren't already taken. I apologize. Of course, you *must* be special to someone."

Kate's eyes met his, widened even more, and filled. Shit. What had he said? Why the tears? Before he could say or do anything more, she took a step away from him.

"No," Kate whispered.

It took Noah everything he had not to move, not to go to her and comfort her. Every instinct told him that would be the wrong move.

"Is that a no to dinner or no to being taken?"

Shaking her head, Kate met Noah's eyes. He drew in a sharp breath. In Kate's eyes, Noah saw overwhelming sadness, loneliness, and resignation. He was wrecked.

"No to dinner. And no, Noah…I'm not special to anyone."

Chapter Four

How long can humans go without sleep before they become desperate enough to cut off their own heads? Kate wondered. A month? That was how long it had been since her last full night of sleep. She was physically and mentally exhausted, and reaching the point of desperation. It didn't matter how tired she was, there was no one to lean on. Every day, despite being dog-tired, she woke up at the crack of dawn and pushed herself to the late hours of the night, in hopes of exhausting herself and earning a full night of sleep.

Over the last week, she tried everything she could think of to make the nightmares stop— rigorous exercise, yoga, red wine, hot baths, soothing music, not-so-soothing music, and meditation. Nothing worked. As she lay in bed each night, she found herself afraid to close her eyes, knowing that she'd be awake soon, but not before reliving the worst day of her life over and over again.

She hadn't had a nightmare in three blissful years, and now they were back with a vengeance. Kate knew why, and she felt weak and stupid for letting the antics of a couple of teenage boys shake her up this much. Still, no matter how often she told herself the present had nothing to do with the past, she couldn't convince her brain of that, and each night the past was resurrected. In time, she would exert her will and conquer the demons once again and another period of reprieve would follow. Until that happened, though, she was a frustrated, exhausted mess.

Kate sighed, shook her head, and refocused on her work. She needed to finish up for the day so she could make her way upstairs and soak in a hot bath. Tomorrow was Saturday, which meant Storytime. Normally, she looked forward to sharing her newest story with the kids.

Now, however, she dreaded the thought of having to wake up at the crack of dawn, bake, and gather enough energy to entertain and engage her guests. Not once since she started Storytime four months ago had she felt like this. Something had to change.

It wasn't just the nightmares keeping Kate from getting any rest. When she wasn't reliving her hellish past, Noah Reed was visiting her dreams on a regular basis. Although the dreams that featured Noah were of the nice variety, sometimes they were also a bit naughty. Kate fantasized about his sexy smile, his strong hands holding and caressing every inch of her until she couldn't think straight. She often woke up hot, bothered, and aroused. Sometimes her dreams were so vivid, she swore she could taste his lips against hers and feel the hardness of his muscular chest and broad shoulders against her small frame.

Kate's mind wasn't always in the gutter where Noah was concerned. When things were slow at the bookstore, she let her mind wander to more conventional dreams and scenes of a life she once longed for when she was younger. Kate's dreams were simple. If she could have a second chance at life, a do-over, she would create everything she didn't have—a family with a man who adored her and was devoted to her and the children they created. She'd be *special* to someone. She'd have ties and dig deep roots for herself and her babies.

But Kate was wise. She knew Prince Charming did not exist outside of fairytales. The bookstore, however, was very real. Fifteen months ago, she drove into Lakes Crossing on her way to the Poconos and saw the *For Sale* sign in front of Dreamscape. She walked in on a whim and fell in love.

At the time, the place was a used bookstore and was a bit of a mess. She spent hours talking to the elderly owners, the Kemptons. One thing led to another and soon she found herself working for them, and then buying the place. At the time, Kate thought she found everything she wanted and needed to be happy for a lifetime. Then Noah waltzed into her world and ruined all her well-laid plans.

A month had passed since Noah asked her to dinner. It was clear the man was not used to hearing the word "no." He drove her crazy over the last month with unexpected visits with Emma in tow, phone calls, and texts, asking her to go out with him. She had no idea how he got her cell number, but that was the least of her worries.

Every week, some combination of balloons, chocolate, and flowers arrived at the bookstore. At first, she was convinced she was only a passing fascination for him. But as he persisted in his efforts to change her mind, he wore her down, and she began to doubt herself. One thing Kate knew, however, if she let herself get sucked into those melty chocolate eyes of his, there would be heartache at the end.

Noah was a charming, good-looking man devoted to his niece and family, but she wondered what he was really like and why he insisted on taking her out. He was a worldly, successful man who drove a BMW. She was a small-town bookstore owner who wore cut-off shorts and old t-shirts from the local thrift store. Her idea of a gourmet meal was anything that came in a take-out box and cost more than Ramen soup. She was a simple girl.

Just last week Emma couldn't stop gushing about her Uncle Reed and the grand plans they had.

"We're going to the City to see *Mary Poppins*. Mommy said she'd take me there, but Uncle Reed said he'd send my chariot." Emma giggled. "It's not really a chariot, it's a big black car. Jake is going to take me to Uncle Reed's apartment in the City. Then we're going to the Sugar Factory for dinner."

"Who's Jake?"

Emma shrugged. "He drives the car. Uncle Reed always lets Jake drive me anywhere I want."

Kate shook her head. Apartments in the City, chauffeured cars, fancy restaurants, and Broadway shows—what in the world could Noah possibly see in her?

Kate tried to recall what little she knew about the Reed family. She knew there were four Reed children, although she'd only met Dee. Rumor had it Noah was married once, but his wife died several years ago in a car accident that had the town of Lakes Crossing buzzing for months. Kate hated gossip and didn't engage in conversations that centered around the misery of others. Therefore, her knowledge was limited.

Kate yawned and rubbed her eyes. As she finished dealing with the day's receipts, she heard a knock at the front door. Groaning, she glanced at the clock and prayed it wasn't a customer. It was 6:30 PM and she'd closed the bookstore half an hour ago. On any other day, she would happily open for a late customer. She needed the income. Tonight, she was too damn tired.

Kate peeked through the front window and froze. Why was Noah Reed standing in front of her door holding a pizza box? She looked like death and felt about the same. She didn't want him to see her like this. For a minute, she considered shutting off the lights and creeping up to her apartment. But even as she contemplated this, her body moved without hesitation toward the door and Noah. Kate straightened her wrinkled clothes, ran her fingers through her hair, and plastered a smile on her face.

"Hello, Noah."

"Hi, Kate."

Noah gave her his signature lazy smile, and Kate's traitorous heart skipped a beat. He leaned against the front porch rail like he didn't have a care in the world— smooth, sleek, and sexy as hell, wearing a beautifully tailored gray suit, a white dress shirt, and a blue silk tie. He resembled a mouth-watering model walking off the cover of *Forbes*. He was devastatingly handsome, and although that was a very good thing, it was also a very, very bad thing in her weak state.

"How are you?"

Kate sighed. "I'm fine. I'm sorry, but the bookstore is closed. Is there something I can help you with?"

"Yup. Can I come in?" he asked, flashing her a toothy smile that made Kate momentarily forget her resolve to keep him at arm's length.

"Well, um, I was shutting down for the evening and about to go up. I'm sorry, but I'm exhausted." Kate shivered in the warm September night.

"I can see you're tired." Noah's smile faded as he studied her face. "I promise not to take long, and I even brought pizza and a bottle of wine." He held up the wine bottle she hadn't noticed.

A slight warm breeze blew, and the mouthwatering smells of spicy pizza sauce and melty cheese hit Kate's nose. Her stomach was a beast and it growled, insistent on getting some nourishment. She didn't realize how hungry she was, but right then and there she had visions of tackling Noah for that pizza. Then there was the wine. How the hell did he know?

There were a few things in life Kate couldn't resist—coffee, red wine, and pizza— preferably with the red wine, dark chocolate—also with red wine, and Dunkin Donuts Boston Cream—add the coffee, delete the wine. She planned on a bowl of cereal for dinner followed by the last of the Godiva chocolate he sent her a few days ago. To make thing worse, she was completely out of cheap wine.

Kate eyed the pizza and wine and licked her lips. "What's on the pizza?"

"Everything but pineapple and anchovies," Noah answered with a small smile playing on his lips.

"I hate olives. Are there olives on that pizza?" she asked in a businesslike fashion.

"I'll gladly remove them for you."

Kate gestured to the wine. "Red or white?"

"Red. A fantastic Pinot Noir you won't want to miss."

Kate sighed, disgusted with herself. She was a weak, weak woman when she was hungry. All she could afford these days were five-dollar bottles of wine and frozen pizzas. This was a treat only a fool would turn away. She opened the door wider and stepped to the side.

"Come on in, but know that I'm only giving in because I'm too tired and hungry to stand here and argue. And I want that bottle."

Noah chuckled and followed her in. "I completely understand. Don't worry, I promise not to keep you up late."

Kate grabbed the pizza box and held it up to her nose. She inhaled deeply. Yum. She was starving, and it smelled like heaven. Her mouth watered in anticipation and she barely stopped herself from opening the box right there and diving into its cheesy goodness. To hell with manners.

Noah closed the door and locked it. He stood with his back to her as he locked and unlocked the door multiple times.

"This lock is pretty flimsy. You need to have a stronger bolt installed," he said, frowning at her over his shoulder.

"Yeah, I know. I'll get to it. It's fine for now. Let's eat." Kate's stomach let out another loud rumble as she started walking toward the kitchen, but Noah didn't budge.

"Kate," he called in a clipped voice.

Kate stopped and glared at him. Why wasn't he following her? He teased her with her two main food groups, and now he stood planted in front of the door denying her sustenance.

"What?" she asked irritably.

Noah tapped on the screen of the security system near the door. "Is something wrong with this thing? It won't even light up."

Kate shrugged. "It died months ago. Don't worry about it. Come on, now. Right now," she demanded. "Have some pity, man. I'm seriously starving."

Noah ignored her protestations and removed his cell from his pocket.

"No security system and a flimsy lock? We need to get this taken care of right away. It's not safe for you to be here without decent security. I'll have one of my guys come by and get this fixed in the next hour."

Kate frowned. What the hell was going on here? Why did this man think he could invite himself into her life and take over? She'd put up with his constant assault on her peace and sanity over the last month because frankly, she was flattered, but enough. No freaking way was she putting up with this ridiculous nonsense. She drew the line at pizza and wine…and flowers, and chocolate, and pretty balloons.

Kate dropped the pizza box on the nearest table with a loud thud. She glared at Noah. "Uh, uh. Stop right there, mister."

Noah froze, his finger suspended over the screen

of his phone. He raised his head and focused on her, quirking an eyebrow.

"I'm not sure what's going on here, but stop. Your intentions may be good, but your execution leaves much to be desired. Thank you for the attention and all the gifts and the pizza and wine, but enough. Just stop."

Kate straightened and scrutinized Noah, putting her hands on her waist. "This is my business, my home. Thanks for your concern, but I'll take care of the lock and the security system when and if I see fit."

Kate and Noah eyed each other for a few minutes, neither giving an inch. Kate held her ground. She kept her head tilted up and continued to stare daggers at Noah, although her neck began to ache. He broke first.

Noah shook his head, slid his cell back into his pocket, and held up his hands in surrender. He gave her an apologetic smile. "I'm sorry, Tiger. Sheath those claws. Message received. Let's have some pizza."

Kate hesitated, not sure what to do. Part of her wanted to kick his overbearing ass out, but she couldn't. The man had driven to her from Manhattan, on a Friday evening in rush hour traffic. He'd brought pizza and wine and now appeared apologetic and somewhat embarrassed. Hmm, something told her he was as surprised by his behavior as she was.

"Okay," she mumbled as she grabbed the pizza box.

Noah sighed. "Where's my friend Shakes?"

"He's in bed already."

"Too bad. I've been reading up on man-eating birds, and I've got a couple of new techniques I want to try out on him. I'm pretty sure we got off on the wrong foot. I need to make my intentions clear, and I'm certain we can come to an understanding."

"Making your intentions clear would be good for

all involved," Kate murmured as she made her way to the kitchen with him following.

They would eat in the kitchen on paper plates. There was no way she was taking him upstairs. That was her sanctuary, and few people were invited there. She didn't know him and didn't trust him enough to let him into her world.

Kate lived on the second floor of the bookstore. When she first started working at the bookstore, she stayed at a bed and breakfast a few blocks over while she searched for a place to rent. The Kemptons offered her the second floor, and she was grateful. No one had occupied the second floor in decades, and the Kemptons used it for storage. It took three months to clean up the place, but gradually it went from an overstuffed storage unit to her very own oasis. Every inch of the place was lovingly assembled and told the story of her life, the parts she wanted to remember anyway.

"I hope you don't mind paper plates," she said as she brought out plates, napkins, and wine glasses from the kitchen cabinet and placed them on the small wooden kitchen table.

"No problem, but do you have a corkscrew?"

Reaching into a drawer, she said, "Weirdly, yes. I spend a lot of my evenings down here, and I enjoy a glass of wine."

Kate sat and studied Noah. He took off his jacket, loosened his tie, and then rolled up the sleeves of his dress shirt and began to open the wine. His arms were muscular and tan, with a smattering of blond hair. He wore no jewelry other than a beautiful Rolex watch, which caught the light with his every move. He was relaxed and seemed to fit in her small space. She was suddenly engulfed in a wave of panic so strong it threatened to take her under.

What the hell was she doing with this man? For the love of God, he wore a Rolex. A *Rolex*! She glanced down at her wrist to the watch she'd purchased for $18.99 from the local discount warehouse store. Then she examined her no-name brand skinny jeans and the espresso Dansko leather clogs she splurged on, also from the wholesaler, for $29.99. She was dressed in cheap, but comfortable clothing while he was—upper class personified.

Kate almost knocked over the wine glasses as she stood and backed away from the table. Her heart beat against her ribs so hard it threatened to leap out of her chest and run out of the room, just like she wanted to do. Her breath was choppy, and a fine sheen of sweat coated her palms and forehead. It didn't happen often, but now and then, particularly when she was overly stressed, tired, or feeling trapped, her emotions got the best of her, and she experienced a full-blown panic attack.

"I'm sorry, Noah, but this…this is a bad idea. I'm not sure why you're here, and it's late, and I'm tired, and…" Kate stopped talking and gasped for breath.

Noah placed the wine bottle on the table and came to her side. He grasped her elbow and placed his other hand on the small of her back.

"Kate, look at me. You are going to be fine. Breathe with me. Come on. In and out."

Noah held her gaze and took slow, deep breaths. Kate didn't know why, but she followed his lead. She didn't want to pass out and make a complete fool of herself. After a few deep breaths, she was less panicked and more in control.

"Better?"

Kate nodded, unable to find her voice.

"Why don't we sit down and we'll talk things out?" When she didn't move, Noah tried again. "We're both starving and need to eat. The pizza is here, as is the wine. What do you say?"

Now that she was breathing a little easier, she felt the panic ease. Kate nodded, and he released her. She walked back to her chair and sat, feeling foolish. She blamed her crazy behavior on three things—hunger, exhaustion, and Noah. He had a way of disrupting her day, hell, her world. He made her long for things far out of her reach. He was a newly printed, crisp, one-hundred-dollar bill and she was a tarnished penny. Other than both being a form of currency, they had nothing in common.

Kate closed her eyes and laid her forehead on the table. "I'm sorry, Noah. I warned you I was tired. This isn't a good idea. I'm not fit to be around you or anyone else at this moment."

"Taste the wine and have some pizza. I'll do the same, and we'll talk. Then, I'll leave you to get some rest. I promise."

Kate opened her eyes and saw the sympathy, but also the determination in his eyes. Noah sat in the chair beside her. She pushed herself into a sitting position and nodded. Maybe if they talked this out, he would back off, and she'd finally be able to get some sleep.

Both the pizza and wine were outstanding, and they ate and drank in silence for a few minutes. He studied her and she focused on the slice of pizza in her hand. She waited for him to speak, telling herself to hear him out and then kick him out.

"Kate?"

Kate glanced up to find Noah's eyes studying her. Their eyes met and locked.

"Here's the thing. You've been on my mind since I first laid eyes on you a month ago. I think you're beautiful, smart, creative, funny, and you're wonderful with kids. I'd like to get to know you better. Correct me if

I'm wrong, but I get the feeling you don't necessarily dislike me, but you don't trust me enough to give me a chance. Am I right?"

Kate's entire body warmed under his scrutiny, and her face burned with embarrassment. She focused on her wine and swirled it in her wineglass, hating her inability to control her body's responses. She felt vulnerable and exposed, it was damn annoying, especially at her age. Kate wasn't used to receiving compliments. Noah Reed thought she was beautiful and smart? Surely there were dozens of beautiful, smart women in his circle who would be more than happy to go out with him.

The thing was, Noah was right. She didn't dislike him; on the contrary, she found him sexy, interesting, funny, and a whole lot of other things she couldn't articulate. But, she didn't trust him and didn't trust herself with him. She had a bad habit of letting men take over her life, and she'd worked hard to break that habit. She didn't want to lose herself again and lose the ground she'd gained.

"Kate? You still with me?"

Kate jerked, and a drop of wine splashed out of her glass and landed on her jeans. Embarrassed, she took the napkins he offered her with a grateful smile.

"Thanks. You're a nice man, but I'm not looking for a relationship, and even if I were, we don't have anything in common. We come from very different worlds, trust me. Thank you for all the gifts. I'm flattered. I'm sorry you came all the way out here for no reason. I appreciate the pizza and wine, but I'm not changing my mind."

Noah didn't appear the least bit perturbed by her words. He grinned. "Actually, we have quite a bit in common. I can even prove it to you. You like pizza. I like pizza."

"Yes, but…"

"I'm not done. You like red wine. I like red wine. You like Emma and Deidra. I love Emma and Deidra. Do you see a trend here?" he asked with a mischievous smile.

Kate smiled right along with him. He was ridiculous. "Okay, well done. But did you hear the part where I said we come from different worlds and the part where I said I'm not interested in a relationship?"

"Yup. I'm choosing to ignore those parts, and I think you should too. You're overthinking this. I'm only asking you to let me take you out on one date. That's it. If you don't have a good time, I'll leave you alone. What do you say?"

Kate studied Noah and sighed in frustration. She was tired of warring with herself and him. "You're not going to give up, are you?"

"Nope," he said, grinning full out, his eyes dancing in triumph.

"Then tell me one thing."

"Sure, anything," Noah said, without hesitation.

Kate pierced him with her green eyes. "I'm certain there's no shortage of women who would be happy to go out with you. Why me?"

Noah's cocky grin faded into a soft smile that stole her breath. His eyes darkened as he focused on her. She could feel the heat creeping up her cheeks again, and she couldn't believe she'd asked him that question. She didn't even know why she had, except that she wanted to hear his answer. If she let herself fall for this beautiful man with the killer smile and the softest brown eyes in the world, she'd fall hard and fast. If she were just a toy to him, one that he got bored of and discarded after a while, she'd be devastated. She had lost so much already and survived, but Kate wasn't sure she could survive his games. If she allowed herself to hope and dream of a life with Noah but then lost it all, she'd crumble, and no amount of superglue would put her back together.

Kate waited for his answer, her eyes locked with his, and he didn't let her down.

"Yes, I won't deny that I've dated other women and there are those who wouldn't turn me down for a date, but they're not you."

Noah reached for her hand, and she let him feel the tremble that ran through her as he engulfed her small hand in his. He raised her hand to his mouth and kissed her fingers, never taking his gaze off her.

"You say you're not special to anyone, but that's not true. *I* see something special, someone special. I know we don't know each other very well, but if you give us a chance to change that, together, *we* may be something special. We won't know unless we try."

Kate's breath hitched, and her heart squeezed. Jesus, the man had a way with words. How did he know what she needed to hear? Now she understood what Roberta Flack meant when she sang "Killing Me Softly." He was clawing at the door to her heart, and she didn't think she was strong enough to resist him, even knowing that she may get shredded if she let him in.

Kate dropped her gaze again as her eyes began to fill. Her breathing was ragged, and her heart broke its confines and was on the run. Whether it wanted to be caught by Noah or not, Kate wasn't certain.

Special.

Kate had waited thirty-one years to hear someone call her special. She struggled to rein in her emotions and push back the tears that threatened to roll down her cheeks. She wanted to go out with Noah so badly it hurt. She wanted to get to know him and to be a part of his world, but she was terrified. Good visited her very few times in her life. The instant it arrived, she began preparing for its departure. Good was a temporary visitor, and a fickle one at that.

"Come on, Kate. I can sense you're afraid. I swear I'm a nice guy. I'll do my damnedest not to disappoint or hurt you. Take a chance. Take a chance on me."

Kate heard the vulnerability in Noah's voice. She explored his handsome face, a face she was sure she would never tire of admiring. All traces of his earlier cockiness vanished. Instead, it was replaced by a rawness, an earnestness, a tenderness she'd never seen before. That was the look Kate would remember for a lifetime. Years from now, she would say that was the exact moment she knew, if Noah Reed asked her, she would be his for a lifetime.

Kate let out a slow breath and with a soft smile, she whispered, "Okay, Noah Reed. I'll take a chance…a chance on you. I'll go out with you."

Chapter Five

Noah spent the week thinking of Kate and planning the perfect first date. The week dragged, but when Saturday arrived, he leaped out of bed at the crack of dawn. As Noah went through his morning routine, he heard the weatherman on TV say it was going to be an unseasonably warm October first. He smiled and prayed the man was right for once. He often thought he should have become a meteorologist. It was the only job he knew where one could consistently be inconsistent and get paid for one's lack of expertise and precision.

Even if the weather turned, nothing would ruin this day. It took a month, but Kate Willowbrook finally agreed to give him a chance. Initially, when she refused to go out with him, he decided to stop making a fool of himself and stop pursuing her. That decision, however, wasn't well communicated to his brain or his dick. As part of his plan to purge Kate and her persistent ghost out of his mind, Noah had gone out on a date with Ava Louise Cunningham, a childhood friend of Dee's. But he had no interest in Ava whatsoever. The date with Ava was a colossal mistake. She'd been all over him, and he spent the entire night keeping her at arm's length and comparing her to Kate. He found Ava remarkably lacking.

After failing at replacing Kate with Ava, Noah took a different approach. Like a lovesick teenager, he spent weeks popping up at the bookstore with Emma and sending Kate gifts. Each time she received one of his gifts, she thanked him and asked him to stop. But he heard the happiness in her voice and saw the delight on her face. Still, she'd refused to go out with him. Four weeks into his plan to win Kate, he admitted defeat and deployed his secret weapon, Deidra.

Noah and Dee were as close as siblings could be, and then some. His big sis was his lifeline. She was born with the wisdom of Solomon and the patience of Job, and she had a soft spot for him, as he did for her. He knew Dee would be ecstatic to hear he was interested in someone enough to ask for her help. The fact that Dee and Kate were friends was a bonus.

Noah called Deidra, admitted his interest in Kate, and begged for her help. Instead of the excitement and support he expected from Dee, he received silence followed by a hesitant, "of course, I'll help you." Deidra didn't ask any probing questions, didn't laugh or squeal with delight, didn't say it was about time—nothing.

In a flat voice, Dee said, "I've only known Kate a few months. I know she loves pizza, wine, chocolate…the usual. She's a very private person. I'm not surprised you're having problems getting to know her. Honestly, I don't know how I can help."

Noah was disappointed and perplexed by Dee's response. His usually warm, helpful sister was acting strange and being evasive. He didn't know what to make of it.

"Dee, I get the feeling you don't approve. What's going on? Kate said you and Emma go to Dreamscape often, and you guys are friends. What am I missing?"

After a minute of silence, Dee sighed. "Be careful, Reed."

What did she mean? *Be careful*? Noah was officially annoyed. He hated playing games, and Dee knew that.

"What the hell, Dee? What does that even mean? Kate's a tiny thing, not a serial killer. I think I can handle myself." Noah gave a forced laugh. "Stop being so vague. What's on your mind? Spit it out."

Dee sighed again but didn't utter a word.

"Deidra," Noah warned, losing his temper.

"Fine, Reed. I like Kate as a friend, but she's not the type of woman you typically go out with. I have a feeling she's been through a lot. She's sweet and great with Emma, but there's something about her that worries me. She's got a past. One that's left its mark on her. You don't know what she's really about, what she's hiding, or what she wants from you. I know you better than anyone. You are a good man and can have any woman you want, and she's not the right woman for you."

Deidra was wrong. She said it herself. She didn't know Kate well. Kate was the right woman for him. She'd brought light into his darkened world, energized him, and awakened desires he thought he'd never feel again. Dee was letting her imagination run wild and making some unwarranted assumptions and judgments. Noah wanted his sister's approval and wished Dee had been in the room to see and hear the authenticity and vulnerability in Kate's eyes and voice when she'd asked him—*why me?*

With those two words, Kate captured Noah's heart.

In all his forty years, Noah never met anyone so genuine. There wasn't an ounce of artifice or deceit in Kate Willowbrook. Kate wasn't trying to be coy or cute. She wasn't fishing for compliments. At that moment, she was exposed and unguarded, and incredibly brave, asking him, no, warning him, not to break her heart.

Kate had focused those expressive green eyes of hers on him and given him a glimpse into her soul. She was taking a leap of faith on him. Noah made a silent promise to Kate. He would do everything in his power to guard and cherish her heart. He would be patient and win her trust and respect, and if she found him worthy, maybe

Noah would even win her.

I see something special, someone special.

Noah told Kate she was special, and he meant it. He spent the past month trying to understand why he was so drawn to her, and at the end of the day, the answer was as easy as it was complex. It was in the way she spoke to Emma and the other children who came into Dreamscape. It was also in the way she took time from her day to bake for the residents of the local nursing home. Then there was her shy smile and the commanding, yet indulgent voice she used on Shakes. All of those things and much, much more made her irresistible.

Take a chance on me.

Noah had asked Kate to be brave, to take a chance on him, but what she didn't know was he too was being brave. He was putting himself out there again.

Was he ready to take a chance with someone new?

Was he ready to trust his heart to another?

If someone had asked him those questions before Kate entered his life, the answer would have been a resounding *no*. Despite the sadness and overwhelming loneliness that colored all aspects of his life, he wasn't interested in moving on and becoming whole again. He couldn't find his way out of the darkness on his own.

Kristin had destroyed him. He had given his heart to her, and she'd shredded it. Life with her was a living hell from the start. The storm that obliterated his life hadn't come out of the blue without warning. No, there'd been plenty of notice to evacuate to safer ground. He'd ignored every warning, every plea from his family and friends to take care, and every sign heralding disaster. He was certain he could wrap his arms around the storm, harness its power, and contain its devastating aftereffects.

He'd been wrong. Never again did he want to

have such little control over his life. Never again did he want to feel that helpless. If he and Kate were meant to be in each other's lives, he would leave nothing to chance. If she were his, he would protect her with everything he had. He would protect her, even from herself.

Noah shook his head and ran a hand through his hair. He spent too much time and energy thinking about and dissecting the past. It had to stop. Instead, he turned his thoughts back to the day's plan. He didn't have the girl yet, and he had his work cut out for him. While he drove out of the City toward Jersey, he reviewed the plan for the day. He'd called Kate on Wednesday to confirm plans, and she attempted to back out. She had no idea who she was dealing with. He'd anticipated this might happen and was ready for it.

"Noah, I'm so busy this Saturday. Maybe we should reschedule?"

"No problem. We can be busy together."

"But I have Storytime and then clean-up, and that can take hours."

"I have plenty to do to keep myself busy. I won't get in your way," Noah replied in a patient, indulgent voice.

"I also have to go to a local farm and the pumpkin patch. It's muddy and messy. I don't want to subject you to that."

Noah laughed. "I love pumpkins, and what's wrong with a little mud? I hear it's good for the complexion."

Kate huffed irritably. "Noah, honestly. The weekend is the only time I have to get things done. After I finish all of that, I still have to decorate the entire place for Halloween."

"Kate, I get it. You're busy, and I accept that.

You're always going to be busy. But you're not getting out of this, and besides, I'm a world-renowned decorator."

Kate sighed. "Fine, but don't say I didn't warn you."

The plan for the day was simple and stress-free. Noah thought it was the perfect first date. Pumpkin picking, decorating, and dinner and a movie. What could go wrong?

Before meeting Kate, Noah spent the morning inspecting the Easton Estate on Forest Mountain Road. It was a large house near Deidra's home. The estate was about five miles from Dreamscape. It was located deep in the forest, built on the highest peak of a small mountain, and it overlooked a lake. It was magnificent and vacant. He'd been searching for a home in the area for months, and nothing seemed right until now. He didn't need to think twice. He put an offer on it and left the details to his lawyer and realtor to work out.

For the last ten years, when he wasn't traveling, Noah had lived in a 4000-square-foot penthouse that overlooked Central Park. He'd bought the place right before he and Kristin married, thinking they would live there forever. He imagined his children growing up with the world's most famous park in their backyard. Kristin fell in love with the penthouse the instant she saw it, and although he wasn't crazy about it, he wanted to give her everything she wanted. Unfortunately, no matter what he provided or how much he indulged Kristin, Noah was never able to satisfy the emptiness inside her. It was thoughts like these that motivated Noah to get the hell out of the penthouse.

Noah shook his head. It was time to bury the past along with all the anger, self-recrimination, and hopelessness that engulfed him every time he thought about the life he'd shared with Kristin. Kate gave him hope for the future. Like Kate, he was going to take a leap of faith and hope he didn't fall flat on his face.

Noah parked his car in front of Dreamscape and made his way up the front steps, ready to begin the day discovering all the things that made Kate smile. He smiled and pushed open the front door. Immediately, he sensed trouble. Shakes was in his cage, but the door was open, and two teenage boys were taking turns sticking their hands in the cage, attempting to grab him before he nabbed them. Another boy had Kate cornered behind the front desk, blocking her small body with his much larger one.

"You know, you're a hot piece of ass, even though you're old enough to be my mother," the kid sneered, reaching for Kate as she cowered away from him.

Noah saw red. He stalked toward the kid and Kate.

"What the hell is going on here?" Noah bellowed, grabbing the kid taunting Kate by the back of his shirt and roughly pulling him away.

The two teenage idiots who were taunting Shakes snapped their heads toward Noah. At that moment, Shakes went in for the kill. In a move that should have been recorded for the record books, Jaws reached out and clamped his beak on the finger of one of the boys, and then the thumb of the other. Both boys cursed and howled in pain. They backed away from the cage, calling Jaws every name in the book. Shakes squawked, puffed out his feathers, and flapped his wings, appearing and sounding possessed. That's when Kate became unglued and flew across the room to Shakes, attempting to calm him with soft words and coos.

Noah quickly scanned Kate from head to toe. She

appeared physically unharmed. He left her to deal with the incensed bird while he took care of the boys. He dragged the boy who'd been harassing Kate out of the bookstore by the collar of his shirt, while the other two ran out ahead. Noah used his size and his booming voice to scare the shit out of them, he hoped. He threatened them with everything he could think of, including having them arrested and doing them bodily harm, not in that particular order. Once they were on the run, he tried to harness his runaway temper.

Noah shook with rage. He didn't want to think about what could have happened to Kate if he hadn't arrived when he did. He kicked himself for listening to her. He should have followed his gut and had the locks and security system replaced.

Noah took a few calming breaths and walked inside. He went to Kate who stood facing Shakes. Noah stood behind her and asked, "Are you okay?"

Kate continued to focus on Shakes and nodded. Noah wasn't fooled. He saw she was trembling. He closed the cage door, put his hands on her shoulders, and turned her to face him.

"Kate?"

She didn't answer him, focusing all her attention on Shakes. He touched her chin with his fingers and tilted her head so he could see her eyes. What he saw in them made him want to go after the boys and teach them a more memorable lesson. Kate was terrified. Her big, beautiful green eyes were shadowed, overflowing with fear, and her small frame shook.

"Oh, Kate, baby." Noah pulled Kate toward him. "You're safe, sweetheart. You're okay now."

Perhaps it was too much, too fast, but he couldn't help himself. Without giving it too much thought, Noah acted on instinct and enveloped her in his arms. Kate didn't resist. On the contrary, she let him hold her, and she buried her face in his chest. His arms tightened around her, and she gripped the front of his shirt.

Noah closed his eyes and breathed out. He let the sensation of having Kate in his arms wash over him.

Jesus! God! He was home.

This was where he was supposed to be, and in his arms was where Kate belonged. Never had he felt like this, not with Kristin, not with anyone. Having Kate in his arms was the most extraordinary feeling. Nothing had felt so right in his entire life. She was soft and so tiny against his much larger frame, yet she fit perfectly. He cuddled her to him and rubbed soothing circles on her back with one hand as he rested his cheek against the top of her head. He felt her heart flapping against his chest, and her fast breaths whispered against his throat.

Noah drowned in a world of sensation he never experienced before. Her silky hair brushed against his face, and when he took a deep breath, all he could smell was cinnamon and sugar—sweetness. For the rest of his days, he would associate that smell with Kate. Pure, delicious sweetness.

"Shh, now. Easy. You're okay. They're gone," he murmured, trying to still her shaking body.

When her grip on his shirt loosened and her trembling calmed, she pulled away, and he reluctantly dropped his arms.

Kate's face was flushed, and her voice shook as she stepped away from him. "Thank you. Sorry for the meltdown."

"Don't apologize. I'm glad you're okay. Is Shakes?"

Kate glanced at Shakes who continued to puff out his feathers and stood solemnly in the corner of his cage.

"He's pissed, but we're both fine. I guess they've

stepped up their game. I shouldn't have let them get to me like that. I froze. Master Lim is going to lose it when I tell him about this."

Noah raked his fingers through his hair. "Whoa. Back up a bit. Do you know those boys? Who is Master Lim?"

Noah's temper bubbled to the surface again, and he fought to control it. This wasn't the first time those boys harassed Kate? She was alone and vulnerable in the bookstore, and he hated the thought of those boys or anyone putting their hands on her, hurting her in any way. Something had to be done.

"Let's sit a minute," Kate said as she sank down on a plush leather couch in the corner of the room.

Noah followed her and sat on the couch next to her.

"Master Lim is my Taekwondo instructor. I've been studying Taekwondo and self- defense off and on for years. I can easily defend myself…when I don't freeze up, that is."

Noah shook his head in disbelief. This delicate, sweet, sexy creature studied martial arts? Jesus, she was one big contradiction.

Kate shook her head and ran a hand through her hair. "I'm an idiot. I can't believe I stood there and let them bully Shakes and me again. It's ridiculous really. They're kids, but…"

Now it was his turn to freeze. He gave Kate his complete attention. His body stiffened, and his face lost all softness.

"Again?" he asked in a low menacing tone. "They've done this before? When?"

Kate's eyes widened and her gaze flew up to meet his eyes. Her pupils widened, and she jerked away from him. Shit, he'd scared her.

Noah forcibly relaxed his posture and softened his tone. "I'm sorry. I didn't mean to scare you. I'm worried about you. Please tell me. How often have those boys bothered you?"

Kate studied him for a few seconds, and then she dropped her shoulders and slouched into the sofa.

"A couple of times. They're usually harmless, but this time they, well... They came in after Storytime. Everyone had left, and I asked them to leave so I could close up. That's when they became difficult. That boy...he cornered me and I...I lost it, I guess."

Sensing there was something more, something important she wasn't telling him, Noah probed a bit. "Why do you think you froze? There were three of them, and they're bigger than you. Was that it?"

Kate focused on her hands and shook her head. "No," she said in a small, haunted voice. "I don't think so. It's that kid...the one who had me cornered. He looks so much like..."

Noah waited for her to continue, but when she stayed silent, he gently prodded. "Who does that boy look like?"

Kate shook her head and said, "Never mind. It's not important. What is important is that Sensei is going to have my hide for this."

Noah didn't like Kate's avoidance of the topic, but she wasn't ready to talk. He understood and respected her reluctance to expose herself to someone she didn't know well. They were only beginning to get to know one another, and some truths were too painful and cut too deep to share with just anyone. Noah decided it was best to back off for now.

"Sensei sounds like an ass. Perhaps this should be our secret," he said with a smile.

Kate gave him a wry smile in return. "He's tough,

no doubt about that. He can be an ass, but I still have to tell him. Master Lim and I have a relationship based on trust and honesty. I must be honest with him, or he can't help me. He's not going to like what I tell him, but he is going to help me make sure this doesn't happen again."

Kate shook her head. "I *have* to be able to defend myself, take care of myself. I can't show weakness or vulnerability. It's a huge tactical error. I know better."

Taking a deep breath, Kate squared her shoulders then stood. "This will not happen again. I won't allow it to. I will do better."

Noah studied Kate and heard the determination and resolve in her voice. While it was good she wanted to protect herself, she was too hard on herself. Why did she say she couldn't show weakness or vulnerability? Was that only about the boys or in general? Noah was relieved to know Kate took her safety seriously and could kick ass if she needed to. But she'd frozen this time, and she'd let the boys harass her in the past. He couldn't get the image of her terror-filled eyes out of his mind.

"Kate, I think you should file a police report and have the sheriff put the fear of God in them."

Kate's gaze darted back to his, and she shook her head. "No, that's not a good idea. That would reinforce the impression I'm scared. I know what I must do in the future. If they come around again, I will show them I'm not scared of them. Anyway, I doubt they'll be back. You and Shakes left an impression on them."

"I know you're capable of taking care of yourself, but you don't have to handle this on your own. Asking for help doesn't make you weak," Noah said in frustration.

Kate stood and glared down at him. "Believe it or not, I know what I'm doing when it comes to those boys. This isn't my first rodeo."

Kate tilted her head and smiled a smile that didn't reach her eyes. "I don't want them to ruin our day. Can we please forget all about this? I'm ready to get out of here for a while. Ready to go pumpkin picking?"

Noah wasn't as convinced as she was about those boys. They may have been deterred for now, but they would be back. If she wouldn't tell the sheriff what's going on, he would. Noah never forgot a face and could describe those boys easily, especially the one who'd cornered Kate. He was going to find out everything about that kid. There was no way he was going to leave her safety to chance, no matter how confident or stubborn she was.

For now, though, Noah could tell Kate said all she was going to say on the topic. Against his better judgment, he gave in, again.

"Okay, let's go, but promise me if they come back and start making trouble, you'll call the police. And I've changed my mind about your Sensei. You should tell him what happened."

Kate nodded.

Noah stood and faced her. "Good. One more thing, let's talk about that security system. I'm going to have…"

Laying a hand on his forearm, Kate squeezed it. "Noah, stop," she said in a soft, but determined voice. "I don't want to argue with you. I'll get things taken care of on Monday. Please, can we go? I need to get out of here for a while."

Kate gave Noah a pleading smile that reduced him to a pile of mush. Why did this woman have this effect on him? He nodded then waited for her to shut off the lights in the bookstore, grab her jacket from her apartment, and feed Shakes. Noah decided his sweet Kate was too used to being alone. She clearly had trouble relying on and trusting others.

His Kate.

One minute she was Kate and the next, she curled into his arms, burrowed into him so deep he swore his heart paired itself with hers, and she was *his* Kate. She was his, and he wasn't going to stand by and let anyone hurt her. While she gathered her things, he made a quick call to Jackson, Dee's husband, who owned a security company in town. Noah would do what he needed to do now and beg her forgiveness later.

Deidra was right. Kate had a story. A burden she carried on her own, eating away at her. One day, he hoped she would trust him enough to share it with him, the good and the bad. Until then, he would help her make some new memories, memories they could share together.

Chapter Six

Noah was nothing like Kate expected him to be, and everything she dreamed he would be. She used and abused him and his poor BMW for most of the day, but he was a great sport and never complained. Noah followed her around the pumpkin patch for an hour until she found the perfect pumpkin. Okay, it was more like fifteen pumpkins, but who was counting? He used those big muscles of his to carry the various sized pumpkins she chose and to lug around bales of hay. They also built a scarecrow, or four, and carved five large pumpkins to put on the front porch.

Noah was a delicious, hot and sweaty sight by the time they were done. Kate enjoyed the show he put on as they decorated every inch of the bookstore. To his credit, he only questioned her sanity once.

"Kate, Halloween is still four weeks away. Is it possible we're doing this too early?"

Kate shook her head. "Nope. It's never too early to celebrate. I love Halloween. Actually"—she smiled and quirked her head to the side—"I love all holidays, including the not so traditionally celebrated ones, like National Donut Day. Get used to it. This is how I roll."

When Kate was a kid, she longed to decorate for and celebrate the holidays like other kids did, but her father despised all holidays and celebrations, including birthdays. He lost his mind if one penny was spent on holiday 'crap.'

Kate's mother sometimes snuck her a small birthday or Christmas present, but the risk of her father finding out was often too great. The one time he discovered a present her mother gave her was memorable. Kate was eight years old, and it was

Christmas Eve.

"Santa came for you this year, baby girl. You were especially good. See what he brought you, baby."

Her mother handed her a clumsily wrapped present. Kate was ecstatic and carefully opened the gift, making sure not to rip the pretty paper. It was a Barbie, the cheap dollar store version, but it was new, and it was hers.

Kate wrapped her small arms around her mother's neck and kissed her cheek. She knew Santa didn't exist. Her life was too real, too raw for her to believe in Santa Claus or the Easter Bunny.

"Thank you, Mama. Please, can I keep the paper? It's so pretty and shiny. I promise to hide it, and I'll be extra good from now on. You and Daddy won't see me, won't hear me. I promise."

They hid the paper between Kate's mattress and the box-spring. That night, young Kate snuck out of bed, took out the paper, and fell asleep admiring its beauty. On Christmas morning, her father found her curled in bed holding the wrapping paper and the Barbie. To say he was livid was an understatement.

He dragged Kate out of bed and to the worn, stained sofa in the living room. He told her to watch and learn what happens when he was disobeyed. Her father proceeded to teach her mother a lesson with his fists, stopping only when the poor woman hit the floor unconscious. Kate crouched in a fetal position on the couch, watching over her mother's unconscious body with tears streaming down her face. Feeling tremendous guilt, Kate spent the next two weeks helping her mother recover. That was the last holiday Kate spent with her mother.

"Well, I think that's it. I'm starving. Have I earned my dinner yet?" Noah said, walking in from the porch where he'd been tying down Mr. and Mrs. Scarecrow to their designated rockers.

Startled out of her dark memories, Kate glanced up and smiled at her starving, sexy helper who had hay stuck to his shirt, pants, and even in his hair. Lord, the man was a mess—an adorable mess in dark jeans, a long-sleeved, fitted gray t-shirt, tousled hair, and a killer smile that lit up his eyes and the room.

Kate walked to Noah and started removing pieces of hay from his clothes, giggling as she did so. "Yes, I think we're done, but are you sure you're not wearing the majority of the decorations?"

She tugged on his shirt, urging him to bend forward. "Come down to my size, will you? You've got hay in your hair. We've got to clean you up somehow before I take you out in public."

Kate ran her fingers through his hair, removing the hay and pushing his hair away from his eyes. The man had thick, luxurious hair, the kind most women dreamed of having. Noah closed his eyes and smiled as he leaned into her touch. Kate melted from the inside out. She wouldn't mind spending the entire day doing this. She smiled. Her Incredible Hulk could be tamed by simply stroking his hair. She would keep that trick in mind, in case she needed it in the future.

"Okay, all cleaned up. Where to for dinner?"

Noah gave a contented sigh. "Are you sure you got it all? Maybe you should do that again."

"Ah, no. I'm certain you're done." Kate grinned and pushed at his chest. "Now feed me."

Noah straightened and reached for his keys and wallet on the counter.

"Darn. Okay. Japanese, Italian, American, or Chinese? I think those are our choices for the evening. We'll have to make it fast, or we'll be late for the movie."

"I'm craving a burger. Is that okay with you? Ray's Monster Burgers is right next to the theater. They're sinfully good." On cue, Kate's stomach growled.

Noah chuckled, shook his head, and held out his hand. "Come on, sweetness. Let's go feed you before that thing gets any more demanding. For a little person, you sure have a loud stomach."

They took Noah's car and twenty minutes later, they were seated with Ray's famous one-pound monster burgers, fries, and sodas in front of each of them. Kate attacked her burger as though she hadn't been fed for a month. She was so focused on her food she didn't glance up until she heard Noah's stifled laughter.

"You know you can slow down. No one's going to take that away from you. I promise to buy you another if you want, although I doubt you'll be able to finish the one you have."

Kate flushed, her face matching the color of the ketchup on her chin and lips. She chewed, swallowed, and then wiped her hands and mouth. "Sorry, I'm a fast eater, especially when I'm hungry."

"Hey, I didn't mean to embarrass you. I enjoy watching you eat." Noah reached across the table and wiped Kate's chin with a napkin. "Honestly, it's refreshing to have a date who eats real food, rather than one who picks at a salad while staring at my food longingly. It's creepy to have hungry eyes follow my every bite."

Kate grinned, picked up her burger, and took another massive bite. Noah smiled and did the same. When she swallowed, she used her most serious voice, staring at her plate and said, "Well, Noah, I'm not like your other dates, and if this is going to work, there's something you should know about me."

Noah put down his half-eaten burger and grabbed

a napkin. He wiped his hands and mouth and gave her his full attention, all laughter gone from his features. "Okay, I'm listening."

Doing her best to keep a straight face, Kate met Noah's serious eyes. "I've always had a scarily massive appetite. I mean it's disturbing how much I can put away. Hell, I eat more than most grown men. I can be a pretty expensive date. So get ready because I want popcorn and Whoppers at the movies, but I'm already half-full, so I'll skip the butter this time."

Noah threw his head back and laughed. "Don't worry. I can afford your grazing habits. I'll even throw in a box of Raisinets."

By the time Noah and Kate arrived at the theater and parked in the crowded lot, they were tight on time. Kate stood in line to buy snacks, while Noah purchased their movie tickets. Kate couldn't remember the last time she'd seen a movie. She told Noah to pick any movie he wanted since she hadn't seen any of the recent releases. That, however, was a colossal mistake.

Kate sat in the dark theater next to Noah as she shoveled popcorn into her mouth. As the previews finished, she read the title of the movie and froze, and her heart sank. *Nowhere to Hide.* It was an action thriller she'd seen advertised—lots of guns, lots of violence. This was not a movie she would ever choose to sit through. Comedy and romance were more her style.

Ten minutes into the movie, the first violent scene began with shoppers in a busy mall being taken down, one by one by a sniper. Every muscle in Kate's body stiffened, and her heart crashed against her rib cage. She inhaled sharply and nearly stopped breathing. Each time the gun fired, Kate jumped. Noah must have sensed her anxiety because his hand slid over her tightly clasped hands, prying them apart. Kate trembled as Noah held one of her hands in his and ran his thumb in soothing circles in her palm.

Saliva filled Kate's mouth, and nausea stirred in her stomach as one by one, shoppers fell to the ground dead, and others screamed in agony. Although Kate couldn't stand to watch anymore, she was frozen, her attention riveted to the screen. She was unable to pull her eyes from the horror playing out in front of her. One of the victims, a young blonde woman, was shot in the head and fell to the ground dead, her sky-blue eyes staring at Kate.

Kate lost it.

Kate's mind snapped back to an earlier time, thirteen years ago to the girl's bathroom at Elmore High School. She reacted on instinct as she had years ago. Kate pulled her hand out of Noah's grasp and stood on trembling legs, toppling the tub of popcorn in her lap onto the floor.

"Are you all right?" Noah whispered, reaching for her hand.

Before he could touch her, she mumbled, "I'm fine, Noah. I'll be back," and quickly stepped into the aisle.

Kate stumbled up the partially lit aisle and out the theater doors, all the while telling herself to keep it together. In the lobby, she leaned against the wall, closed her eyes, and took deep, cleansing breaths, attempting to control her racing pulse and choppy breathing. Lord, she was a mess.

Kate opened her eyes and scanned the lobby. She needed fresh air. Once she got her shit together, she'd suck it up and go back into the theater. No way was she letting the past take over her life again. This was all those stupid boys' fault. She should've drop-kicked them when she had a chance to.

In her line of vision, she saw the door to the women's restroom. Even in her agitated state, Kate recognized that was a poor option. In the opposite direction was the exit to the parking lot. Relieved, she drew one more deep breath and let it out. Kate fled through the lobby and out to the parking lot at a fast, measured clip.

The cool night air fanned Kate's clammy skin. She leaned against the side of the theater and stared into the starry sky. She closed her eyes again and for a minute, she allowed the self-pity to bubble to the surface. Lord, why now? When was it going to end for good? She'd been free of nightmares and panic attacks for three years, and now when she had a home, a business, and even possibly a man, they were back? Life was so fucking unfair. She was getting tired of fighting the past, but fight she would.

"Kate?"

Kate jumped, straightening away from the wall and into a defensive posture. In the same instant, her eyes flew open and she immediately scanned her surroundings. When her eyes met Noah's, she let out a relieved sigh and sagged against the side of the theatre.

"Are you okay?"

The tenderness and compassion she saw in those eyes killed her. How was she ever supposed to explain her complicated mess of a life to him when she didn't even understand it all herself? This was why she didn't want to dive into a relationship. She wasn't fully healed yet. She'd come a hell of a long way, but she wasn't completely healthy yet. It was unfair to burden another with her baggage. One day she would be ready, but today wasn't the day.

Kate nodded. Suddenly, the exhaustion of the past week, the drama with the boys, and the strenuous activities of the day, hit her hard. She felt like one of those inflatable punching bags. She'd taken too many hits today, and all the air whooshed out of her. She couldn't do or say one more thing.

Noah studied her, and then reached and pulled her into his arms. Kate went willingly. She needed his soothing touch. She laid her forehead against Noah's chest, and her entire body slumped against him. His arms tightened around her. God, they felt good. He felt good. She couldn't help herself. She melted further into him and absorbed the warmth of his body. She inhaled his scent, let it surround her and relished it. Kate desperately wanted to close her eyes, forget everything, and sink into Noah's world for a little while.

Noah, however, was probably regretting the moment he met her, and she didn't blame him. This was the second time in less than eight hours that she'd unraveled in front of him. It was time to put an end to this dating experiment. She was being selfish, taking and taking, unable to give back. There was nothing she could offer Noah in return.

Kate sighed. "I'm sorry I ruined the evening. Can you take me home?"

"Hey now, you didn't ruin anything. I guess the movie was too violent?"

Kate nodded. She pulled away from his hold and turned toward the parking lot. Noah caught her hand and tugged on it. Kate stopped walking but kept her gaze downcast. She was disheartened and couldn't bear to meet his eyes. She didn't have him for long, but letting Noah and the dream of any future with him go was painful.

"Look at me, Kate," he commanded in a firm voice.

When she didn't, he said, "We'll figure this out,

okay?"

Kate nodded again.

Sighing, Noah led her toward the car. "Let's get you home."

At the car, Noah opened the passenger door and waited for Kate to slide in before closing the door. He rounded the car and the minute his car door closed, Kate laid her head against the seat and closed her eyes, fighting back tears. The entire way home, Kate's eyes remained closed, and she was lost deep in thought. She didn't realize Noah had parked the car in the circular driveway in front of Dreamscape until she heard him whisper her name and felt him lightly caress her cheek with his knuckles.

Kate turned her head away, opened her eyes, and unbuckled her seatbelt. She sat up and reached for the door handle. "Thank you for today. I'm sorry the day began and ended with drama. You've been wonderful, and I appreciate your kindness, but…"

Kate never finished the sentence. Before she knew what was happening, Noah's hand reached across the seat and grabbed her hand. He tugged her toward him as his other hand slid her hair off her shoulder, came around her neck, and pulled her gently, but steadily toward him. Before she could protest, firm lips claimed hers in a kiss that had her forgetting her name, let alone anything she had to say.

Noah's lips were warm, plump, and sensual. When the tip of his tongue traced the seam of her lips, she parted her lips in a surprised gasp. His tongue went in and explored every inch of her mouth. The kiss grew from tender and sweet, to deep and demanding in seconds.

At first, Kate had no idea what to do. She'd been kissed before, but not in a long time and never like this.

She never saw this coming. At first, her brain short-circuited, and she froze, letting him do all the work, but God he was good, and she was starved. Starved for so much the list was too long to consider.

All Kate wanted to do was to feel and to forget. She was tired of remembering and sick of thinking. She wanted to lose herself in him if only for a few minutes. She melted into him, moaned into his mouth, and kissed him back, letting her tongue dance with his. He nipped her lower lip and immediately licked the sting away as she ran her fingers through his hair and pulled him closer, deepening the kiss even more.

It had been three years since she was in a man's arms, three long years. Had kissing a man been this spine-tingling good? Since Jeff, there'd been no one, and Jeff seemed like a lifetime ago. Now all of that pent-up need and emotion came crashing down.

When Noah pulled away, they were both panting. Their faces were flushed and their lips were swollen. He laid his forehead against hers and whispered, "I was right."

Frowning, she asked, "About what?"

"I thought you'd taste as sweet as you smelled, and I was right—cinnamon and sugar. Pure sweetness."

Kate closed her eyes and attempted to gather her senses. God, he was delicious, and God, she wanted him. Every cell in her body cried out for his touch. But Noah was a dream, and he deserved someone normal, untarnished, and uncomplicated. Kate straightened.

"Noah, I…"

"Uh-uh. Not a single word. Stay there. I'm coming to get you. I have a bottle, actually an entire case of that wine you liked last week, in the trunk. We're going in and having a drink."

"I don't think that's such…"

Noah brushed her lips with his and smiled. "I know, sweetness. I know what you're thinking. Right now, thinking for you is strongly discouraged. We're going inside to have a drink and talk and maybe even kiss a time or two. Stop fidgeting and stop fighting me. You don't have to say or do anything you don't want to. I don't want to leave you alone right now. I need to know you're okay. Try to trust me. Please?"

Through the glow of the front porch light, Kate found Noah's eyes. In his eyes she saw so many possibilities, so many wishes and dreams. He'd kissed her and called her sweetness, even after she behaved like a lunatic. All day he did anything and everything to make her happy, to make her smile and laugh. It had been years since she felt as carefree as she did today, despite beginning the day being bullied by the teens.

Noah asked her to trust him and for the life of her, she couldn't deny him, despite the doubt that continued to make its presence known deep in her belly. She licked her lips, tasted the remnants of him, and nodded. Kate prayed she wasn't making a mistake.

Inside, Noah guided her to sit on one of the deep, overstuffed loveseats while he opened the wine and grabbed the glasses from the kitchen. Once he was seated next to her, he tucked her into the crook of his arm and held her close. As she sipped her wine, he said, "Okay, so today there were a few unexpected events. That was partly my fault since I totally jinxed us this morning."

Puzzled, she glanced up, taking in his amused expression and half smile. "You jinxed us?"

"Well, on my way here this morning I ran through our plans for the day and congratulated myself on planning the perfect date. But what sealed our fate was when I asked out loud, 'what could go wrong?' Those are apparently fighting words where you're concerned," he said with a small smile playing on his lips.

Kate took a deep breath and tried to pull away, but Noah's arms tightened around her.

"Nope, stay where you are. No running, sweetness. Tell me everything. Tell me nothing—whatever. But stay where you are and relax. Let me help you feel safe. Listen for a minute, okay?" He kissed the top of her head and squeezed her shoulders.

For the life of her, Kate didn't know what it was about this man that made her go soft all over—including soft in the head. Every time she was in his presence, and now in his arms, she lost the ability to have rational thoughts and conversation. She closed her eyes, sank back into the crook of his arms, and nodded.

"Good choice," he said, giving her another tender squeeze. "Kate, it doesn't take a genius to see you've had a rough life. Something in your past still has a hold on you and scares the hell out of you. I know we're getting to know each other, but I want to help if you'll let me."

Kate glanced up and frowned. "Why? Isn't one day filled with drama enough for you? Honestly, you're a nice man. A really, really nice man with a wonderful family."

Kate sat up and this time he let her.

"I told you why, and today didn't change my mind. Just the opposite. I am a patient man. I'm not going to push you into anything."

Shaking her head, Kate recalled the words her father used to tell her on almost a daily basis. *You're nothin' special, Missy. Nothin' special at all.*

Noah had said the words she'd longed to hear since she was a young girl, but she had a hard time accepting or believing them. Perhaps if he knew her whole truth, he'd think differently.

She stood, placed her empty wine glass on the

side table, and walked to the window, laying her forehead against the cool glass.

"Noah, my past is like Hurricane Katrina. It was bad right from the start, and though no one thought it could possibly get worse, it did. Even years after the storm, people are still trying to rebuild their lives, while others gave up and moved on. But even if everyone rebuilds, no one will ever forget. The damage was devastating."

Noah stayed silent, but Kate felt the waves of pity coming off him. She hated to be pitied.

"I'm not telling you this so you can feel sorry for me. I'm proud of myself and all I've overcome. I still have a way to go and I'm working on it, but part of me will always be damaged. That's a fact. The best thing I can do for you is to tell you to run."

Kate turned, and her gaze traveled to and locked with Noah's with such force, a jolt of electricity zinged between them. "Run, Noah. Run," Kate whispered.

Noah's understanding eyes never left her. He put his glass next to hers, rose, and walked to her.

"You know, I'm a grown man and can make my own decisions. You don't have to protect me. Your past doesn't scare me. We all have pasts. Hell, mine isn't lily-white. Why don't you let me be the judge of what I can handle? I swear I won't let you down."

Noah held out his hand for her to take.

Kate studied his outstretched hand, and her palm itched to take it. He offered her things that she always dreamed of, things that she desperately wanted—a future with some who thought she was special. But was it fair to burden Noah with her life and her past? If she'd been able to completely work through the past and was a normal, functioning adult, then maybe. But hell, the list of things she couldn't do was extensive.

She still couldn't sleep through the night without waking up screaming.

She couldn't enter a public restroom, especially if it smelled like disinfectant.

She couldn't watch violent shows or movies, which pretty much wiped out almost everything on TV or in the theaters these days.

She couldn't have children—not because there was anything physically wrong with her, but because she didn't want to pass on the cesspool of a gene pool she was gifted with from her poor-excuse-for-human-being parents.

And she couldn't lay all this shit on anyone, especially not on a great guy like Noah.

Kate glanced from Noah's outstretched hand to his beautiful face and said, "But I'm pretty sure I'll let you down."

Chapter Seven

Noah waited until Kate locked the door behind him before walking to his car. He'd tried his best to talk some sense into her, but it was a losing battle. She was physically and emotionally exhausted. Rather than arguing with her, he kissed her on the forehead and told her they'd talk later. She said little in return, neither agreeing nor disagreeing.

Noah sat in his car and watched the lights go off on the first floor; a few moments later the second-floor lights came on. She didn't invite him up, and he figured she had a right to her privacy. Still, he worried about her safety and her peace of mind. He hoped Kate would be able to find sleep and that the morning would bring clarity for both of them.

The drive to the penthouse seemed longer than usual, giving Noah plenty of time to think. It was almost midnight by the time he made it home, and he was no closer to figuring out what to do. Earlier in the day, when he walked into the bookstore to find the boys harassing Kate, all his protective instincts kicked in. And when Kate ran out of the theater like she was being chased by an ax murderer, he didn't even stop to think. He followed her, ready to fight any battle with her, for her. He'd never forget the expression on her face or in her eyes when he caught up with her—pain, fear, loss, and desolation. She tried to hide her emotions, but he'd seen each one of them.

The storm that had hit Kate's world shattered it. He didn't know what happened or how much she recovered from that initial devastation, but she wasn't fully healed. He should take her advice and run. Maybe another man would have, but for some inexplicable reason, he was drawn even more to her. Noah wanted to soothe, protect, and shelter her. He wanted to make her smile and take the pain out of her eyes. She was one hell of a fighter, though, and resisted him every step of the way.

Then, there was that kiss. Why the hell had he kissed her? Noah had no idea where it came from, except that it came naturally. He didn't think it through, it just happened. It was the same when he held her after the boys fled, and when he found her outside the theater. He was compelled to go to her, to wrap her in his arms, and to protect her. He couldn't help himself.

Noah was showered, dressed in boxers and in bed with a glass of brandy when he made the decision to call her. He didn't like the way the evening ended. Kate's eyes were desolate, and he couldn't sleep knowing her night would be less than peaceful.

The phone rang twice before Kate's sweet, melodic voice graced his ears.

"Noah? Is everything okay?"

Noah smiled and sighed. Relief washed over him as he heard her voice. "Hey there. I hope I didn't wake you."

"No, I'm awake. Are you okay?" Kate said in a puzzled voice.

"Yeah, sweetness. I'm fine. I wanted to check on you before I went to sleep. How are you doing?"

"You called to check on me?"

Noah heard the surprise in Kate's voice. Did she think she succeeded in scaring him off?

Noah took a long drink from his glass and in a gravelly voice said, "Sweetheart, don't sound so surprised. You had a tough day, and I wanted to make sure you were safe and sound and able to get some sleep."

Kate sighed, and when she spoke next, her voice was husky. "I'm fine. It's good of you to call, but there's no need for you to worry." She cleared her throat, and he was sure, if he could see her, she'd be sitting straighter, shoulders drawn back, head held high. "I'll be fine. I've been here before, and I'll be fine by tomorrow."

Noah shook his head and raked his fingers through his hair. This woman was so used to being on her own, protecting herself from everyone and everything, getting over the fifty-foot wall she built around herself was going to take stamina. What Kate didn't know, however, was Noah worked out daily, ate his Wheaties, and took his vitamins. He had the endurance, grit, and determination needed to scale that fortress, and he had every intention of doing so.

"Here's the thing, Kate, I know you'll get through the night and the next day and the day after that. No doubt, you're a survivor, and I couldn't be happier about that. But, baby, I'm a big boy. You've issued the warnings, and I've heard them. Consider yourself off the hook. Know that I don't scare easily, and you're not getting rid of me anytime soon."

For a few minutes, all Noah heard was Kate's even breathing.

"Okay," she whispered.

"Okay?" He repeated in shock. He couldn't believe what he was hearing. Was Kate agreeing to give them a chance without a fight? Holy shit, it felt like he'd won the lottery.

"Yeah, Noah. Okay." Now she sounded as if she was getting annoyed.

"Good, sweetheart." Noah couldn't help the grin that covered his face.

His gut told him now that they were in a good place, and she seemed to be in a relenting mood, he should come clean and tell her she would be getting a visit from Jackson in the morning, but he couldn't do it. She was going to throw a Kate-size fit—small, yet powerful, and he didn't want to break the hard-won truce they'd forged.

Noah took a deep breath. "Now that we've got that settled. How are we going to get you to relax for the night so that you can get some sleep?"

"That's not going to happen for a while, so I'm taking advantage of the situation and catching up on my baking. I'm trying a new recipe. Piñata Surprise cupcakes."

"Baking? So late? Do you do that often?"

Kate sighed. "I bake when I can't sleep. It works. By the time I'm done, I'll be too tired to think. It's the only thing that works."

Noah sucked in a breath. Kate let him in a tiny bit. It was a gift, and he would tread carefully. She had trouble sleeping, and she escaped through baking. Well, baking was better than other forms of escape; better than drugs, better than alcohol.

"Okay, sweetness. Go bake and try to get some sleep. I'll call you tomorrow."

"Goodnight, Noah."

Noah hated feeling helpless. He was a man of action. It wasn't in him to stand around doing nothing when someone he cared about was in danger or hurting. And Kate was both. He didn't know her past, and there was nothing he could do to erase it or to help her cope with it, not now anyway. But the future, he could certainly do something about.

For the life of him, Noah couldn't understand why she refused to file a police report against the teenage boys. They weren't going to give up. They'd be back. Something had to be done. He would risk her wrath.

Although it was late, Noah called Sheriff Billy Jordan. The good sheriff was a friend of the family, which was the only reason he tolerated Noah's after-midnight call. After Noah described what happened and gave him a thorough description of the boys, Jordan agreed to investigate the matter.

Noah crossed that issue off his list. He felt better after speaking with the sheriff. Still, there was Kate's past. She wasn't ready to talk, and he knew he wasn't patient enough to sit back and wait. He'd done that with Kristin, and there was no way in hell he was going to do that again. How could he help her fight her demons if he didn't know the enemy?

If this were a business matter, he'd have one of his investigators research Kate's past. As CEO of Reed Technologies Group, an enormously successful company that developed and manufactured aerospace and military technology, Noah had unlimited resources at his disposal. But Kate was not a business matter. He had a feeling if he violated her privacy in this manner, she'd never forgive him.

Noah was at a loss. His hands were tied, and he didn't like that feeling at all. He tossed and turned through the night, but with morning came blessed clarity, or so he thought.

The answer to his problem came in the form of Deidra. Although she was less than enthusiastic about him dating Kate, he thought it was her overprotective side making a showing and nothing more. He gave Dee the benefit of the doubt and put their previous conversation out of his mind. The Reeds were a tight-knit group who loved and supported one another, but Mama Dee was the one they all went to for advice.

In fact, the entire town seemed to go to Dee for advice. For fifteen years she had run the Lancaster

County Crisis Center. She officially stopped working when Emma came along, but her phone never stopped ringing, and her house was always filled with people young and old seeking her wisdom. Even the police called on her now and then for help.

Noah brewed a pot of strong coffee, and although he knew it was very early, he couldn't wait any longer. He dialed her number.

"Good very early morning to you, brother," Deidra said and yawned. "What can Deidra's sunrise counseling service do for you on this fine day?"

"Hey, Dee." Noah glanced at the bedside clock and winced. It was 6:00 AM. "Sorry for the early mayday. Want me to call back? Did I wake you?"

Dee's distinctive husky laugh filled Noah's ears and put a smile on his face.

"No need to call back. Your niece has been up for an hour, demanding breakfast. But you should know I've only had one cup of coffee, and the caffeine has yet to penetrate my brain. But I'm all ears. Tell Mama Dee your worries and I'll wipe them away."

Noah didn't need much prodding. He told Dee everything that happened the day before. If Kate and Dee weren't already friends, and if he wasn't desperate for some guidance, he wouldn't have shared the details.

"Dee, I don't know what to do, how to help her, how to get her to trust me."

Deidra took a deep breath in and let it out slowly. "Reed, are you sure this is what you want? We've talked about this before, but please consider it again. Are you sure that she's the right person for you? I don't know the depth of her problems; neither of us does."

"Dee, we've been through this already. I…"

"Noah," Dee interrupted him. "I've got three words for you—damsel in distress. Are you sure you want to travel down this road?"

Not this again!

Noah couldn't believe Dee was bringing up this nonsense again, about Kate of all people. When he was a kid, his siblings swore every girlfriend he brought home had some sob story and Noah was their knight in shining armor. The whole family referred to his attraction to needy women as a deadly affliction. Luke, Dee, and Clare found this hilarious and would rib him for hours. The hilarity, however, ended with Kristin.

Noah sighed. This was unbelievable. Deidra didn't like Kate, not for him anyway. She wasn't going to change her mind, and she wasn't going to be of any help to him. He was disappointed in her. She'd been on him for years to get back out there, find a woman, and start again. Now that he had, she was finding every excuse, including his childhood misadventures, to deter him. He didn't understand her behavior and couldn't believe she was going to be a bitch about this. Didn't she want him to be happy?

Noah understood Kristin had put them all through the wringer, but Kate wasn't Kristin, and he wasn't that man anymore. Kristin changed him forever. He'd made serious mistakes with her that ultimately cost three people their lives; Kristen and two innocent teenagers. Their deaths took a toll on him, marking him forever. He carried the weight of their loss everywhere he went. So, yeah, he'd changed, he grew, and he learned many painful lessons along the way. Dee knew all of this. She was his confidante, his strength through it all. The fact she was using his past and his failures against him, was hurtful.

"Dee, in case you haven't clued in, I'm not that kid or that man anymore. I think I've learned enough lessons. Don't you think? I don't need you or anyone else reminding me of the past. I live it every fucking day. Do you think I've suddenly developed amnesia? I'm sorry I called you. Goodbye."

"Whoa, there. Hang on, Reed. Don't you dare hang up."

Only the plea in Dee's voice stopped him from disconnecting the call and throwing his phone across the room.

"You called me, and now that I'm asking some tough questions about a woman you've only known for a few weeks, you're going to hang up and what…pout? For God's sake, Reed. This is me you're talking to. I love you, and I want to see you happy, but I have a right to worry about you. What's going on here?"

Noah stood and walked to the floor-to-ceiling windows that overlooked Central Park. He laid his forehead against the cool glass and closed his eyes. He searched for the words to explain himself to Dee. This isn't how he hoped this conversation would go. He needed her to understand him, to support him. She wasn't just his sister, she was his best friend and biggest supporter, his lifeline.

If he were honest with himself, he could see how Kate fit the role of a damsel in distress. But unlike Kristen, Kate didn't want him to take care of her and to solve all her problems. On the contrary, she was tough and capable of taking care of herself. Every time Noah let himself think of Kristin, he felt impotent once again. He remembered how helpless he was and how he was unable to stop the train of destruction and sorrow that started down the tracks early in his marriage. His relationship with Kristin became a runaway locomotive demolishing everything in its path.

With Kate in his life, history was not repeating itself. He wouldn't allow it. While he couldn't be a hundred percent sure, he would bet his entire company that unlike Kristin, Kate's problems didn't come in the form of drugs and alcohol. He didn't know Kate well, but his gut told him, she didn't have a selfish bone in her body. She would never compromise everything she had and everyone that loved her for a fix. No, Kristen and Kate were as different as the sea and the sand.

Noah walked back to the kitchen in silence and poured himself another mug of coffee. He took in a long, deep inhalation of the potent brew, hoping he could get a caffeine high from the scent until he poured enough in his system to baptize all his cells with it.

"Dee, I'm sorry I snapped at you. I know your concern comes out of love, but I know what I want." Noah took in a long, deep breath. "No one in a long, long time has made me feel as alive as Kate does. When I wake up, she's the first thing on my mind, and she haunts my dreams at night. I don't know where this will lead. I only know I want to find out. I need your trust and support, but even without it, I'm not backing away from Kate. I can't. I won't."

Dee was silent for a few minutes, but something Noah said must have touched her because she sighed and relented. "Okay, Reed. You win."

Noah smiled and breathed out in relief as the tension that built during his intense chat with Dee slipped away. "Thanks, Dee. Now help me, for the love of God."

"I know very little about Kate. She showed up in town a little over a year ago and stayed. The Kemptons kind of adopted her, and she spent most of her time in the bookstore. The place was a run down mess and sold used books. I never went in there until she bought it and transformed it into a children's bookstore. She never talks about her past or her family with me or with anyone. She's friendly, but has few friends. If I had to bet, what

Kate needs the most is to feel like she belongs. She needs friends and a sense of community support. Be her friend first. Help her feel safe and secure. When she's ready, she'll open up to you."

Noah knew Dee was right. She had an uncanny way of understanding what people needed. She'd tried to help Kristin, but was rejected over and over again.

"I'm not good at the waiting game, Dee, and I'm only one person. If she's been in Lakes Crossing for a year and still hasn't made friends, how do I get around that barrier?"

"That's where I come in, I guess," Dee said with a resigned sigh. "I'll help you on one condition. Promise me you'll take this slow. If you've healed enough and are ready for a fresh start, and I want that for you, Reed, promise me you'll keep an open mind. There are so many good, uncomplicated women out there who would be good for you. All I ask is think before you leap, and consider all your options."

Dee was at it again, trying to talk him away from Kate and into the arms of some other 'uncomplicated' woman, probably Ava, if she had anything to say about it. Noah needed Dee's help. Her posse of friends, other than Ava, were exactly what Kate needed. He chose to take the high road.

"Fine, sis. I promise to tread carefully with Kate, but that's all I can promise you. Right now, I'm not interested in any other women. One woman is keeping me busy enough."

Noah ended the call with Deidra, smiling and thanking God and his parents for creating the wonder woman that she was. That wasn't the first time he thanked God for her and his family. He was certain it wouldn't be the last. She may not be completely sold on Kate, but she was always on his side and had his back. In time, Dee's worries about Kate would float away. Kate was a gentle spirit—a beautiful butterfly on the cusp of flying away to higher ground. It was impossible to stay away from her, impossible not to like her.

His beautiful, gentle, butterfly, however, called him three hours later living up to every bias written about redheads and their temper. Jackson was at her doorstep, and she was flaming mad.

"Noah," she gritted out. "Jackson is at my doorstep insisting on installing a security system. Since I didn't order a security system, and I told you not to do so, I assumed he was at the wrong place. I've given him coffee and muffins, and he still won't go away. He says he can't leave without installing the system. Do you know anything about this?"

Noah couldn't help himself, a smile stretched across his face. Even crazy mad, she was adorable. He took in a breath and plowed ahead.

"Sweetheart, calm down. I only wanted to…"

"Uh-uh. No way. Stop right there or I swear, I'll hang up. Do not sweetheart me and do not make light of this. I'm an adult, damn it. I can make my own decisions, and you will learn to honor them, or I swear, Noah, I swear I will…"

Noah's smile faded. Shit. She was boiling mad, and he had to do some quick explaining before this got out of hand. She was blowing this all out of proportion.

"Kate, easy now. Hang on. I know I said I'd leave you to handle it, but it's difficult for me to know you need something and not provide it. Were you planning on actually fixing the lock and the system? Because you didn't sound convincing when you told me to let it be."

Silence.

When Kate spoke, it was in a frigid voice that sent shivers down his spine. "What I was or wasn't going to do is none of your business, Noah. I told you I would take care of the problem and I will, in my own way, on my own time!"

Noah knew he wasn't handling this well, but he couldn't seem to stop his mouth from spitting out the words and his temper from spiking.

"And what way was that? You're making this a bigger deal than it is. I identified a problem, and now I'm addressing it. Let go, and let me take care of you."

The second the words left his lips he wanted to swallow them back. Why the hell had he let his temper get the best of him? Now he was regretting it.

"Okay. Now you listen, Noah Reed, and you listen very carefully. Dreamscape and I are not a *problem* that needs addressing and fixing."

Noah stood and started pacing. This conversation was like a car that lost its steering and brake system. He had no idea how to control it or redirect it. It was headed, *they* were headed, for a crash and burn and he was helpless to stop it.

"I am not one of your business transactions gone awry. I can and will handle this on my own. If you want to know the truth, I can't afford to fix the system or to pay monthly for the system at this time. But I have a plan, and I don't need you to save me. My life is mine, and I solve my problems on my own. I always have and always will. If you can't respect that, and it's evident you can't, this won't work between us."

This was the root of the problem. Kate was used to being on her own, in survival mode all the time. She never had anyone to share her burdens with, and she was terrified of letting anyone in. How was he ever going to get in there? On top of that, she didn't know him well enough to realize that she was asking the impossible of him. He needed a measure of control in his life. He needed to know the people in his life were safe and well taken care of. How the hell was this going to work if she never gave an inch?

Noah took in a deep breath and let it out slowly as he regained control of his temper.

"Kate, of course you're not a problem. That's not what I meant. I'm sorry if you feel strong-armed. All I was trying to do was provide you, and me, with peace of mind and security. You're putting yourself at risk without the proper security system installed. As for the cost, there is none. Lexington Security is a subsidiary of Reed Technology Group. It costs me nothing to give this to you."

Silence once more descended and all he heard was Kate's labored breathing.

"You want to give me something I need?"

Noah sighed and raked his fingers through his hair. Finally, he was making headway. "Of course. Anything for you, sweetness."

"Good, I need space—wide-open space to breathe without feeling suffocated and controlled. You can't seem to give me that, so allow me to show you what that entails. Goodbye, Noah."

Chapter Eight

Noah was one miserable son of a bitch. For the last week, Kate refused to see or speak to him, no matter what he did. She was stubborn and hot-tempered. Why didn't he see this when they first met? Where had she been hiding that volatile temper? His kitten had claws.

He spent the week dissecting their conversation. At first, his temper flared, and he decided the ungrateful woman wasn't worth the effort and he didn't need her in his life. That lasted twenty-four hours. Then he realized, like him, she needed to have a measure of control over her life, and they needed to find a middle ground. First, though, he had to get her to talk to him again.

Noah started campaign number two, to win Kate over. He seemed to be doing that a lot. Never had he worked so hard to get a woman's attention and keep it. It was a humbling experience. Noah decided he had to approach this campaign differently than the last. Kate loved holidays and gifts, so he spent a few hours on his computer researching "silly national holidays." He was rewarded with a list he thought he could work with, but one that took some ingenuity to fulfill.

On Tuesday, National Bow Tie Day, Noah sent Kate fifty teddy bears of various sizes. Each bear wore a different bow tie and held a sign with a message.

How can you be angry at a face like this?
I can't bear the silence.
Forgive me. I'm just a big dumb bear.

Dee informed him Kate removed the signs and gave the bears away to her tiny customers. However, she kept the largest one at the front desk, the one holding the sign that read, *I'm just a big dumb bear*.

On Wednesday, National Magic Day, Noah sent a

magician to Dreamscape to put on a show for the entire day. Noah sent a note saying, *We could be magical together. Forgive me?*

The magician spent the day entertaining kids and their parents at the bookstore. He made a pair of doves appear, followed by a rabbit and a duck. Although Kate appeared entertained, she made the man take back all the animals when he left, especially the duck that fell in love with Kate and followed her around the entire day.

Thursday was National Bird Day. That day was a no-brainer. The last time Noah was at Dreamscape, he noticed Shakespeare's cage was a bit run down. This ridiculous holiday was the perfect opportunity to spoil Kate's man-eating bird. He was her baby, and Noah was convinced the way to Kate's heart was through Shakespeare. Noah had two new state-of-the-art cages, one for the bookstore and one for her apartment, tree-stands, and toys of all varieties delivered and set up. He even sent a bird vet and groomer to Dreamscape to pamper the creature.

Friday was National Make a Hat Day. That day took a bit more thinking than the others. Noah's sixty-year-old British administrative assistant came to the rescue. Every customer who came to Dreamscape, male or female, young or old, was gifted with a hat. While most of the kids, and some adults, took part in decorating their hat with feathers, flowers, or glitter directly outside the bookstore, others chose one from the endless racks of hats Noah had delivered. Word got out, and Kate was flooded with customers, each wearing a lovely British-style hat.

Saturday was Take Your Pants for a Walk Day. Noah could be creative, but this holiday was ludicrous. Instead, he substituted another holiday from the endless list of National Holidays and decided it would be

National Kiss and Make-Up Day. He contacted the Hershey Store in Times Square, and a one-pound chocolate kiss was delivered to Dreamscape with a special note sticking from the top reading, *Forgive me and kiss me. I'm yours.*

The massive chocolate smooch was accompanied by twenty-five pounds of small Hershey's kisses. Each chocolate kiss had the message—*Forgive Noah*—and was distributed to every person who walked in the store. Customers were asked to unwrap the chocolate and give the note to Kate.

By Sunday morning, Noah still hadn't heard from Kate. He called Dee once more, begging for help. This time, Dee did not let him down. An hour later, he received a group text from Dee that read, "It's on." Everyone included in the group text message knew what the message meant.

Sunday lunner was on.

Dee's Sunday lunners were legendary. They didn't happen every Sunday, but when they did, no one who had the distinct privilege of being invited refused the invitation. Basically, Dee would wake up on any given Sunday, and if all the stars aligned, she would text family and friends, "It's on."

Like hungry hyenas, people would converge at Dee's house at 1:00 PM sharp, bringing whatever struck their fancy. Feasting began at 1:45 and went on for hours, eventually leading to dinner time. She used the term "lunner" to describe this odd feeding pattern that spanned the time between lunch and dinner. Everyone who came was considered family, and although she'd invited Kate before without much success, this time Kate agreed to come.

It was a perfect fall day, warm and sunny. The great transformation had taken place. New Jersey's lush green landscape was replaced with the vibrant hues of fall. Copper, crimson, and orange adorned the trees. Dee always set up lunner in her backyard so everyone could enjoy nature at its finest. Today would be no different. Soon the trees would be naked, and everyone's good mood would be replaced with whining and complaining as the bitter cold of winter swept across the state. Every second of fall had to be relished.

As guests arrived, they would set their contributions on picnic tables, and when given permission to feast, they'd pounce on the food and drink, devouring everything along their path. After bellies were filled, some would gather around the fire pit chatting, while others passed out in cozy deck loungers in food comas. Kids would run around playing tag, climbing trees, and having a great time, while the football addicts made their way to the den to watch the game. It was quality family time that everyone cherished.

When Kristin came into his life, Noah stopped attending lunners with any regularity. When he did attend, he rarely stayed for more than a few hours. Still, he remembered the perfection and beauty of those afternoons. Kristin didn't enjoy family gatherings and whined incessantly each time a family event came up.

"God, not another lunner. Noah, why do we have to go? We saw everyone two weeks ago, and you're always on the phone with one of them. When is it my turn?"

At first, Noah thought Kristin's aversion to family was because she didn't grow up in a big family and didn't have siblings, but that wasn't it. Kristin was a selfish child who never grew up. Her problem with family could be summed up in one simple word—jealousy. She was jealous of everyone and everything that took Noah's attention off her, even if it was for a millisecond.

Kristin acted out, picked fights, and got drunk at almost every family event. Due to Kristin's embarrassing behavior, Noah spent less and less time with family. Where there used to be love, distance grew. Dee brought him back into the fold after Kristin's death. Right now, family and friendship were what he and Kate needed.

Noah heard lunner in full swing as he got out of his car and made his way around the house to Dee's backyard. His arms were full of fresh Italian baked bread, olive oil, cheeses, and a couple of bottles of Kate's wine. He wondered if Kate had arrived yet, and if so, he hoped she wasn't overwhelmed. This group was friendly, and they embraced newcomers, but they could also be a bit intrusive to the innocent.

Noah added his contributions to the already loaded tables and scanned the crowd for Kate. In a long cranberry cardigan sweater and slim-fitting dark jeans, Kate stood among Dee's posse with her cinnamon hair framing her face and falling in waves around her shoulders and down her back. She threw her head back and laughed. Noah froze in his tracks, enchanted by the sight of her. The sound of her musical laughter floated through the trees and carried in the breeze until it hit his ears. Lord, she was gorgeous, so damn sweet, and he was magnetically drawn to her.

He watched as she stood chatting and laughing with Dee's posse—Aimee, Jules, Lexi, and his baby sister, Clare. He'd met the women in Dee's life at various functions and liked them. Dee thought the world of them and they were a tight bunch, each with their own story and each ferociously loyal to one another. They were what Kate needed. These ladies would be a great support system and would expand her world beyond the bookstore. Noah indulged in a mental fist pump.

Jules' toddler, Lilly, pulled on Kate's cardigan,

and her whole face lit up as she picked the child up and showered her with kisses. Then he saw her face transform again as Jules' husband, Ethan, pounced on his wife, gathered her in his arms, bent her back dramatically, and kissed her without a care to who was watching. Noah's chest tightened, and he inhaled sharply at the exquisite expression of need and envy written all over Kate's face.

Noah couldn't wait anymore. He walked toward Kate in long, sure strides. As if sensing his presence, she glanced his way and caught his burning gaze. Her face flushed, and her green eyes widened in surprise as her lips formed the word, "oh." Noah's face split into a wide grin. Kate was adorable in her flustered, surprised state. He saw the panic set in as her gaze darted around the backyard searching for an escape. It appeared she wanted to make a run for it.

Noah was at Kate's side before she had a chance to move. He shook hands with Ethan and said hello to the other women as he slid a possessive arm around Kate's waist and pulled her to his side. She stiffened and tried to pull away, but he chose to ignore her resistance and tightened his arm around her. He dropped a kiss on the top of her head as the breeze rifled through her hair, filling the air with her sweet scent.

Noah didn't care who was watching. In fact, he wanted everyone to know she was his. The sooner that happened, the better. He turned his body into hers, giving her his complete attention.

"Hi there, sweetness," he said in a low voice, pressing a quick kiss to her lips. "It's time to forgive me. I'm sorry. Okay?"

Kate's breath caught. She slid her tongue over her lower lip and took her lip between her teeth. Noah used his thumb to pull her lip away from her teeth and kissed her once more.

"Sweetheart, don't damage that lip. I'm going to need it for later." Noah smiled into her beautiful eyes.

For a few seconds, they stood lost in each other's eyes, sharing a conversation that no one could hear but them. Finally, Kate reached between them and rested her hand on his chest and her lips curved into a faint smile. She nodded.

"Okay. Anything to stop your antics. Seriously, Noah, no more sweets, bears, hats, or animals. I'm running out of room. But what are you doing here? I thought you couldn't make it."

Noah shrugged. "Hmm, is that what Dee told you?" He feigned innocence. "I don't come as often as I should, but today somehow I felt I'd be missing out on something special if I didn't make it."

Kate dropped her head as color rose and hit her cheeks. Noah felt her body relax in his arms, and he wanted to pull her even closer and give her a proper kiss, but they had an audience. He could feel all of their eyes on them. He and Kate were entertaining the group.

"Come on, sweetness. Let's get some food."

Noah dropped his arms and took Kate's hand. As they turned toward the picnic tables, he came to a dead stop. Dee appeared with Ava Cunningham beside her. What the hell was his sister up to? Ava rarely attended lunner. To her, lunner was bohemian, and she often said it wasn't her scene. She was more of the charity ball, five-star restaurant sort, not the eating off paper plates on picnic tables kind of girl. So, what the hell was she doing here?

"Hey, everyone," Dee said with a big, cat–that-ate-the-canary smile. "Most of you know Ava. This is her first lunner in years, so behave yourselves and leave some food for her so she'll want to come again."

Ava was a tall, willowy blonde dressed in a plum-colored wrap-around dress that hugged her bony body. She resembled a runway model and was completely out of place in Dee's backyard.

Turning to Noah, Dee's smile widened. "Reed, you know Ava, of course. Be hospitable and guide her through the grab-and-go process, will you? I've got to go set up the dessert table."

Dee took off before Noah or anyone else could get a word in. After introductions were made, Ava turned her attention to Noah, gifting him with a seductive smile.

"It's nice to see you again, Reed," she said in a breathy voice that Noah was sure some men found sexy, but it grated on his nerves. "I haven't had a chance to thank you for our lovely date. I had a wonderful time. Will you be attending the Boys and Girls Club Charity Ball at the MoMA next week? It's my turn to ask you out."

Noah felt Kate stiffen, and his blood began to boil at his sister's antics.

"Excuse me. I'll let you two catch up," Kate said with a forced smile as she stepped away from his side and pulled her hand out of his. "It's a pleasure to meet you, Ava."

Noah reached for Kate's hand again. "Kate, wait."

Without acknowledging him, Kate turned. "I'm starving. I'm going to get something to eat. I'll see you later."

Kate walked away, head held high. But she wasn't fooling him, she was hurt. He heard it in the tremble of her voice and saw it in the slight sag of her shoulders. Damn Dee and her interference. He had enough trouble getting Kate to trust him. He didn't need another obstacle.

Noah was pissed. A few minutes later, he extricated himself from Ava and made it clear that he wasn't interested in furthering their relationship. He scanned the yard and located Kate sitting on an Adirondack chair, far from the crowd, eyes closed, with her face turned up to the sun. She was stunning and seemed peaceful with her hair falling in a thick curtain around her. He grabbed a couple of plates and walked to her side, kneeling beside her.

"Kate," he said, brushing her cheek with his knuckles.

Kate's eyes flew open.

"Easy, sweetness. I didn't mean to startle you." He kissed the tip of her nose.

He handed her the plates. "Come on, time to eat. Make us a couple of plates while I get us some wine. I'll eat whatever you put on that plate except deviled eggs. They freak me out."

"Where's Ava?" Kate sat up, surveying the yard.

"Ava can fend for herself, but I can't. Please feed me. Come on, I haven't eaten all day, and I'm feeling weak. Have pity on me, woman."

Despite the confusion and distrust clouding her eyes, Noah saw a small smile begin to form on her lips.

"All right, but don't skimp on the wine," she muttered.

Noah managed to snag a blanket and found them a spot under a big tree in the corner of the backyard. Once they were settled and enjoying the delicious food and wine, Noah thought it was time to deal with the elephant in the backyard. He didn't want them to spend the rest of the afternoon tiptoeing around one another. Poor Kate was tightly wound as she sat stiffly, concentrating on her plate and picking at her food.

"Kate?"

"Mmh?"

"What's going on in that lovely head of yours?"

Kate stopped pushing the food around her plate and glanced up. "I think I should go. It was nice of Dee to include me, but I don't belong here. I don't know what we're doing, you and I."

Noah put his plate down and picked up her hand, massaging the back of it with his thumb. "I'm glad you're here. You belong here as much as anyone does. Are you still angry with me?"

Kate shook her head and pulled her hand away. "No. It's not just that. You and I don't work, no matter how hard we try. We both want and need different things. We come from different backgrounds, and I'm a mess. Obviously, you and Ava have a thing, and I have no right to intrude on that. Besides, I think she's more in your league." Kate raked a hand through her hair. "Like I said, it was nice of Dee to include me today, but…"

Noah reached up and cupped Kate's cheek with his hand. "Okay, listen to me. Let's break this down and clear the air. I think we want the same things. We have to learn about each other and make compromises. That's not any different than any other couple. As far as coming from different backgrounds, does it matter where we come from as long as we know where we're going, and we travel there together?"

Kate's eyes softened, and she sighed. "Oh, Noah, that's sweet, but…"

Noah's hand snaked into Kate's hair to her nape, and he applied pressure, bringing their foreheads together. "I'm not done yet, sweetness," he said cutting her off and kissing the tip of her nose.

"I'm sorry about the security system, but honestly, I can't help wanting to protect you. I can't lie and tell you I won't do it again because I need to know you're safe. And finally, I went out with Ava on one date. That's it, and that's all it will ever be. One date."

"That's it?" she asked, her eyes shining.

Bringing her hand to his lips, Noah placed a light kiss on the back of it and smiled at her. "That's it. Now eat because you're going to need your energy for what's coming after lunch."

Kate searched his face, seeming to consider his words. Then she gave him a soft smile that made his heart skip a beat. "Okay, Noah, but understand one thing." Kate paused and licked her lips. "I've had my will taken from me in the past. I won't allow it again. You have to respect my decisions. I have to be in control of my life. Please try to understand." Kate's eyes pleaded with him.

Noah studied Kate. He understood, and he didn't. There was so much he wanted to ask her, so much he needed to know, but he was determined to tread carefully and at her speed.

Noah smiled and nodded.

While they ate lunch, Noah told Kate about the Easton Estate. He wanted Kate to see it. Her opinion mattered to him, and he hoped she loved it as much as he did. He called the realtor, and she agreed to meet them at the house whenever he was ready for another viewing.

After they finished eating, Noah and Kate strolled hand-in-hand around the lake, enjoying the beauty of the fall foliage reflecting off the glassy surface of the lake. People were out in droves enjoying the unseasonably warm day. Couples strolled and chatted while others walked their dogs or rode bikes with their kids. This was a family community with five beaches built around the lake. Each beach had a designation—one for families and children, adults only, fishing, and sand volleyball and competitive swimming with sectioned lanes. One beach had a wooden dock that extended into the water toward the center of the lake. Along the dock, there were racks lined with brightly colored canoes and kayaks. It was like living at summer camp, permanently.

"It's beautiful here," Kate whispered.

"It sure is. I grew up here, in the house Dee lives in. I always wanted a place of my own right here on this lake." Noah stopped walking, and Kate followed suit. He met her eyes and said, "It's the perfect place to raise a family. Here kids can run free and grow up breathing clean air. To me, it's as close to paradise as there is."

They continued walking hand-in-hand, and Noah led Kate up a steep, private circular path. The Easton Estate sat at the top of the mountainous property overlooking the lake on five fenced-in acres. By the time they made it to the top, Kate and Noah were breathing heavily. The expansive two-story, four-car garage house had a log cabin appearance that blended with the heavily wooded property. There was a deck facing the front of the house and a much larger one at the back of the house, off the kitchen. The property had an in-ground pool and tennis courts.

The realtor met them at the front door, unlocked the house, and told them to take their time exploring. Noah took Kate on a tour of the house and told her its story. The house was custom designed and furnished for one of New York's top Italian chefs and wine connoisseurs who retired and moved his family to Tuscany. The family used the estate as a weekend getaway and was selling it fully furnished.

Kate was captivated as she followed Noah around taking it all in. Hardwood cherry floors, high-beamed cathedral ceilings, a stone fireplace, and an open dining space and deck made for great entertaining space. The kitchen was gourmet all the way, with top-of-the-line commercial-quality appliances and beautiful marble counters. The master bedroom was as big as a soccer field and had its own private deck that jetted out into the forest. There was an en-suite master bathroom covered in the same marble matching the kitchen and included a custom-designed Jacuzzi tub and stall shower.

Noah and Kate toured the other six bedrooms, children's playroom, family room, living room, and formal dining room. As Noah spoke with the realtor, Kate wandered from room to room. A few minutes later, he found her standing in the kitchen, admiring the expansive back deck with a whimsical smile on her face, sighing every once in a while.

Standing behind her, Noah touched her shoulder. "Kate? Are you still with me?"

She turned her head and smiled. "Sorry, I was lost in all of this. This place is amazing. What a treasure!"

"That's what I thought. I'm glad you like it. Do you want to sit on the back deck for a while? The realtor will close up the place, and when we're ready, we can leave from the back."

Smiling, she nodded and went out to the deck. They sat side-by-side on the loungers.

"We can stay as long as we want. I've got good news. My offer was accepted. The place is mine. Well, it will be soon."

Kate gifted him with a mega-watt smile that lit up her face.

"That's fantastic, Noah. Does Dee know you're going to be neighbors? Does Emma?"

"No, it's a well-kept secret. I wasn't sure how fast I would find a place. All the properties I've inspected, up to this point, have been disappointing. The second I saw this place, I knew it was perfect and put an offer on it. Once I make up my mind on something, I'm pretty persistent," he said as his eyes locked with hers.

"I've noticed that," she murmured as a small smile played on her lips. "But why do you want to move?

Emma tells me you have a beautiful place. Aren't you happy in the City?"

Noah shrugged. "I love the City, but it's time I made a change. It's time I put the past behind me."

Noah took a deep breath and focused on the trees in the distance. It was time to share some of himself with Kate. He couldn't expect her to open up to him if he wasn't willing to do the same. This was a lot harder than he thought it would be. Resurrecting the past, resurrecting Kristin, was going to cut deep.

In his past relationships, he didn't talk about Kristin. Those were temporary interactions, not worth dredging up the past and painful memories. But Kate was different. Kate was worth it. Wasn't she?

Noah's chest ached. He searched Kate's beautiful eyes that were the same color as the forest that surrounded them. He knew the answer. He'd known since the first time he laid eyes on her. Kristin was his past, but Kate was his future.

Chapter Nine

Kate met Noah's eyes, and she recognized the pain she saw in them. She reached for his hand and squeezed. "We don't have to talk about this if it's going to bring back bad memories."

Taking her hand in his and gazing into her eyes, Noah took a deep breath. "I rarely discuss my past with anyone. It's not a place I like to travel to often. I've tried to put it behind me, and for the most part, I've been successful. I think parts of it will always haunt me. You probably know I was married, and my wife passed away. Right?"

Kate nodded.

"I bought the penthouse in the City right before Kristin and I got married. She fell in love with it and, at the time, I thought we would live there forever and raise our children there. Man plans, God laughs. Right?" Noah's harsh laugh rang out in the silent forest.

Kate's smile faded as understanding dimmed her eyes. She got it. She understood what he was feeling.

"I'm sorry, Noah. You must have loved your wife very much. I understand being haunted by the past."

"I loved Kristin, but sometimes love isn't enough to save someone. It's been five years since she died, but sometimes the memories are so vivid, it seems like it was yesterday."

Noah pulled his hand away from hers, stood, and went to the railing of the deck. He gripped the wood with such force Kate heard the wooden railing squeak in protest. Noah let go of the railing and rubbed the back of his neck. Lost in his own reflection, Noah startled when Kate wrapped her delicate arms around his waist and squeezed.

"You know how you said I could tell you anything? I could trust you, and you wouldn't judge me or let me down?"

Noah nodded.

Squeezing him again, Kate said in a soft voice, "I'm here, Noah. You can trust me. With me, you are safe. I won't judge you, and I'll do my very best never to let you down."

Noah breathed in. He took her hands in his and brought his lips to them. The gesture was so tender it brought tears to Kate's eyes.

Just a few days ago Kate had warned Noah off, not confident she should get involved with anyone. She was getting her life together, and she wasn't sure there was room in it for another. But as she stood with Noah in her arms, her world and her heart expanded to let him in. This amazing man had heard all her warnings but refused to walk away. Now he stood open and vulnerable, showing her he too had demons. Noah needed to know that he could trust her, that with her, he was safe. She wouldn't let him down.

Kate took a deep breath and closed her eyes as she rested her cheek against his solid back. Her arms tightened around her big bear of a man. This is what she could give him back. This is what she could share with him. She knew what it felt like to be tortured by the past. She was stronger than ever. She wasn't a cowering little girl who hid from her father in corners trying not to be seen or heard. She wasn't a young woman running for her life or hiding from her past. She could be strong for him, support him, and comfort him.

Kate felt Noah's chest expand and contract on a deep sigh. They stood for several minutes in silence, listening to the sound of the leaves falling from the trees as a breeze blew. Kate shivered against Noah's back and pressed herself closer to his heat. The sun had gone down, taking the temperature with it. Noah turned to face her and gathered her in his arms. He dropped a soft kiss on her lips and a second one on the tip of her nose.

"Thanks, sweetheart. Are you sure you want to hear this? It isn't a pretty story with a happy ending."

Kate glanced up and met his soft brown eyes. "If you want to tell it, I want to hear it."

"Okay, but let's walk and talk. It's getting chilly out here, and soon it'll be dark. This is a nature preserve area, so there are no street lights. Black bear, deer, and fox claim this area as their home and consider humans interlopers. You look pretty tasty, and I wouldn't want you to be a critter's dinner."

Kate laughed and took the hand he offered as they walked down the deck stairs and to the path leading to the main road.

"When I married Kristin I didn't know she struggled with drugs and alcohol. She had a tough childhood. Her mother was a single parent, a waitress. They barely survived paycheck to paycheck."

Noah rubbed the back of his neck and winced. He sighed and continued. "We met at a restaurant in the City. She was the hostess, and we instantly connected. It was a whirlwind romance, and we eloped in Vegas three months later."

Kate stiffened, stopped walking, and studied their joined hands. She knew it was unreasonable to feel jealous of a dead woman, but she couldn't help herself. For Noah, there had been another, someone he loved enough to elope with. Kate didn't know him then, and even now she had little claim on him. Still, she couldn't help feeling a tiny twinge of the green-eyed monster.

There had never been another man for Kate, not really. She and Jeff dated for two years, but she never gave herself to him. Jeff never knew the real Kate Willowbrook, he just thought he did. He spent two years in a one-sided relationship never knowing Kate's real name. He knew her as Meghan Summerville, a person Kate made up after she fled Chicago. Jeff didn't know the woman he held, kissed, and made love to didn't exist beyond the small town of Canton, Texas, not until the day she broke down and told him about herself. Then he'd reacted as she feared he would.

Noah squeezed Kate's hand, and she raised her head. He raised her hand to his lips and kissed it. "We don't have to talk about this, Kate. Not if it's going to bother you."

Kate shook her head. She was an idiot. Kristin was part of Noah's past, as Jeff was in hers. "No, no. I'm good. Please continue. How old was she when you married?" Kate asked quietly.

Noah shook his head ruefully with a sad smile. "She was barely twenty-three. Thinking back at it now, I can see all the mistakes I made. She was too young and too troubled to be in any relationship, let alone married."

"The alcohol and drugs?"

"That was only a part of it."

Noah cleared his throat, and they resumed walking. "Kristin had a hunger that was impossible to fill. No matter how much attention I paid her or what I provided, it was never enough. There was a deep hole in her, and I wasn't enough to fill it."

Noah rubbed his forehead and continued in a defeated voice. "I thought if I loved her, and gave her everything she dreamed of, things would be okay."

"How long were you married?"

Noah sighed. "That depends on how you define marriage. Our first year of marriage was fantastic, but things went to hell after that."

They'd reached one of the beaches that were built around the lake, and as they stood on the dock watching the sunset, Noah pulled Kate into his arms, her back to his front. Kate knew he was leading up to a difficult part in the story because his voice was flat, almost dead, and her heart ached for him.

"We were married for three years before I saw she was in trouble. She was using long before that. I couldn't see it; or rather, didn't want to admit it. Anyway, the following two years were hell. I tried to get her the help she needed, and she fought me every step of the way."

Noah was silent for a few minutes. Kate felt the tension in his body, and she wished she could do something to ease his pain. She held onto his arms that were around her waist and waited for him to find his voice once more.

"A week after our fifth wedding anniversary, I was in London when I received the call." Noah's voice was husky. "She was involved in a head-on collision and was killed on impact. The autopsy report showed she was intoxicated and was using cocaine."

Kate turned in his arms, reached up, and placed her palm against his cheek. The pain in his eyes shredded her. She felt completely inept at comforting him. It was obvious he had loved Kristin, despite the hell she put him through. He was an extraordinary man. Kate wondered if Kristin had known how privileged she was to have had the love of this man.

"I'm so sorry, Noah, so very sorry. I'm sure you did everything you could to help her."

Noah closed his eyes and rested his forehead against hers. "No, I failed her," he said in a resigned voice. "I was too busy with work. I was blind to her wants and needs. I should have listened to everyone who told me she was in trouble. I shouldn't have given in to her so often. I shouldn't have believed all of her lies. I should have done something to stop the destructive path she was on."

Kate heard the self-recrimination in Noah's voice and could relate. This beautiful man, with a huge heart, lived with the crippling weight of guilt for the last five years, not unlike the weight she bore. If only there was something she could say or do to lessen his burden. Kate stood on her tiptoes and kissed the underside of his jaw, and then brushed his lips with hers. Laying her cheek against his chest, she wrapped her arms around him and sighed.

"I am sorry. I know I wasn't there and don't know everything that happened. I do know that sometimes, no matter what we want for someone else, no matter how much we try to help them, unless they want help, there's nothing we can do to save them. It sounds like you did everything you could. It's not your failure. It's a tragedy that's all too common."

Noah touched her cheek with the back of his hand. "Sounds like you are speaking from experience. Were you in a similar relationship?"

Taking a deep breath, Kate rested her forehead against his chest. It was time. He opened the door, and it was time for her to share a little piece of her life with him. It was time to take a tiny step forward. She took another deep breath in and willed her body to stop trembling.

"No. I've never been married. I…" Kate's voice wobbled, and her mouth felt dry. She licked her lips and tried again. "I…my parents, we, they…"

Noah placed two fingers under her chin, urging her head up. "Look at me, Katie."

Kate's eyes widened, and her heart skipped a beat.

Katie.

No one had called her Katie since she was a little girl and then it had only been her beloved Nana, her mother's mother. Kate's family moved from Kentucky to Chicago when Kate was five, and she never saw her Nana again. That nickname and the other endearments Noah called her never failed to warm her all over.

Noah held her and looked at her as though she was the most important person in his universe. Kate felt something she never felt before. She felt cherished. If she were brave enough to share a bit of herself with him, he'd keep that part of her safe. Kate peered up to see him smiling at her, the pain that was in his eyes all but washed away.

"Talking about the past is never easy. I rarely talk about Kristin. But, I trust you, and it's not fair to expect you to share your story with me if I'm not willing to do the same. In a strange way, it feels good to talk to you about it, liberating in a way."

Noah was right. Kate resolved to open her mouth and crack open the door to her heart. But she was terrified. She'd done this with Jeff. She found her voice, trusted him, and let him in. She told him some, not all, of her story in hopes he would understand her better. She was so very wrong. He rejected her in every way possible and what they had, shattered. Kate trembled again. Noah just entered her life, but if he rejected her, the pain would be devastating.

"Kate, stay with me." Noah rubbed her back. "I'm not pushing you to tell me anything. Not now. Not until you're ready. I didn't tell you about my life to force you to tell me yours."

Noah dropped his forehead to rest against the top of her head. "It felt right telling you. It's never felt right with anyone before. Your past is your story. You tell it anyway, anyhow, anytime you want."

Noah raised his head, kissed her forehead, and rested his chin on the top of her head. "Okay? Breathe. You're safe. I swear to God, Katie, in my hands you will always be safe."

Kate didn't know what to say, so she said the first thing that popped into her head. "I'm scared," she whispered. "I'm scared I'll never be able to put the past completely behind me. I've had to do some things that I'm not terribly proud of to survive. My life now is good, it's simple. But my past is hard to stomach. You don't know me at all, and if I tell you, you won't want to know me."

Kate turned her face away from him. She refused to cry in front of him. She learned long ago crying was a useless waste of energy.

"You and your family, this town, are the closest things to a good and happy life, a beautiful life, I've ever known. My whole life I've dreamed of having this. I want to enjoy every second of it because sometimes happy doesn't last forever. The second you know all of me, you'll see me differently. You may decide it's all too sordid, too much."

Kate reached up and fisted her hands in his shirt. "In some ways, I want you to know everything now, because if you walk away from me now, it'll hurt." She met his eyes. "But I won't lie. If you walk away later, Noah Reed, once you have my heart in your hands…if you walk away later, it'll devastate me. I won't survive."

Noah tightened his arms around her and spoke in a soothing voice.

"Oh, Katie, sweetheart. We all have a past we wish didn't exist, but that's why it's called a past. It's not the present. Whatever happened, happened. I too wish I could have a do-over, but there's no such thing. I know you have no reason to trust me, but I swear I won't judge you. I don't know what's in our future, but what I can say is, I won't hold your past against you. I will do my very best never to hurt you. I'm not that man."

Kate heard and weighed every word that came out of Noah's mouth. She recalled every interaction they had since the beginning and every detail of the time they spent together. If there was someone in this world she was going to take a chance with, someone she would trust with her past and her heart, it was going to be Noah.

"I know you're scared. I can feel your body trembling. You have nothing to fear from me, not now, not ever. If you let me in, I promise to catch you."

The understanding and support Kate saw in Noah's eyes did her in. She studied him for a long moment, luxuriating in the warmth of his powerful body surrounding her and his delicious masculine scent. She made a decision, one she hoped she wouldn't regret. She would share with Noah the one secret, her biggest regret. She would tell him the one thing he deserved to know before their relationship went any further.

If Noah was going to push her away, judge her, and view at her with disgust, then so be it. Kate knew what it felt like for someone to say they loved her and would never hurt her, and then discard her the second she laid her heart in their hands. If Noah was going to turn out to be less than she hoped and dreamed he was, it was best she experienced that loss now.

Kate took in a deep breath and let it out. "I was eighteen when I was forced to leave home without warning or planning. I had nothing," Kate said in a hollow voice as her big green eyes searched his. "No family or friends to help me. No money, no skills to get a job. No way to feed myself, except one."

Kate paused, her gaze never leaving Noah's.

"I was in a strange city, homeless, cold, and starving. I'd run out of funds, and no one would give me a job. I couldn't go to a shelter, couldn't show my face. I had to be nameless and faceless. But that's a story for another time."

Kate licked her lips.

"Three days. I hadn't eaten anything in three days. I-I was so weak, so cold, so damn tired. I didn't care anymore—about anything. It… It was…"

Kate's voice broke. She stopped, took a stuttering breath, swallowed, and willed the tears back. Noah's arms tightened around her, and a muscle twitched in his tight jaw. Then he snaked a hand through her hair, pushing it back from her face. He cupped her cheek and rubbed his thumb over her cheek.

"Shh, sweetheart. It's okay."

Noah's eyes were soft, liquid milk chocolate, filled with compassion. God, his eyes were her undoing. She took another breath and pulled away from him, taking a step back. She turned and stared out into the water, wrapping her arms around herself.

In a hollow tone, she pushed the words out in short, clipped sentences. "I didn't have any other options. He took me to a filthy motel room. He pushed me face down on the bed. I… I couldn't breathe. He was rough. I was terrified. I begged him to stop, but it was too late. It hurt. It was my first time. I was a virgin. I cried the entire time. It didn't help."

Before the last word was out of her mouth, Noah's hands grasped her upper arms, turned her, and engulfed her in his arms.

"Jesus. Jesus. God. It's okay, sweetheart. It's okay, baby. I'm here. I'm sorry."

The agony in Noah's voice, as he repeated the words to her and rocked her as no one ever had, broke her. Years of pent-up emotion burst free, and Kate cried. She cried for her innocence and for the pain and shame she'd carried for thirteen years. She cried for the girl who never had anyone fight for and protect her. She cried for the girl who never had a chance at beauty, not until now.

One of Noah's arms banded around her waist, while the other held her head to his chest. He held her and swayed side to side with her. She heard his harsh breathing and the rapid beating of his heart, and she held on and sobbed into his chest, letting him comfort her.

Minutes passed, and Noah never loosened his hold. Every once in a while, he squeezed her tighter, rubbed her back, or kissed the top of her head. In time, Kate sunk into Noah's body, relishing the feel of his toned, muscular chest that she was becoming addicted to. He never pushed her away and never raised his head to glare at her with disgust, as Jeff had when she shared this with him.

After several minutes, their breathing and heartbeats slowed to a normal pace, and fell in time with one another. Noah pulled her away and studied her.

"Thank you," he whispered as he wiped the last few tears from under her eyes.

Kate forced herself to glance up and meet his eyes, embarrassment sinking in. She furrowed her brow and cleared her throat. "For what?"

"For trusting me. This changes nothing between us. It doesn't change the way I feel about you in the least bit, except I think you may be one of the bravest people I know. You did what you had to do to survive. No one can fault you for that."

Kate was speechless. He thought she was brave? She'd been young, stupid, and incredibly lucky not to have been killed on the street, but brave? Kate shook her head and frowned in confusion. Maybe he was romanticizing the whole thing. Maybe he thought she'd told him her entire past. It couldn't be that easy, could it?

"Noah, that's only part of my story. It's not the whole thing, just a chapter of a horror novel."

Noah smiled.

"I'm sure there's more. We all have more. But for right now, you need to decide. I'm not running, Kate. But I can't do this alone. You've got to want this too. Let me in, sweetheart. Let me try to be a real part of your life. Can you do that?"

Kate didn't hesitate, how could she? This amazing man had done the unexpected. He listened and comforted her, and he declared her worthy, something she hadn't believed herself. Kate met Noah's eyes and nodded. This was the first time in her life she was willing to fight for her happiness. She was willing to dredge up the past, to deal with it head on, and to rid herself of the demons she carried with her, since the day she was born.

It was time for her to learn how to breathe free and easy. It was time to make her dreams a reality.

A smile spread across Kate's features as she held Noah's eyes. "Yes, I want this. I want to try. There's still much you don't know. So much I have to work through. I swear, Noah, I'll give it all to you one day. Be patient with me. The last time I opened myself up to a man, I regretted it the instant the words left my mouth. You're different. I know that now. Don't give up on me. Okay?"

Noah's smile turned into a huge grin that lit his eyes.

"Baby, I'm not going anywhere, no matter what you tell me. But, I'm not the only one who's going to need some patience. You're going to have to have some staying power too."

Chapter Ten

Staying power. This was a new trick Kate would have to learn. She stretched, stood on her tiptoes, and touched her lips to Noah's in a feather-light kiss. What started out as soft and gentle soon changed into a hungry, greedy kiss with Noah taking charge and claiming her. He ran one hand through her hair, holding her head close, while his other arm held her against his warm, hard body. His lips were firm and possessive against her soft lips.

Like a starving man, he deepened the kiss, his tongue caressing and tangling with hers. God, the man could kiss. She moaned into his mouth and melted further into him. Kate held onto his shirt with one hand. Her bones liquefied while her muscles turned to mush. Her fingers dove into his thick hair. She let the strands sift through her fingers and held his nape, urging his mouth to stay on hers.

Kate's body was on fire. She was surprised at how quickly her body responded to Noah's touch. She'd never had this with Jeff. She was an avid reader and read about the passion, desire, heat, and intimacy that could exist between lovers. She'd never experienced anything close to it. Making love with Jeff had been pleasant, but her head and her heart weren't fully vested. She'd always felt somewhat disconnected when Jeff held her, kissed her, and even when he made love to her. Kate assumed she was broken, dead inside, from what she'd seen and experienced at a tender age.

With Noah though, Kate was anything but broken or dead. Her body was alert and alive, burning and needy. As Noah kissed up her neck to right beneath her ear, then bit her earlobe, she shivered. Her nipples hardened, and wetness gathered between her legs, soaking her panties.

Need raced through Kate's blood, fogging her brain. She didn't care where they were or who could see them. At that moment, all she knew was that she was hungry for Noah, and she finally understood what the word *desire* meant.

Kate wanted the kiss to go on forever. The warmth of his body enveloped her, and she no longer felt the chill of the cool October night. Noah was a big man, a wall of stone. She loved the feel of his body against hers. The spicy scent of his cologne, mixed with his all-male scent, intoxicated her, and the salty flavor of his skin drugged her. She couldn't get enough. When he pulled his lips away, she let out an involuntary whimper of protest and burrowed closer into him. Noah smiled against her lips.

They were both breathing hard and gasping for oxygen. Embarrassed at her behavior, Kate buried her hot face in his neck and inhaled him. As she took in his delicious scent, she couldn't stop herself and kissed his neck, letting her tongue dart out to taste him once more. She heard him groan, and she smiled, loving the effect she had on him.

"Sweetness, you're going to kill me. I can't go back to Dee's like this," he said as he pushed his hips against her. She felt his hard erection press into her belly, and that made her want him more. But he was right, they had to stop or they would make a scene upon their return.

Reluctantly, Kate pulled away from Noah. "Sorry, I don't know what got into me. I'm not usually that, um... It's been a long time, and you're hard to resist. I guess I got carried away."

Kate smiled and flushed. She was incredibly aroused and flustered. Hell, she was acting like a teenager, not a thirty-one-year-old woman. She bet most teenagers these days had more experience than her. She put her hands to her burning cheeks and scolded him.

"If you weren't so damn sexy, I wouldn't be in this state and neither would you, I might add," she said, glancing down pointedly.

Noah threw back his head and laughed as he hugged her tight to him.

"I'm not complaining. I'm only sorry we're not in a place where we can continue this. But we have time, lots of it. Now, though, we better get back before they send a search party after us. We've been gone for a while."

Noah touched his lips to hers and took her hand as they started making their way back to Dee's.

"And for the record, sweetheart," he said, bringing her hand to his mouth and kissing it, "you are one gorgeous, sexy woman. I've wanted you since the second I laid eyes on you. I was too terrified of your man-eating bird to make much of a move. I'm braver when your guardian isn't in the picture."

Kate let out a sigh as she let Noah's words sink in. He thought she was gorgeous and sexy.

By the time Noah and Kate made it back to the house, the party was winding down, and clean-up was in full swing. Kate joined the clean-up crew as Noah disappeared to watch football with the guys. As she cleaned, she chatted with Aimee and Jules and found out they were childhood friends who grew up together in Indiana. Jules was a respiratory technician at Lakes Community Hospital, and her handsome husband, Ethan, was a pediatric oncologist.

Jules was a tall, blonde woman with wholesome good looks and a welcoming smile. She had a gentle way about her and was always running after her daughter, Lilly. Lilly resembled her mother so much everyone called her mini-Jules. The child was beautiful, but a handful.

Kate noticed Jules wore a stunning, heart-shaped locket. When Kate commented on it, Jules told her Ethan gave it to her when they were in high school. It was obvious Jules was very much in love with her husband because when she talked about him, or when he was near, her eyes softened, and she got a dreamy expression on her face. It was sweet. Kate wondered if she appeared like that when she talked about Noah.

It felt good to be part of a group, to have girlfriends to laugh and let go with. Kate hadn't allowed herself to get close to anyone since Jaz. Thirteen years had passed and still Kate could remember almost every conversation she'd had with her best friend. Kate met Jasmine Lions her freshmen year of high school, and although they had little in common, they quickly became inseparable. Jaz was Kate's only friend, her protector, in a world dictated by gangs and violence. Kate loved Jaz unconditionally, something Jaz never experienced before Kate.

Kate closed her eyes and allowed herself to remember Jaz's soulful dark brown eyes and smooth cocoa skin. Kate wrapped her arms around herself and remembered the feel of Jaz's powerful arms around her as they hugged one another for the last time.

Jaz whispered in her ear, "I can't protect you anymore, Kate. You've got to be strong. You've got to stop cowering. Remember what I taught you. I love you, my soul-sister. Now go. Run like the wind. We'll always be together in our hearts."

Kate opened her eyes, swiped at her wet cheeks before anyone could notice, and continued putting away the leftover food. Jaz was gone, dead. Someday Kate would forgive herself for causing her death. She'd punished herself for years, denying herself all the good things in life—family, community, friends, even love. Maybe it was time to bury the past and move on.

Kate was glad she accepted Dee's invitation to lunner, but she wondered why Dee had been so standoffish all day. She wasn't rude, but she wasn't her usual friendly self. In fact, she barely said two words to Kate all day. Everyone, friends and family, saw the possessive way Noah touched, kissed, and claimed her. Kate wondered if Dee objected.

"Hello. Kate, isn't it?"

Kate stopped loading the potato salad into the plastic container and glared into Ava's ice-cold, aquamarine eyes and shivered.

"Hello, Ava."

"I see you and Reed have hit it off," Ava remarked as she studied Kate like she was a bug invading the picnic.

Kate wasn't experienced in dealing with women like Ava, and she wasn't interested in learning how. In high school, she did everything she could to hide in plain sight. Not that there were any girls like Ava in the inner-city Chicago high school she attended. Since escaping Chicago, Kate lived in small towns and kept to herself. At the end of the day, though, it didn't matter where she grew up. Kate was a woman, and she understood what this was—cattiness and jealousy.

Over the years, Kate developed a skill that never failed to end any conversation she didn't want to be in. The ultimate conversation ender was based on a simple concept. It takes a minimum of two people to have a conversation. She learned a long time ago, if she wanted a conversation to end, don't engage. Most people can't stand silence and have no idea how to deal with it. Kate lived in silence for years and welcomed it. It was home.

Kate regarded Ava, shrugged, and went back to

her task.

"Have you been seeing Reed long? You're not his usual type," Ava said with a sickly sweet smile.

Kate raised her head once more and blinked in Ava's direction. She flashed a quick smile at her, and continued with her task.

Ava let out an annoyed huff. "Take some advice from a friend. Reed's not your type. You seem like a nice enough woman. Dee tells me you own a bookstore. That's sweet, but Reed's out of your reach. He and I have been dating for a while, and we have everything in common—literally, everything."

Kate smiled to herself. This woman had it bad for Noah, and she couldn't blame her. If Kate hadn't spent the last two hours in his arms, she would have fallen for Ava's bullshit. Instead, she was entertained. Kate finished putting away the potato salad and started on the macaroni salad without glancing up or missing a beat.

"You aren't much of a conversationalist, are you?" Ava asked. Her voice rose as if Kate was deaf.

Kate granted Ava one response. She stopped what she was doing, wiped her hands on a napkin, and stood straight. Kate met Ava's icy glare and in an equally frigid voice said, "No."

Before Ava had time to respond, Emma's speeding body and excited, little-girl squeals came at Kate.

"Miss Kate, Miss Kate! Where have you been? Where did you and Uncle Reed go? I've been searching for you guys everywhere. Wanta see my new bookshelf Uncle Reed got me? It's so cool. He said he would help me fill it with dreams. He means books." Emma rolled her eyes and giggled.

Kate's face lit up with a huge smile. She kneeled to catch Emma in her arms, laughing at the child's antics.

Standing up with Emma in her arms, she swung her around and kissed the top of her head. "Hi there, cupcake. Man, I've missed you."

Kate stood the giggling girl on the seat of the picnic table and glanced up, meeting Ava's glare. Kate quirked an eyebrow at her, and then dismissed her with a jerk of her chin. She turned her full attention to Emma and ignored Ava's annoyed huff.

"Where have you been all day, Em?" Kate stroked Emma's wispy blonde hair off her face and watched Ava's retreating figure in delight.

"I've been taking care of Lilly. That kid's trouble. I'm pooped. Where'd you and Uncle Reed go?"

Kate couldn't stop smiling. It was clear that Emma was having a good day among her family and friends. She could be herself, and there was no sign of shy, self-conscious Emma.

"Noah and I took a walk around the lake. I'd love to see your bookshelf, though. Is it in your room?"

Emma furrowed her brows. "Why do you call Uncle Reed, Noah? No one does, not even Grandpa Joe or Uncle Luke."

"No one calls him Noah?" Kate asked, intrigued.

"Nope. Mommy says he doesn't like it when people call him that, 'cause he's always been Reed. So why do you get to call him Noah?" Emma pinned Kate with her inquisitive stare.

Amused by the blunt little girl, Kate shrugged. "I guess he looks like a Noah to me and not a Reed."

Emma giggled. "He *looks* like a Noah? Like Shakes looks like a Shakes, 'cause he shakes his head a lot? Does he like it? Should I call him Uncle Noah?"

"Well, Shakes is actually named after a very famous writer, Shakespeare. As for your uncle, I'm not sure you should call him Noah, not if he doesn't like it.

Hmm. I didn't know he didn't like being called Noah."

"Are you gonna call him Reed like we all do now? Maybe he lets you call him Noah 'cause you let him kiss you. I saw him kiss you. Do you let him do that a lot? Mommy says I shouldn't let boys kiss me. Uncle Reed doesn't count. Why did you let him kiss you? That's so gross."

Kate was at a loss for words. Emma wasn't, though. She'd barely taken a breath since she flew into her arms a few minutes ago. Kate had no idea how to answer Emma's questions about Noah. How could she have dealt with mean-girl Ava, but have trouble answering questions from an inquisitive eight-year-old?

"Hi, beautiful. Where have you been all day, and why are you torturing Kate?"

Both Kate and Emma startled and turned to find a grinning Noah standing behind them. Obviously, the rat had been listening in on their conversation and was enjoying Kate's flustered state.

"Uncle Reed." Emma squealed in delight and leaped off the picnic table bench and into his open arms. Like a koala bear, she wrapped her tiny arms around his neck and her legs around his waist.

"How come Miss Kate gets to call you Noah and I can't? She says you look like a Noah. I don't get it. Is it 'cause she lets you kiss her?"

Noah chuckled and rubbed his nose against Emma's.

"You know how I call you beautiful?"

"Yup."

"Do you know why?"

"Uh-uh." Emma wrinkled her brow and studied her uncle.

"Em, I call you beautiful because you are. To me, and to so many others," Noah replied in a quiet voice, as he gazed into his niece's blue eyes. "You're Beautiful to me, as I am Noah to Kate."

"But I'm not beautiful, not like Tina or Anna or Jenny. They're so, so pretty. Not me, though. Not with this," Emma whispered to her uncle, her eyes filling with tears as she touched her upper lip.

Noah stroked Emma's hair and sat down on the picnic bench with her in his lap. He wiped her tears as they spilled down her cheeks and kissed the top of her head.

"Beautiful—baby, look at me."

Emma lifted her head.

"There are all kinds of beautiful in this world. Some people are beautiful on the outside, but not on the inside. Others, like you, have a special kind of beauty. It's like a bright light that shines all around them. That light comes from the inside"—he pointed at Emma's chest—"and it pushes its way out. It's so bright, it's blinding, like the sun shining in your eyes. That's you, gorgeous. So beautiful inside and out. So beautiful, it's blinding."

Kate stood, rooted in her place, listening to Noah comforting Emma. By the angelic smile that filled the child's face, he'd struck gold. Kate's heart did a summersault and ached at the same time. One day, this man was going to be an awesome father. He'd be gentle, kind, and loving, all the things Kate dreamed and prayed to have in a father, as a child, but never got.

As Noah talked with Emma, Kate turned and walked to the edge of the yard, trying to gather her emotions. She didn't want Emma or Noah to see the tears stinging her eyes. It had been a long time since she thought about the people who'd given birth to her, neglected, abused, and abandoned her. She wondered where her parents were. Did they ever think about her?

Did they ever wonder what happened to her? She doubted it.

Today had been an eye-opening, emotional day. She found the strength to share one of the most horrific parts of her life with Noah, and she made the commitment to stop running and try this thing called a relationship with him. That meant it was time to stop shoving the past to the side, hoping to forget it. It was time to tie a noose around its neck and do away with it permanently.

Her parents were part of the past, and it was time to find them and get some closure. They gave her life and then set her on the road to hell. But she was the one who pulled herself out of that fire-pit. She had help, thank God. But essentially, she pushed, shoved, and clawed her way to a better life. And she knew in her heart that the good she created here at Lakes Crossing had the potential to become great.

"Kate? You okay?"

Kate turned her head and smiled at Noah. He wrapped his arms around her waist. Noah pulled her body back toward him and nuzzled her neck. Apparently, this was his favorite way of holding her, and she had no complaints whatsoever.

Kate sighed, wrapped her arms around his, and held on, enjoying the feel of his hard torso against hers. "Yup, I'm fine. Just giving you and Emma some alone time. You're so good with her. She is one lucky little girl to have so many people who love her."

"That's a good thing, right? So, why do you sound so sad?"

Kate tilted her head back and kissed his chin.

"That's a very good thing. Seeing you with her, though, brought back some not-so-good childhood memories. I wasn't as lucky as Emma."

Noah frowned. "I take it you had a difficult childhood?"

Kate took a deep breath and settled back against Noah. It surprised her, but talking to him about her life was becoming easier and easier.

"I didn't have a childhood. I lived in hell. My father was a drunk who enjoyed hurting my mother, and my mother found comfort in a variety of pill bottles. When she had enough, she left, and he turned his rage on me."

Noah's arms tightened around her, reminding her she was safe. "How old were you when your mother left?"

"I was Emma's age. She told me to be good for daddy and said she was going grocery shopping. She never came back. I was devastated." Kate sighed. "She wouldn't win mother of the year, but she wasn't a bad mother. When she was around and awake, she fed me, held me, and kissed me. I loved her, and I think she even loved me—not enough to take me with her and not enough to save me from him."

Kate stood still and allowed the painful memories to wash over her. Remembering the past hurt, but she was still standing, and she wasn't crying. She'd done plenty of crying for the day. She wouldn't waste any tears on the sperm and egg donors who'd created her.

"Katie. I'm sorry. You survived, though. Thank God. That, in itself, is a miracle."

Noah kissed the top of her head and held her close to him. "Where are your parents now?"

Kate sighed. "I have no idea where they are or if they're even alive. I never saw or heard from my mother after she left. I was eighteen the last time I saw my father. If he's alive, he's probably in Chicago where I grew up."

Kate turned around in his arms and smiled.

"Because of you, now that I have you by my side, I've decided to do some digging and find my parents. I've never wanted to before now. But, it's time. I don't need a thing from them except closure."

"I think that's good, but why because of me?" Noah asked with a small, quizzical smile.

"I want to be healthy and whole for me and for whatever we may become. Part of that is dealing with my past. You are the first person in a long time that I've opened up to. I didn't believe I could do it without crumbling. But I did it, because of you."

Noah smiled and kissed her forehead.

"I'm proud of you, sweetheart. I have a slew of private investigators. I bet they can locate your parents in no time at all. Do you have brothers or sisters? Other family members you keep in touch with?"

Turning around to face him, Kate shook her head.

"Uh-uh. No way, Noah. My past is my business. I appreciate the offer, but I'm doing this on my own."

"Kate, don't be stubborn. I understand you want to do this on your own, but I have the resources to help you."

Kate pulled away and stood straighter. Meeting his eyes and with a firm voice, she said, "You want to help, fine. Be there for me by listening and supporting me. This is the way I want to do things. I've been on my own, pretty much since I was born, and I'm good at taking care of myself. I need to do this on my own, stand strong against my demons."

"Kate, for God's sake. I'm not trying to take your independence or power away. I'm trying to help you."

Kate folded her arms on her chest. "Help me by being understanding and respecting my wishes. My past is mine. I deal with it the way I want to."

Noah's jaw tightened, and his face was grim.

"Noah, please try to understand," Kate said, relaxing her stance and her voice. "It's not that I don't want your help. That's not it at all. In fact, it would be so much easier to have you handle everything."

"Exactly my point."

"No, Noah. That's my point. I need to stop cowering. I must stop living half a life. Today alone, I came a long way, but now I need to stand up all the way, on my own two feet. I need to use my strength and my voice to exorcise my demons. If I give in and let you handle everything, I will lose myself in you."

"And where do I come in, Kate? Where do I fit into your life plan?"

Kate heard the hurt and doubt in Noah's voice, and her heart ached. Her face softened, and she dropped her arms. She didn't want to hurt Noah. That was the last thing she ever wanted to do. She took a few steps, closed the space between them, and wrapped her arms around him. She stood on her toes, reached up, grasped his shirt, and pulled him to her.

"You, sweet Noah, are a dream. You're everything I've ever dreamed of having and never thought I deserved."

Chapter Eleven

Over the next two weeks, everything in Noah's life clicked into place. He was convinced that God and the universe were finally giving him all the good he'd missed out on, in the tiny package named Kate. He and Kate spent every possible moment together, discovering each other and settling into each other's lives with remarkable ease and speed. They were two puzzle pieces that fit seamlessly together.

Even Shakes warmed up to him. Instead of hissing and lunging at Noah, he now threw objects at him—peanuts, various toys, and once spaghetti, complete with sauce and cheese. His relationship with Shakes wasn't perfect, but they were making progress.

One thing Noah and Kate didn't have to worry about was physical attraction. The chemistry between them was evident in each look they exchanged and each touch they shared. When their lips met, Noah's brain crashed against his skull, stopping all cognitive function. He was reduced to a puddle of red-hot lava of desire and found it difficult to control himself. Noah was convinced if Kate didn't let him in soon, he'd have a permanent case of blue balls.

Every time they were together, they barely kept their hands off one another and today would be challenging because Emma was with them. They had to behave. After Storytime, Noah took Kate and Emma out for lunch, followed by a haunted house and then shopping for Emma's Halloween costume. By the end of the day, the kid and the adults were wiped out, but he and Kate had plans. After he dropped Emma back home, he and Kate were going to dinner at Carlos's, an Italian bistro that opened the week prior.

Noah parked in front of Dee's house and peered over his shoulder to find Emma curled up, fast asleep in the backseat. Emma didn't stir as he scooped her up and carried her to Dee's front door. Dee had the door open and was waiting for them on the front porch.

"Hey there. I wondered when you guys would make it home," Dee whispered as she led Noah up the stairs to Emma's room.

Noah tucked the child in and kissed the top of her head. He took a moment and studied the sweet girl, sleeping peacefully. This little princess had his heart, and she knew it.

"Why don't you stay and have a drink with Jackson and me? We were about to open a bottle of wine," Dee said, as she closed Emma's door and followed him down the stairs to the front door. "I never see you anymore."

Noah shrugged. "Sorry, Dee. I've got to go."

Since pulling that stunt with Ava at lunner, Noah hadn't spoken with his sister much. They exchanged some heated words the day after, and on a number of other occasions. Noah warned Dee to stay out of his love life, and in response, she told him he was moving too fast with Kate and reminded him that he promised to keep an open mind. They talked circles around each other and agreed on nothing.

"Meeting up with Kate, again?" Dee said in an exasperated voice. "Weren't you with her all day?"

Noah stopped with his hand on the doorknob. He took in a deep breath in an attempt to control his anger, then spun around and studied Dee. He wasn't sure why or when his sweet sister turned into a bitch where Kate was concerned. He'd made an effort to be understanding and to reassure her that Kate was nothing like Kristin, but she wasn't interested in hearing anything good about Kate.

143

He was tired of having to defend their relationship. Noah wasn't going to allow Dee to ruin the evening for him.

"Dee, I love you. I've been tolerant, but you're pushing the envelope. Kate makes me happy, and I haven't been this happy in a long time. If you love me, and I know you do, then do better. Be better. I'm counting on you to make Kate feel like an important part of our family because my gut tells me she will be one day soon."

Dee's mouth hung open and her pupils dilated. Before she could say anything further, Noah gave her a peck on the cheek and walked out, closing the door behind him.

As Noah drove to Kate's, he put Dee out of his mind. He had bigger worries. On Monday, he had to leave for a ten-day trip to London. He hated the idea of leaving Kate and put off telling her. Every day he told himself he'd tell her, but he wasn't sure what her response would be and experience taught him to be wary. Kristin used to have mega-size meltdowns each time he left on a business trip.

"How can you leave me again? Why did you bother to marry me if you were going to lock me away in this house and travel the world, partying it up without me? Don't you care about me? Don't you love me? I miss you so much when you're gone. I need you. Please, Noah, don't leave me again."

At first, Noah thought Kristin's meltdowns and her need to be close to him all the time were kind of cute, and he relented. For the first year of their marriage, he took her everywhere he went, but she didn't understand the concept of a business trip. She wanted him to play with her all day, every day. She was a huge distraction, and it was impossible to get anything done.

When she wasn't whining and pouting, she was

shopping, spending thousands of dollars on things she didn't need. When she wasn't shopping, she was out partying, getting wasted and getting into trouble. Eventually, Noah refused to take her with him, and her destructive behavior kicked into high gear.

Noah reminded himself that Kate was not Kristin, but he was human, and the past messed with his head. He had nothing to worry about where Kate was concerned, however. After a wonderful dinner, they went back to Dreamscape. They settled in on one of the overstuffed couches, and he broached the subject.

Noah explained how Noah Reed Senior established Reed Technology Group over forty years ago, but when Noah's mother passed eight years ago, he left the company in Noah's and Luke's hands and moved to Florida.

"The company is strong and stable financially, but it's a complex operation that requires a lot of my attention. It has twenty-two offices in seven countries, although the hub of its manufacturing is in Cleveland."

Kate listened to Noah as he spoke with pride about his company. She asked intelligent questions about the business, but when Noah started going into detail, explaining the importance of the business trip, Kate laid a hand on his chest and smiled.

"It's okay, Noah. I'll be fine, and I'll see you when you get back."

Noah was puzzled. He quirked his head to the side, not believing Kate's reaction.

"My travel doesn't bother you? It's okay. You can tell me, and we'll talk about it."

"I'm fine. I'll miss you, but we can call, text, and Facetime."

Frowning, she reached out and smoothed out the worry lines on his forehead in a soothing gesture.

"What's this all about?"

Noah contemplated not answering the question and changing the subject, but he wanted Kate to know everything about him. She needed to understand his fears. Honesty was the only way they were going to make it. He stood, walked to the window, and peered out into the night.

"When we first married, Kristin and I traveled everywhere together. I showed her Paris, Rome, London, Greece—all the places she dreamed of. I neglected the business and my family. But I didn't care. I was doing my best to keep Kristin happy. Then mom got sick, and everything changed."

Noah raked a hand through his hair and continued pacing. "I worked long hours so Dad could be with her. I traveled a lot. Although she wanted to accompany me on every trip, it didn't work out. Kristin wanted a play buddy, and I had to work. I left her in New York so I could focus on my work, and she lost her mind. She couldn't deal with the reality and rhythm of everyday life and couldn't deal with, what she referred to as, my family obligations. Our lives quickly unraveled in every way possible."

Noah stopped pacing and met Kate's eyes. "My job is demanding, Kate. There's nothing I can do about that. I don't want to make the same mistakes again, though. You'll always come first. I promise."

Kate sighed and smiled. She patted the loveseat. "Oh, Noah. Come here."

Noah walked back to Kate and sank down next to her. She cupped his cheeks in her hands. "I'm sorry you had to go through that with Kristin. I'm sorry for your pain."

Kate touched her lips to his. "I'm not Kristin. You don't have to worry about being with your family or traveling as you need to for work. I'm used to being on my own. I'm glad I'm not anymore, but I'm a big girl with a business of my own to run. Go. Run your empire and I'll run my little shop. I've traveled enough and am happy to stay put. I'll be here when you come back."

Was it as easy as that? Kate wasn't going to mope, whine, or complain?

Noah was speechless. He reached for Kate and pulled her into his embrace. He gave her feather-light kisses on the tip of her nose and her soft lips, and Kate returned each of his kisses with one of her own. She kissed his chin and his bottom lip, nibbling on it with her teeth. Her tongue darted out to run along his lips.

"Mmh," she whispered against his lips.

Kate was so small, so soft, and the perfect fit for him. Noah wanted more. He pulled her into his lap, and she straddled him, molding her body to his as his strong arms crushed her to him. He deepened the kiss, and when their tongues touched and then tangled, she moaned and arched further into him. He felt her breasts press to his chest and he sank his fingers into her lush hair. She wrapped her arms around his neck, pulling him closer. She ground herself onto his rock-hard erection. Noah groaned as he heard the sexy as hell, needy, mewling sounds that came from her when his hand snaked under her thin sweater and up her back.

Kate's skin was warm and soft as satin. His hands had a mind of their own as they explored every inch of her. They made their way from her back, across her rib cage, to her chest. When his hand closed over her breast, he brushed the nipple with his thumb through her thin, lacy bra. She gasped and pressed further into his palm. Even through her bra, he could feel the softness, the perfection of her plump breast. He swiped his thumb again over her hardened nipple and pinched it gently.

Kate's soft, small hands were killing him. He felt them everywhere—in his hair, over his shoulders and back, up his abdomen and over his chest. She dug her nails into his shoulders and pulled him even closer. Jesus, he was going to lose his mind. She moaned again into his mouth. She was the sexiest thing he'd ever experienced.

Noah pulled away, taking in great gulps of air, and she protested with a little whimper and an adorable pout. He touched her lips with his and sank his face into the side of her neck, breathing in her sweetness and kissing a path to her ear.

"Sweetness, I want you so bad."

Putting his hands on her hips, Noah guided her down onto his erection as he pumped his hips up, grinding against her hot core.

"The thing is," he said, as he licked a trail from her neck to her earlobe. "If we don't stop, we're going to put this couch to use in a way I don't think you anticipated. I'm game, but I want you to be sure you're ready."

Noah kissed Kate and between kisses, said, "I want our first time to be perfect, in a comfortable bed, not on a lumpy couch."

Kate's body trembled in Noah's arms. She was as far gone as he was. Her chest rose and fell with exertion, and she was flushed. He kissed her chin and deliciously swollen lips. Kate closed her eyes and rested her forehead against his.

After a minute, she pulled away, straightened, and stood. Noah felt her loss. He glanced up and found her giving him a shy smile. She held out her hand to him and asked in a husky voice that had his rock-hard erection straining even more against his pants, "Want to see my place, upstairs?"

A huge smile spread across Noah's face. Kate was

letting him in. Thank God!

"Yeah, sweetheart. I'd like that very much."

Noah took her hand and stood. He pulled her into his chest and kissed her breathless once more, enjoying the delicious taste of her.

"Lead the way, baby," he whispered in her ear.

Hand-in-hand, with her leading the way, they went up the rickety wooden stairs that led to the second floor of the bookstore where Kate lived. The place wasn't large or fancy by any means. The single bedroom, sitting room, tiny kitchen, and dinette were designed in an open floor plan with Kate's four poster bed in the corner of the room.

The apartment was decorated with unique pieces of furniture that appeared like they came from antique shops and thrift stores. The place was very feminine, decorated in various shades of dark rose, gray, and cream. The walls and various surfaces were covered with pictures and trinkets that told a story.

As Noah scanned the room, he understood why Kate was protective of her personal space. These rooms showcased the story of her life. She didn't have much, but it was evident that this is where Kate revealed herself and felt safest. Here was where she called home.

Kate walked around turning on lamps in the small sitting room that flowed into the dinette and kitchen. Noah followed her. Pictures of Kate in front of the St. Louis Gateway Arch, at the Grand Canyon, the Golden Gate Bridge, the Space Needle, and in Central Park adorned the walls. The coffee table that sat in front of an old leather couch was littered with a variety of baking books.

On an end table was a picture of a younger Kate seated next to an elderly woman with kind eyes. He wondered who the woman was. Kate never mentioned having any family, other than her parents. Maybe a grandmother? Kate was remarkably different in the photo with short hair and a sad smile.

Noah had a thousand questions for Kate, but he promised her she could tell him what she wanted, when she wanted. He bit his tongue, cataloged his questions, and filed them away for a later time. Kate studied him from across the room as she chewed on her lower lip. He wouldn't let her down, and he sure as hell wouldn't push her away. It took six weeks to get an invitation into her world, and no way was he blowing it.

"Your place is lovely, Kate," he said as he met her troubled eyes with a warm, genuine smile. "It's all you, every bit of it. I can see *you* here. This is more than a home, it's your refuge, isn't it?"

Exhaling, Kate gifted him with a smile that lit up his world. "I'm glad you like it. Yes, it's my little oasis. I've lived here since I moved to Jersey a little over a year ago. I love it."

Kate's eyes sparkled, and she turned in a circle, her arms outstretched. "It's not big or fancy, but it's comfortable, and it's mine. Dreamscape and this tiny apartment are the only real home I've ever had. They're the only places I can call my own."

Noah walked to Kate, pulled her into his arms, and brushed her lips with his.

His eyes met her gorgeous green ones. "Thanks for sharing it with me, for trusting me."

Noah's mouth closed over hers in a demanding kiss. Kate melted into him, eagerly returning the kiss, opening her mouth to him, and welcoming and tasting him. Their tongues touched and danced with one another. She ran her fingers through his hair as he crushed her to him.

Kate pulled back, and her breath was choppy and

erratic. He could feel her heart galloping alongside his. She was trembling, whether out of passion or nervousness, he couldn't be sure. She rested her cheek against his chest and sighed.

In all their conversations, Kate never mentioned previous relationships. She said she wasn't married, but that was it. Noah, however, could tell his green-eyed girl wasn't very experienced and was wary where men were concerned. Who could blame her? He wanted their first time together to be perfect. He ached for her, but he wouldn't rush her. They had all night, and if she wasn't ready tonight, there would be other nights.

Noah hummed "The Way You Look Tonight" and slowly swayed them to the music. Kate sighed again and relaxed against him. He caressed her cheek with the back of his hand and ran his fingers through her hair. Then he kissed the top of her head and continued the song and sway routine.

In time, Kate raised her head. Noah smiled and waited for her to make the first move, but she licked her lips and blushed. Noah urged her chin up with his fingers. He traced her lower lip with his thumb and then bent and took her lips in a slow, sensual kiss that had her standing on her tiptoes and clutching his shirt.

She tasted like chocolate and peanut butter, probably because they'd consumed two of her phenomenal buckeye cupcakes for dessert. Kate moaned and sucked on his tongue. It was his turn to moan, unable to stop the sound from escaping. One of his arms held her close and stroked up and down her back while his other hand dove into her hair, his fingers weaving through its long strands.

When they separated, Kate shivered in his arms, and both of their breaths were labored. He felt way too warm in his clothes, and by Kate's flushed features, he bet she felt the same. He wanted to reach down and help her out of her sweater so he could see those soft breasts that fit perfectly in the palm of his hands. But he was afraid of pushing her too far, too fast. She had a complicated past and sometimes he felt like he was stumbling around in the dark where she was concerned.

It was apparent, however, that Kate had no idea how to move this forward. There was no doubt in his mind she wanted him, but maybe she wasn't ready yet? When they made love, he wanted their time together to be only about pleasure, with no doubts or hesitation between them.

"Katie, look at me, sweetheart." When she raised her eyes to meet his, he whispered, "It's okay if you're not ready. I can feel you trembling, and I want you to know it's okay. We have all the time in the world. I don't want you to have any regrets. I want you to want this as much as I do."

Kate's eyes were filled with apprehension, and the blush rose higher on her cheeks.

"I…I'm totally inept at this seduction stuff, Noah." Kate licked her lips, her gaze drifting away from his. "I know at my age, I shouldn't be. But that's what happens when you've lived a screwed-up life. You miss out on…well, everything. I want you. I want this, but I have no idea what I'm doing. I want this to be good for you too, but…"

Noah felt like an idiot. Kate wasn't trembling out of fear or indecision. She was trembling with desire. She was ready to take their relationship further, but she didn't know what to do and she didn't want to let him down.

Kate started to pull away, but his arms tightened around her. He wasn't going to let her go. He got it. He understood her fears, wants, needs, and her utter panic. He'd take over. He only needed to know this is what she wanted. Now that he did, game on.

Noah cupped her face with his hands and brushed her lips with his. "This is going to be perfect. You're beautiful and sexy, and I find you utterly captivating. There isn't anything you could say or do that's going to change that. Trust me to take care of you? Let me show you how good it can be, how good we can be together."

Kate didn't hesitate. She turned her face into his palm and kissed it. She whispered, "Yeah, baby."

Noah froze.

Baby?

She called him baby. Yes! Now he knew he was definitely in Kate's head and maybe even in her heart, as she was in his.

Chapter Twelve

Kate relished in the feel of Noah's hard, warm chest as she ran her fingers over it and around to his back, while his mouth continued to consume hers. She wanted to feel him, skin on skin, unhindered by his sweater. She whimpered in frustration and disappointment when she finally made her way underneath his sweater, only to find his t-shirt in the way.

Noah smiled against her lips and broke the kiss. He pulled his sweater and t-shirt off together and tossed them on the floor. Kate drank him in through hooded eyes. His blond hair was tousled. He sported a sexy smile and a five o'clock shadow. Noah was toned, tanned, and delicious. For his height and weight, he was perfectly proportioned, not overinflated like a steroid-addicted athlete.

She glided her hands up his chest, over his broad shoulders and muscular arms, and then down his back, feeling his muscles tense and ripple underneath her hands. His skin was warm, and the light scattering of hair tickled her hands as she explored every inch of him. He stood confident and sexy in only his jeans. She was lost in the wonder of him.

When her hands slid to his abdomen and began exploring every ridge there, they were seized in Noah's hands. Kate gasped, and her eyes flew up to meet his.

"You're killing me, sweetheart. It's a beautiful way to go, but I'd like to enjoy you too."

Blushing, Kate tried to pull her hands out of his grasp. "Sorry, I…"

"Shh, sweetness," Noah said, silencing her with a kiss. "Don't apologize. I'm enjoying every second of your touch. I love the feel of your hands on me, but I want to touch you and taste you without layers between us."

Kate's body warmed and tingled all over at the gentle caress of his words and the heat in his eyes. He made her feel wanted and sexy. Noah kissed her hands as he devoured her with his dark chocolate eyes. He swooped down and cradled her in his arms. She gasped in surprise, and he covered her mouth with his, swallowing the sound as he made his way to the side of her queen-size bed.

Noah put Kate down to stand at the side of the bed, sliding her body down his, never breaking their kiss. He grasped the hem of her sweater in his hand and pulled it over her head, dropping it to the ground. He gathered her thick hair in one hand and draped it over one shoulder, dropping wet kisses down her neck to her exposed shoulder then to her breast.

Kate shook with desire, and her hands went to his shoulders to steady herself as Noah kissed the top of her breasts. She wove her fingers through his hair, held him to her breast, arching toward him as his tongue traced the outline of her bra.

Moaning, Kate's fingers tightened in his hair and she tugged him closer. Noah seemed to get the message and sucked one nipple into his mouth over the thin lace of her bra as his hand kneaded her other breast. He blew on the wet material and then gave her other breast the same treatment. Kate's nipples puckered and hardened. A shiver ran through her from head to toe. She was in heaven.

Pressing her legs together, Kate tried to satisfy the ache that was swiftly building in her core. She needed more. She writhed and whimpered in Noah's embrace. Noah worked one of his legs in between hers, pressing right into her apex.

Kate didn't care anymore about anything except the man in front of her and how he made her feel. She moaned and held on to him, riding his leg and mewling in pleasure. She threw her head back and closed her eyes, allowing herself to sink into the pleasure—to just feel. She'd never felt this way before. With Jeff, she never needed, wanted, or ached in the way she did for Noah at this moment. Kate wrapped her arms around Noah and dug her nails into his back, kissing him with all she had.

Noah unzipped her jeans and slid his hands around and down her buttocks, sliding down her jeans and caressing every inch of her along the way. Kate wiggled out of her jeans and toed out of her flats while she reached for the button and zipper of his jeans. Her hands shook, and she didn't get far. Noah helped her and in seconds he stood, wearing only his black boxer briefs.

Kate gaped, her mouth open, her body swaying toward him. She had no idea why she didn't see how attractive he was the first time she saw him, but at this moment he took her breath away—toned, muscular thighs, trim waist, flat abs, the list went on and on. He was mouth-watering, and she licked her lips when she noted the sizable bulge of his erection.

Noah's hand touched her cheek, and Kate jumped. She met his eyes and stood under his assessing gaze in nothing but a cream-colored lace bra and pink cotton bikini panties with a cream lace trim. Her underwear was nothing special. She didn't have the money to throw away on frivolities, even if she wanted to.

Kate was sure Noah was used to seeing his women in sexy lingerie. She couldn't compete with them. She was by no means supermodel material. In fact, she was the opposite. She'd always been slim, with disproportionately large breasts, no curves, and a tiny waist. In other words, just like her undies, she was nothing special.

Standing in front of Noah with virtually nothing on, Kate felt vulnerable and exposed. She felt the heat of his stare on every inch of her body, and heat crept up her cheeks. He stepped closer to her, and ran the back of his hand down her cheek, to the tip of her chin, down her neck to the V between her breasts. Everywhere he touched, nerve endings fired and her skin tingled and burned on contact.

"God, Kate, you're beautiful. You're absolutely breathtaking."

The genuine appreciation and stark need in Noah's voice had Kate peeking up to meet his heated gaze. In his eyes, she was beautiful, and he wanted her as much as she wanted him. It was evident in every touch and every glance. Noah's hands shook the tiniest bit as he ran his fingers through her hair.

"You have the most beautiful hair—thick and soft."

He took her hands, brought them to his lips, and then kissed each of her fingertips. She was aroused, hot and wet, but she was also horribly embarrassed and nervous. Her entire body trembled and felt like a quivering pile of Jell-O. No amount of deep breathing was going to help this, and there was no hiding it from Noah.

Noah sat at the edge of her bed and pulled her into his lap, cradling her close to his body and running his hand down her hair and on to her back.

"Easy, sweetheart. I've got you. Do you want to slow this down? We don't have to do anything more than this."

Kate considered his words. She felt his hard erection straining against her side and heard the excited gallop of his heartbeat. Her mouth went dry, and her palms began to sweat. Panic filled her, and she had to fight the urge to bolt. Using words to express her needs and wants was beyond her at this juncture. She didn't have the words to tell him how much she wanted him, yet how inept she felt.

Kate wasn't experienced with men or sex. Beyond the God-awful times she'd sold herself to survive, she'd only been with one other man, Jeff. One man in thirty-one years, that was it. The last time she and Jeff were intimate was a little over three years ago, and there'd been no one since. Kate didn't believe in casual sex, and since things ended badly with Jeff, she hadn't made another attempt to try again with anyone until Noah came and swept her off her feet. Part of her believed she was too damaged to be in a long-term relationship, and she assumed she'd be alone forever.

Then there was the issue of sex. She didn't enjoy sex with Jeff, and that fact had been impossible to hide. She never felt clean or deserving and couldn't let go. But she couldn't tell Jeff that. He never knew about her past until the very end, and then he judged her and insinuated she was dirty and damaged. Jeff had a long list of reasons why she didn't enjoy sex, and none of them were based on his ability to arouse or please her. She wasn't adventurous enough. She was too much in her head and needed to learn to let go. The list seemed endless.

What Kate felt with Noah right at this moment was foreign to her. She was incredibly aroused, and every time he ravaged her with his hungry eyes, she felt sexy and beautiful. Still, in the back of her mind, she worried Jeff was right. What if she couldn't please Noah? What if she did something wrong?

Taking a deep breath, Kate straddled Noah, wrapping her arms around his neck and her legs around his waist. She had to conquer her fears. She didn't want to lose him.

Kate rested her forehead against his and closed her eyes. "Noah, I've never wanted anything more. It's just that I haven't been with anyone in a long time. I don't want to let you down, and I'm not...well...it's... Oh, hell, I can't talk about this when you're looking at me like that. I..." Kate gave up trying to explain herself and buried her now-burning face in his neck.

Chuckling, Noah pushed them further up the bed, using one hand to pile some pillows behind his back, while swiping the rest to the floor. Once he had them in a comfortable position, he began drawing small circles on her back with his fingers. "Okay, gorgeous. Here's what we're going to do. You can continue hiding for now," he said, as he pushed her hair away from her neck and shoulder and peppered the side of her face and neck with kisses. "Keep talking so I know what's going on in that beautiful head of yours."

Kate was drowning in delicious sensation, losing herself in his touch and the feel of his skin against hers. His erection pushed against her center, and she wanted to grind herself against him. She held back, uncertain of her actions.

"I don't have a lot of experience," she blurted out. The words escaped her mouth and took off on their own before she could harness them.

"Okay."

"No. You're not getting it. I'm not making sense." She shook her head and mumbled against his neck.

"Want to come out and tell me?" he said, humor still lacing his words.

"No. No. This is good."

"Okay, sweetness, go ahead. I've got you. Get it out." He continued playing with her hair and dropping kisses to the top of her head.

Kate laid her forehead against his chest. "When I say I haven't been with anyone in a long time, I mean a *long* time…three years. I've only been with one person, one relationship, and it wasn't good. I couldn't, well…"

Kate's face flamed with humiliation. She shook her head and buried her face in his neck again. She took a breath and said, "I didn't like it. I wasn't good at it. I want you, but…shit! Never mind. Make love to me, will you?"

Kate felt Noah smiling in her hair. "Is that it?"

Kate nodded.

Holding Kate by the shoulders, Noah coaxed her to a sitting position. He brushed the hair away from her face, and then touched his lips to hers. "Katie, sweetheart, here's the thing you have to know. There's nothing you can do to disappoint me. Today, right now, right here, is about making love, not having sex."

Kate's breath caught and her eyes filled with moisture.

"Don't bring anyone else into this bed with us. Today is about us, not about the past. We'll go slow and discover each other, together. All I want to do is to hold you."

He cupped her face and ran his thumb across her full lower lip.

"And kiss you."

He placed the lightest of kisses on her lips.

"And taste you," he said as ran his finger over the swell of her breasts, making her shiver with anticipation.

"I want to watch your eyes and your face as you come apart in my arms. And when we're through, I want to watch you sleep, as I hold you and guard you, banishing your nightmares and making sure you have the sweetest dreams to escape to."

In that second, every doubt Kate ever entertained

about Noah vaporized. Over the last two weeks, she suspected she was falling in love with him. Now, she knew without a doubt she wasn't falling in love with him, she was already there. It had happened quickly, but Noah Reed captured her heart in his hands, and she didn't want him to let go. She suspected he was on his way to loving her as well, at least she prayed he was.

This good-looking man who held her so tenderly and told her he wanted to make her dreams come true, had no idea *he* was her dream. He was the man she saw in her dreams when she dreamed of a perfect life. He had no idea how far she'd go not to disappoint him. She'd risk everything. In fact, that is what she was doing. Slowly, but surely, she was trusting him with her past, her present, and her future.

"One more question, sweetness, and then no more talking, just feeling."

"Mmh?" she said as she pulled him to her and kissed the side of his mouth.

"This might be a stupid question given what you've told me, but by any chance, are you on the pill?"

Kate let out a long breath. "I am and I'm clean, but are you?"

Noah sighed and smiled. "Yeah sweetheart, I'm clean. I had a physical a few months back, and there hasn't been anyone in almost a year."

"Good, and baby?" she said as she coiled herself even tighter around him and ground herself against him.

"Yeah?" He groaned.

"No more talking. I've waited a long time for you, for this," she murmured against his lips.

Noah closed his mouth over hers, kissing her long, wild, and deep as he reached around her and undid the clasp of her bra. He flipped their positions, and she gasped as he pinned her below him and pulled away her bra, revealing her breasts to his hungry eyes. He cupped and kneaded one breast while he took the other nipple into his mouth, licking, sucking, and tasting her. Kate arched her back, writhing, clinging to him, and chanting his name.

"Beautiful," he said, his voice filled with awe.

Kate's hands ran over Noah's massive body. She kissed and licked his neck, shoulders, and chest. She ran her hands over his chest, down his abdomen and around his back, sliding her hands into his boxers and over his firm, tight ass. Noah's entire body trembled under her exploring hands. Her other hand slipped between them and closed over his erection. Her man was huge and was both hard as iron and soft as velvet.

Kate explored his length, listening to the sounds he made and learning his every response to her touch. She smiled as he groaned and drove himself into her hand. She raised her head and saw the ecstasy all over Noah's face. Jeff was wrong. She didn't suck at sex. Sex with him had sucked.

With a groan and a gasp for air, Noah stopped moving. He opened his eyes, grabbed her hands and brought them to his lips. His breathing was ragged, and his chest heaved.

"Katie, I love these tiny, wandering hands of yours, but if you keep that up…this night is going to end a lot faster than I want it to."

Before she could protest, Noah caught her lower lip between his teeth, bit, and sucked it. He took her mouth in a scorching kiss as his fingers danced over her skin, traveling over her breasts and abdomen, to the top of her panties. As he took her breast into his mouth once more, biting gently down on her nipple, his fingers found their way into her panties. He slid his fingers over her sex, parting her. Kate arched her back and rubbed herself against his fingers as she clung to him and moaned in his mouth.

"God, sweetness, you're so wet for me."

Noah found her clit and started rubbing it in small circles with just the right amount of pressure, teasing her to the brink. Kate's eyes rolled to the back of her head. She was losing her mind, drowning in pleasure, but she needed more.

"Noah," she whimpered and clawed at his back. "Please, baby. I need…"

Noah slid one finger into her, and Kate bucked at the delicious invasion, digging her nails into his shoulders. When he slid another finger deep into her, she froze and whimpered. He stopped moving.

Noah kissed her nose and her mouth as he let her body adjust to his invasion. "God, you're tight."

Kate dug her fingernails into his back and squirmed, needing to move and wanting him to move, to relieve the pressure that was building inside her before she exploded.

"Shh, easy, baby. I don't want to hurt you," Noah said against her mouth as he took her mouth in a deep kiss. His tongue plunged in and out of her mouth mimicking his fingers.

Kate rode his fingers with reckless abandon and threw her head back. Noah hit a spot deep in her no one had ever touched before. Kate's gaze locked with Noah's as she took a sharp breath in. She needed to let go, but held back, unsure of how to and at the same time wanting to so badly.

Tears of ecstasy filled her eyes. "Noah, baby. Oh, my God. Oh, God."

Noah kissed her lips, her eyes, and cheek, and whispered in her ear. "Let go, Kate. I have you, sweetness. I have you now. I have you always."

When Noah's fingers thrust deep inside Kate once more, she unraveled. Every one of Kate's sensory nerves fired at the same time and exploded in a million sensations. She arched her back and clenched around his fingers, holding him in her as she climbed and soared. She clung to Noah, trying to find anchor as her body tensed and shook. The strength and suddenness of the climax stunned her and left her dazed and breathless. Noah held Kate, rubbed her back, and ran his fingers through her hair until she came down.

Kate reemerged slowly and opened her eyes, trying to focus on Noah. She'd let go and let Noah and nature take over. She'd experienced something she had never experienced before. Kate had only climaxed a few times in her life, and only after she had enough alcohol in her system to drop her inhibitions. But this was something entirely different. This was nirvana.

Noah touched his lips to hers as he slid his fingers out of her. "That was undoubtedly, the sexiest, most beautiful thing I've ever seen."

Kate buried her hot face into Noah's neck as he turned them, so she was on top. She breathed in his spicy scent and sighed.

"Come on, sweetheart, let me see those beautiful eyes."

Kate kissed Noah's neck, up to his jaw. She licked his jaw, tasting the saltiness of his skin, and then nipped his lower lip, as he'd done to hers. She lazily stretched out on top of him satiated. She didn't remember ever feeling this good in her entire life. It was time to make Noah feel just as good.

At some point, Noah had divested them both of their underwear, and they were skin to skin with nothing between them. It felt divine. Kate peered up at him and smiled as she pushed up on his chest and straddled him.

She slid her wet core over his hard erection that stretched almost to his navel. She leisurely rubbed herself up and down the length of his shaft.

"Hi," she said with a sexy smile, as she pushed her wild mane of hair off her face.

"Hi, gorgeous." He smiled back.

Noah held onto her hips, pushing his throbbing erection as close to her wet entrance as possible. She set a teasing rhythm, enjoying the tensing of his muscles under her hands and the arching of his back. She bent and took his mouth into a deep, exploratory kiss, wrapping her tongue around his and running her fingers through his hair.

Kate rubbed her sensitive nipples on his chest and felt the hair on his chest tickle them. She reached between them and stroked him from root to tip, feeling his length and thickness. He was a big man, and she felt a bit hesitant, wondering how she was going to take him without pain. But her man was beyond ready for her with pre-cum coating the head of his erection. She longed to run her tongue along his length and taste him. That would be a first for her with any man, and one day she'd give that to him.

Focusing on Noah's melty chocolate eyes, Kate positioned his length at her entrance. Noah held onto her hips, allowing her to lead at her own pace. He reached up and kissed her belly, running his tongue around her belly button. She shivered and began to take him in her. When he breached her entrance, she stopped and moaned, which was accompanied by his.

God, he felt so good, so right. She did her best to work herself on him, moving up and down his length, taking more and more of him, never breaking eye contact with him. He had a death grip on her hips, and his jaw was tight. They were both covered in sweat, but neither seemed to care.

When she was fully seated on him, and he was lodged deep inside her, she closed her eyes and threw her head back, loving the feel of him. She was tight, and he was enormous. She felt like she was being split in half, so full, so good. She was lost in sensation, unable to move, needing him to take over and make love to her. She let out a needy, low whimper and tried to move, tried to find a rhythm that would please them both.

"Noah, baby, please…I can't," she panted, meeting his eyes. "I need you."

Noah didn't need any further encouragement. He sat up, taking her with him, urging her to wrap her legs around him.

"Oh, God." Kate gasped as he lodged himself impossibly deep. She wrapped her arms around his neck and tightened her legs around him. She felt him everywhere—in her, around her, planted deep in her body and soul. He rolled them until he was on top and let go, thrusting into her with abandon, while he took her mouth, destroying her every inhibition.

Kate clung to him, kissing him, giving him every piece of her. She was barely coherent, lost once more to another world where only Noah and the building pressure in her existed. She couldn't believe she was this close to climaxing again. She dug her nails into Noah's back and buried her face into the side of his neck. Kate sucked on the skin where Noah's neck and shoulder met, to keep from screaming.

Noah reached between them and found her clit as he pumped over and over inside her. He applied just enough pressure on it and ordered in a ragged, husky voice, "Come for me, Katie. Let go."

Throwing her head back, Kate screamed his name, and saw stars. Her body shook as the climax raced through her like wildfire, spreading to every nerve and muscle fiber of her body as Noah continued to thrust into her. Kate was transported to a different place and time. Her body was no longer hers. It was his to do with whatever he liked. Noah gave a few more thrusts and then rooted deep inside her, and with a powerful groan, he let go. She felt him pulse inside her, spilling into her.

Kate was a boneless rag doll, unable to control any aspect of her body. Noah slid to the side, taking her with him so that their bodies stayed connected. Her chest rose and fell with his ragged breaths and her sweat-soaked body nestled against his. Noah kissed her nose and lips and stroked her damp hair away from her face.

Kate cuddled closer to Noah, and he tightened his arms around her. In her entire life, she'd never felt as cherished and as loved by another as she did this very second. Even if he never said the words, she knew how Noah Reed felt about her.

Kissing the side of his neck, Kate pushed away so she could see Noah's eyes. She couldn't give him anything of material value. He could afford anything he wanted, but she could give him this. She could give him herself and prayed he would give himself to her in return.

Kate cupped both of Noah's cheeks in her hands. She lightly kissed his lips and whispered, "I love you, Noah."

Immediately she found herself crushed to him and under his warm, strong body. Noah kissed every inch of her face, and she felt him harden inside her once again. He brushed the hair off her face and said, "Look at me, sweetheart."

When he had her eyes again, he said, "You're not alone here, Katie. I've loved you for weeks now. I've been waiting for you to catch up, slow poke." He grinned.

Noah took her mouth in a possessive, needy kiss

that left her aroused and ready for him once more. He stilled her restless body. "Eyes, sweetheart. Let me see those beautiful eyes."

When Kate raised her head and her green eyes connected with Noah's browns, he said, "You're mine now. Every inch of you is mine, as I'm yours. I love you, sweetheart. I love you."

Chapter Thirteen

Noah didn't want to leave Kate, not even for a second. But his commitments to the family business left him no choice. He begrudgingly took his first-class seat on the airplane headed to London and tried not to pout like a toddler. He'd put off this trip long enough. Luke was going to have his head and his ass if he rescheduled one more time.

Resigned, Noah buckled his seatbelt and ordered a double Scotch from the flight attendant, who within the last fifteen minutes came to 'check on him' three times. This was going to be a long-ass flight if she kept this up. He wasn't interested in getting to know her or his seat mate.

The only person Noah was interested in getting to know better was working her tail off this very minute at Dreamscape. He and Kate spent a beautiful weekend together, idyllic in every way, with Kate opening up about her only other relationship with a man named Jeff Harrison, over dinner Sunday night. They were lounging around on her couch, barely dressed, eating pizza and drinking wine when they somehow made it to the topic of past relationships.

Nestled in the crook of his arm, Kate spoke in a faraway voice. "Jeff came into my life when I was a different person. We started as friends. We met at a coffee shop I frequented. He showed up there a lot and asked me out repeatedly until I agreed to go out with him. When he wanted more, I gave in."

Noah glanced down at her, quirking an eyebrow. "What do you mean you gave in? Did he force you?"

"No, no, baby." She patted his arm that wrapped around her. "It wasn't like that. It's hard to explain. He was older, authoritative, controlling even. Jeff was an established accountant in the small town we lived in, Canton, Texas. He was active in the community and at the local Baptist church. He led an ordered, predictable life and nothing in my life, up until that point, could be described that way. He was safe and at first, being with him was easy, too easy. I lost myself in him."

Kate stopped talking and took in a deep breath. Other than Edith, she'd never spoken to anyone about Jeff. But he was an important part of her past, and she wanted Noah to know about him.

Kate sat up and turned toward Noah. "I was a different person then, using a different name, hiding from myself and the world."

"Why…" Noah began to say but stopped when Kate placed one of her tiny fingers against his lips.

"Baby, that's a different story, for a different day. Just listen. Okay?" she asked, quirking her head to the side.

Noah smiled and nodded.

Kate sighed. "I wanted a normal life, but I had no idea what that was. I let Jeff make all the decisions. I gave him all the power. He was old school, and he liked the control I freely gave him. He didn't want me to grow, change, or leave Canton. For a while, I was content with that."

Questions bounced around Noah's brain like ping-pong balls. He was trying to piece Kate's present and past together, taking the crumbs she gave him and forming a loaf of bread. It was a daunting task, but he swore to himself and her, he'd let her lead and open up at her own pace, and it was working. Every day she was giving him more and more of herself. He had to have patience.

"What happened? Why did it end?"

Kate settled back against Noah, and his arms

came around her once again. "One day, Jeff and I got into one hell of an argument. He wanted me to move in with him. I refused. Over the two years we spent together, I'd grown. I'd become more confident and started to find my voice. Jeff didn't like it. He thought I needed more guidance, more stability. What it came down to was, he was uncomfortable with change, and he wanted more control."

Noah's bodied stiffened around Kate's, and he pulled her closer. "Did he hurt you, sweetheart? It's okay, you can tell me."

Kate swallowed and cleared her throat. She pulled away from Noah and faced him again, bringing her knees up to her chest, hugging them to her. She rested her chin on her knees, and her thick hair surrounded her. She resembled a lost little girl.

"No, not physically," she whispered.

Kate slid her gaze up to meet Noah's. "I made a lot of mistakes with Jeff. He had no idea who I was or where I came from. I guess I never totally trusted him. I don't know why I did it. I don't know why I kept so many secrets. Part of it was self-preservation. I know that now, but still, I was wrong. I shouldn't have let it go on for so long, especially when, truth be told, I never developed deep feelings for Jeff."

Kate licked her lips and glanced down. "I've been lying to myself for years, thinking I told him about my past so he could better understand me, but that wasn't the case. The day it all came out, he kept pushing and pushing, and I wanted him to stop. I wanted the lectures about how I should dress and how I should behave to stop. I wanted him to stop pushing me to do things I didn't want to do. I wanted to stop cowering away from him. He pushed and pushed and before I could stop myself, the words poured out of my mouth. I didn't tell him, I screamed it at him. I raged at him."

Kate was breathing hard and trembling, and Noah's arms ached to hold her, but he held still and waited for Kate to say and do what she needed, to expunge this part of her past.

Kate raised her head, and her wide, pain-filled green eyes met his. "I didn't tell him everything. I didn't need to. I told him enough to repel him, enough for him to throw me out of his life and never look back. I told him my real name was Kate, not Meghan. I told him the trash heap I came from, and he wasn't my first or my second. I confessed that for three months, I sold my body. That wasn't my entire past, but he'd heard enough."

Noah could no longer hold back. He reached across the sofa and pulled Kate onto his lap, and she came willingly, straddling him, wrapping her legs and arms around him and laying her head on his chest. In the short time he spent with her, he recognized this was her favorite position, the one that soothed her the most. He loved it too. This way she was wrapped around him and he around her.

"Know what, Noah?"

Noah tilted his head down and kissed her forehead as he ran his fingers up and down her spine.

"What, sweetheart?"

"He did what I expected him to do. He turned his back and walked away."

Noah startled out of his thoughts as he felt the plane abruptly launch itself into the air. His body slammed against the back of the seat as his drink sloshed out of the glass and onto his lap. So much for a smooth taxi and takeoff. He shook his head and settled back in his chair and sighed.

Noah closed his eyes, willing his body to relax and his brain to slow down. The more Kate told him about her past and present, the more he worried about her. He wanted to, no, needed to protect her. Noah understood that his past experiences with Kristin impacted his actions, but he felt powerless to throw off the panic that gripped him when he thought of anything happening to Kate.

The problem was, Kate didn't want protecting. In fact, she insisted on handling everything on her own, and that didn't work for him. Surely now that she admitted she loved him and knew beyond a shadow of a doubt, he loved her as well, she'd let him help her.

Since Kristin, he'd become a protective son of a bitch over all his loved ones. He'd let drugs, alcohol, and a variety of unsavory people invade his life and take away Kristin, submerging her in a world he didn't know and had no wish to enter. He vowed he wouldn't let anything like that happen to Kate.

On his way to the airport, he'd called Sheriff Jordan for an update. He hadn't heard from the good sheriff, and Noah wanted to get some reassurances Kate was safe. Unfortunately, what he heard from Jordan only agitated him more.

"The leader of the pack is Kyle Granger. He's trouble, Noah, and so is his posse. The kid's got quite the rap sheet for a sixteen-year-old."

Noah ran his hand through his hair. "So why is the little shit running around? I don't get it."

The sheriff sighed. "The kid comes from a wealthy family. The family moved here about six months ago. Dad's running for state Senate and is rarely home. The kid's mother died three years ago, and that's when he went off the rails."

"Yeah, that's all real interesting, Jordan." Noah ground his teeth and tried to control his rising temper. "That doesn't answer my question. Why is the little infestation running around? Why aren't you doing your job?"

"Settle down, Noah. I'm on your side. Kid's been picked up multiple times for a variety of reasons. When it comes right down to it, none of his victims follow through and file charges. I suspect his father has deep pockets and takes care of his kid's indiscretions, but I can't prove anything. My hands are tied. Kate must file a formal complaint, or I can't do a damn thing about it, other than have a word with him. I gotta tell you, that'll probably piss the kid off and he'll go for her again."

Recalling that conversation made Noah's anxiety level peak, and the seven-hour flight to London felt more like twenty-seven hours. Jordan promised to check in on Kate today and to try to get her to file a complaint. After speaking to Jordan, Noah called Kate to warn her about Jordan's visit, but she didn't give him a chance to get a word in. Kate was overwhelmed with customers and told him to have a good flight, and then quickly hung up.

By the time Noah made it out of the busy Heathrow airport and to his penthouse in Knightsbridge, it was 11:00 PM in London and 6:00 PM in New Jersey. Noah knew Kate would be in the process of closing the bookstore. He decided to give her time to finish out her day before he called. He spent the time unpacking and checking his messages. Then he foraged for food.

God love Luke. He always had the place well-stocked for him. Noah fixed himself a drink and a sandwich and sat on the cream-colored leather couch to call his sexy siren. The phone rang and rang, finally going to voicemail. He waited another half hour and tried again without any success. He texted her but got no response.

By 1:00 AM, Noah was exhausted and was still unable to reach Kate. He lay in bed, trying not to let his imagination get the best of him. Eventually, exhaustion won, and he fell into a fitful, dreamless sleep. Four hours later he was wide awake, thinking of Kate once again.

Noah made his way to the kitchen and started the coffee machine. He needed a significant hit of caffeine to clear the cobwebs. Ten minutes later, he sat with a steaming cup of industrial strength Java and dialed Kate again. It was midnight in Jersey, and he felt guilty calling so late, but he needed to know she was all right before he started what was sure to be a busy day. Assuming she wouldn't answer, Noah was surprised when she picked up on the first ring.

"Hello, Noah," Kate said in a clipped, tight voice.

"Kate, sweetheart, hi." Noah sighed in relief and sank deeper into the couch. "Did I wake you? I'm sorry I'm calling so late, but I tried earlier and couldn't get you. Everything okay?"

"Everything is fine, and no you didn't wake me. I know you called earlier, but I was too damn angry to speak with you." Kate sighed. "Anything you want to tell me, Noah?"

Noah sat up and shook his head. What had gotten into his sweet Kate to make her sound so prickly? Then, it hit him.

Jordan. Fuck.

Taking a deep breath, he dove in, hoping she was in an understanding and forgiving mood.

"I take it Sheriff Jordan paid you a visit."

"Yup. He sure did. I don't get it. We discussed this, and I told you I didn't want the sheriff involved." Kate's voice rose. "I told you I was going to handle this my way. You didn't listen to me, didn't respect my wishes. What gives you the right to interfere in my life this way?"

Whoa.

Noah placed his mug on the coffee table, stood, and started to pace. Kate was a lot more worked up than he thought she'd be. Somehow he'd stepped into a huge pile of shit, again. He needed to calm her down and be the reasonable one. He needed to control his rising temper. He didn't appreciate her accusations. Both of them couldn't lose it, though.

What gave him the right? Was she serious? She was his. His to love. His to protect. The thing with the security system was way before they declared their love for one another. This was different. He had to get her to see reason.

"Kate, I'm sorry. I tried to tell you when we spoke earlier, but I didn't get a chance. I spoke to the sheriff, and those boys are trouble. They're not going to go away. The kid that cornered you, Kyle Granger, he's bad news. He's been in a lot of trouble and his father always bails him out. He's not harmless. I was trying to protect you. I…"

"I know that kid is trouble. I know all about kids like him. I grew up with kids like him in the toughest, most gang-ridden area of Chicago where kids killed each other over a pencil, or a cookie, or just for breathing. I know how to handle his type and much worse. What I don't know, is how to handle you," she barked out.

Kate could handle gangsters, but she didn't know how to handle him? With those few words, so many things clicked into place. Kate was used to violence, abuse, and neglect, but she had no idea how to interpret affection, caring, concern, or kindness. She'd been on the defensive her whole life, always fighting for survival. Nothing else made sense.

Now that he understood where she was coming from, he wouldn't assume again that she would interpret his actions appropriately. God, he loved this stubborn woman. He'd have to spend time explaining his actions until he could right her world, and she learned this new language of love. But, he would protect her, even from herself. He had no choice. He couldn't live any other way.

"Noah, are you listening to me?"

"Yes, of course. I hear you, but calm down and listen," he said, gentling his voice.

"No, I will not calm down. You had no right, no right at all to disregard my wishes. I'm not a helpless twit who can't take care of herself," she yelled, her voice rising again. "I won't have you making decisions about my life without me. I've been there before. I told you. I need to do things my way. I don't need you to save me."

Was she fucking serious? Despite Noah's best efforts, his temper rose again, and the words were out of his mouth before he could stop them.

"I have no right? Are you kidding? I heard everything you told me, and I've tried to be patient and understanding, but when will you bend? When will you understand my feelings and compromise? I asked you before, and I'll ask you again. Where the hell do I fit into this picture, this life you created where no one is allowed in and no one is allowed to care about you or help you?"

It was as if Kate never heard his questions or the anguish in his voice. She bulldozed on, never backing down for a second, fighting for something he couldn't understand.

"I don't need taking care of. That's not what we're about. I thought you understood that. You've seen me at my worst, and you might think I'm a mess, that I'm weak. But let me assure you, I'm not. I've survived things you couldn't even fathom."

Kate was incensed, panting. He imagined all five feet four of her standing rod-straight, red hair flowing around her, fire in her eyes, and her hands fisted as she raged.

"I've had my power stripped from me before, and I will not allow it to happen again. This isn't going to work, Noah. I'm not the right woman for you. I can't do what you're asking me to do and be the woman you want me to be. I need to be in charge of my life. I can't have you plotting and planning behind my back."

This was about power, control, and survival for her. Kate wasn't scared of those boys half as much as she was scared of losing control over her world. In fact, she was terrified of that happening again. Noah thought he was protecting her, keeping her safe, but she wasn't ready to trust him with herself yet. She wasn't prepared to give someone else the privilege of taking care of her. He had to get her to listen to him before they lost all the ground they'd gained.

Kate had no clue what a healthy relationship was about—the give and take, the sharing of good and bad. She couldn't understand that letting someone care for her was not the same as giving up her power.

Noah rubbed his neck and breathed out. He had to approach this problem from a different angle. He had to have patience, go slow, and lead his injured girl out of the darkness and into the light.

Kate had been silent for a few minutes, and he heard her ragged breathing slow.

"Kate, baby, stop. Now I get it. I know you're hurt and angry and maybe even scared, but stop now, and listen to me. Okay?"

Hearing no reply, he continued. "I'm sorry, sweetness. I'm sorry. I was only trying to keep you safe. I didn't want those boys to hurt you. I'm far away, in a different country, and I couldn't stand it if anything happened to you. The last time I was given a chance at happiness with someone, I fucked it up. I didn't keep her safe, not even from herself. I lost her, Katie, and I can't get her back." Noah's voice broke.

"I can't lose you too. Don't you get it? I too am struggling, here."

Noah raked his fingers through his hair and sat down on the couch.

"Katie, sweetheart, this has nothing to do with stripping you of your power and everything to do with keeping you safe. I don't think you're weak or helpless, not at all. On the contrary, you're the strongest person I've ever met. I don't want to take over your life. I want to be a part of it. Please, don't end us. Just hold on. We'll figure things out together."

More silence.

Noah waited, hopeful that she would accept his apology and understand where he was coming from. If she could do that, if she could meet him half way, there was hope for them. This was the first of many missteps to come as they learned to navigate the waters around each other. They'd each come into this relationship with weighty baggage, and until all the bags were opened and unpacked, they would have to afford each other some grace if this was going to work. Noah was willing to make the effort and do the work. But was Kate?

She didn't let him down. Her voice came through the phone, soft and deflated. "I'm sorry. I don't know how to do this, Noah. I'm broken. I told you. I'm…I'm not used to having anyone care for me, think about me without trying to control every aspect of my life. How do I do this, so I don't destroy us?"

Kate started to sob, great, big heaving sobs, and Noah felt his heart break a little. He felt like absolute shit. She was crying, and he wasn't there to hold and comfort her.

"Hey now. Easy, sweetness. Don't cry. It's going to be okay. I can't stand to hear you cry. You're killing me here. We're going to be okay. We're going to find our way around each other, with each other. We have to allow for mistakes and mix-ups and not think the worst or give up on each other when they happen. This is new for both of us. Okay?"

After a few minutes, in a more composed voice, Kate said, "Okay."

"I love you, Kate. Please don't cry. I never want to make you cry."

Kate took in a stuttering breath. "I'm sorry. I love you too, Noah."

Smiling in relief, Noah let out the breath he'd been holding. This battle was fought and won, and they'd survived. He knew there would be more battles to come, and some would be bloody, but for now, he was going to celebrate this small win. "Okay. Now tell me why you're up so late, other than being pissed at me. What're you doing?"

"I'm baking. When things get tough, and I can't sleep, I bake," she said with a smile in her voice. "I'm making red velvet cupcakes with a cream cheese filling and frosting. They're phenomenal."

Noah sighed and settled back against the couch. "God, that sounds good, but I'm sorry I drove you to bake in the middle of the night. You're going to be wasted in the morning. You have to open the bookstore in a few hours." He lifted his coffee cup and drained its contents and then made his way to the kitchen for another cup. She wasn't the only one who was going to be wasted.

"Nah, I'll be fine. I'm used to this. It happens all the time."

"Really? Getting so few hours of sleep can't be

good. What has you up so often?"

Kate had previously told him she baked when she had a lot on her mind and had trouble sleeping, but he thought there was more to the story.

Kate sighed. "I have nightmares. I thought I got rid of them, but I was wrong. Sometimes I wake up and can't go back to sleep, and sometimes I'm too scared to close my eyes."

Noah sat down heavily on the couch again, closing his eyes, absorbing the pain in his girl's voice. He tried to make sense of all the things she was not saying. "Are the dreams about your childhood?"

"Yes. There's a lot of content there to keep me going for a long time, but thankfully there are a lot of recipes I haven't tried yet. So, it all works out in the end. I bake, and I sing horribly off key to Shakes, and he sings with me."

Kate was making light of it, but Noah wasn't fooled. One day, he'd ask her to tell him all about her dreams, but she wasn't ready for that yet.

"Never mind me and my obsessive baking. Shouldn't you be at work or something?"

"Actually, yeah. I should probably get going. But I want you in bed first. Are you done baking yet?"

"Yup. The kitchen is closed, and I just made my way to my room. I'll lie down for a while. You go to work. I'll be fine."

"Nope, that's not how this works. I'm going to tuck you in and give you something to dream about. Let me know when you're in bed, and I'll work my magic on you. I have special powers that have nothing to do with baking and everything to do with taking you to a fabulous new location."

Kate laughed. "Okay, dream-weaver. I'm in bed. Now what?"

"Now, snuggle under the blankets and close your eyes. Have you ever seen the sunset on the beaches of Costa Rica? They're the most wonderful thing, a true miracle of nature."

"No, I've never traveled out of the U.S. Tell me about it," she said with a yawn.

Chuckling, he said, "Close your eyes, sweetness, and imagine you're walking on a white sandy beach with the bluest, clearest ocean on one side, and a tropical rainforest on the other. The sand is so fine, it's like sugar. As the sun makes its dramatic exit, the sky explodes in many colors, layering the sky in deep golds, purples, varying blues and grays, pinks, oranges, and yellows. The sun appears like a giant golden orb as it makes its descent through the clouds and for a few minutes, it appears as if it's bouncing on the surface of the ocean.

"The warm breeze kisses your face and lifts the hair off your shoulders. The smell of the sea fills your nose, salty, crisp, and clean. The sound of the waves crashing to shore fills your ears, but if you listen carefully, you can also hear the sound of the rainforest nearby. There is nothing more perfect, more pure, or more miraculous than standing so close to the equator, but never being burned by the sun. Here the world and all its inhabitants come together and are at peace with one another. Here you are safe, and nothing can harm you."

Noah stopped speaking, hoping he'd accomplished his goal and that his girl found some peace. When the only thing he heard coming from the other side of the phone was the sound of her deep, slow, steady breathing, he smiled. For now, she found sleep in the beautiful dream he created for her. Today he could keep the boogie man away long enough so she could find a few hours of peace, but that wasn't good enough. He wanted to banish all her nightmares permanently. He wanted to make all her dreams a reality. This was only the beginning. He had a lot of work to do.

Chapter Fourteen

Kate's eyes fluttered open. She smiled and stretched. She'd only slept for a few hours, but she felt rested. She could still hear Noah's soothing voice in her ear, as he transported her from her small bedroom above the bookstore to the breathtaking beaches of Costa Rica. His rich, deep voice was hypnotic. He managed to wipe away not only the anger and confusion that came with the sheriff's visit, but also her nightmares.

Tuesday was Kate's favorite day of the week. Mrs. Greco, her part-time help, came in at 10:00 AM and stayed until closing. This allowed Kate to get some paperwork or shelving done, have an occasional lunch out, run errands, or spend some time at the dojo with Master Lim.

Kate got out of bed and went through her morning routine. She dressed in dark denim jeans that fit her small body like a glove, a colorful striped sweater, and a black quilted vest. She pulled her mass of hair into a high ponytail and slipped her feet into tall, black leather boots that had a quilted pattern to them. She was ready to conquer the day.

She worked through the morning with a smile on her face. What did she have to frown about? She had a man in her life—a man who cared about her, who was patient, kind, and didn't run when she lost her temper and screamed at him. She was ashamed of her behavior and vowed to make it up to him. Noah constantly surprised her. Just when she thought she scared him off, he turned things around and reeled her back in.

"Well, hello there. Isn't this a cute little place? Simply charming."

Kate jumped, almost knocking over the display

she worked on all morning. Turning toward the front door, her welcoming smile froze on her face. Decked in a black cashmere turtleneck, a tiny black leather skirt, and four-inch black leather boots, Ava resembled the witch she was.

"Good morning, Ava. What do you want?"

Tucking her sleek, straw-colored hair behind her ear and putting her index finger to her cheek in a thoughtful pose, Ava smiled. "Well, that's not a very welcoming way of greeting your customers. I was in the area and dropped by to see what all the fuss was about, but if you're going to be nasty…"

Kate glared at Ava in silence and shrugged. Ava gave an exasperated sigh.

"I see you're going to give me the silent treatment again. Well, that's fine with me. Perhaps your vocabulary is lacking. You should expand your reading choices beyond the children's section." Ava said.

Kate controlled her facial expression, making every effort to appear unaffected by Ava's words. All she wanted to do was slap the condescending smile off the bitch's face. Instead, she turned her back on Ava and resumed working on the display.

"I have a lot of work to do, Ava. If you need assistance, Mrs. Greco can help you."

"Ahh, she speaks. I don't need assistance, but I think you could use some advice. Dee tells me you and Reed are an item now. Spare yourself the effort. He's been down this road before, and it ended in a disastrous crash with several fatalities."

Kate froze. Was Ava comparing her to Kristin? She needed to put an end to this conversation. She didn't want to listen to anything Ava had to say, didn't want to give Ava a hint of encouragement, but she couldn't help herself. Kate was curious about Kristin. How were they alike? She wasn't out of control and into drugs and alcohol.

"Reed doesn't need another poor, needy damsel in distress in his life. I've known Reed since we were children, and he always falls for the wrong type, like his daddy did—both bleeding hearts."

Damsel in distress? Kate turned slowly to face Ava. Ava's face had a triumphant expression on it as she took a step toward Kate.

"Leave Reed and his family alone. They're good people, but they've been through enough with the last poor choice he made. We've all decided we're not letting him make the same mistake again."

Kate stood, rooted to her spot. What did Ava mean by *we*? Did Dee and Clare feel the same? Did she remind them too much of Kristin? Is that why Dee was treating her so coldly? Regardless, Kate couldn't allow Ava to speak to her like this. If Dee, Clare, or anyone else in the family had something to say about her and Noah, they would have to do it in person. She wasn't falling for this bullshit.

Kate opened her mouth to tell Ava off when she caught movement at the door. Emma. How did Emma always appear out of the blue each time she and Ava were at each other's throats? It was uncanny.

Emma's eyes were huge and troubled. Kate wondered how much the poor kid heard of Ava's bitchy comments. Kate ignored Ava and smiled at Emma.

"Hi-ya Em," Kate said, trying to keep her voice light and playful. "Did you drive here on your own or did Mom bring you?"

Emma glanced at Ava, and then back to Kate. She came to stand by Kate and reached for her hand.

"M-mom's outside. She wants to know if you can come to lunch with us. We're meeting Aunt Jules and

Lilly." Emma pulled on Kate's hand. "You've got to come now. Right now."

"Hi there, Emma. How are you doing, princess?" Ava said in a sickly, sweet tone. "How's every little thing? Come give Aunt Ava a hug."

Emma took a step back and hid behind Kate.

Ava's eye's widened, and she huffed.

"For goodness sake, Emma. What's this about? I'm not going to bite you. That's very rude behavior, young lady. Your mother would be horrified."

Emma tucked herself even tighter into Kate's back. Kate had never seen Emma behave this way and was stunned. She felt Emma tug on her hand.

"We have to go," Emma insisted in a trembling voice.

Kate turned and squatted, so she was eye to eye with the child. "Emma, look at me, baby. Everything's okay. Why don't you go outside and tell your mom I'll be out in a few?"

Emma shook her head. "Y-you have to come now." Emma's eyes filled with tears, and her lower lip trembled. "Please."

Kate had no idea what had her so worked up, but she couldn't stand to see Emma upset. Sighing, she stood and peered over her shoulder at Ava.

"Like I said, Mrs. Greco can help you. As always, it's been a joy chatting with you."

Not waiting for a reply, Kate took Emma's hand and walked out to find Dee approaching the front door.

"There you are. I was wondering what was keeping you guys." Dee smiled at Kate.

Before Kate could answer, Emma ran to her mother and blurted, "Aunt Ava is in there. I told you she was mean to Miss Kate. She did it again. I don't like that, Mommy. Why is she so mean?"

Dee's eyes met Kate's, and Kate shrugged and winced. So, Emma had heard Ava. Emma was a smart kid and had plenty of experience with bullies. Of course, she would be protective of Kate, while being scared at the same time. Children like Emma were sensitive and knew who to trust and who not to. Ava was Dee's friend, however, and Kate did not want to cause problems between the women. Since lunner, Dee had been treating Kate differently, and the last thing she wanted to do was make things worse.

"Hey, Emma. I don't want you to worry about any of that. I'm fine. Ava and I were having a difference of opinion. Nothing for you to worry about. Okay?"

Emma studied Kate for a beat and then gave her an uncertain smile and nodded. Dee didn't say a word and didn't make any effort to go and greet Ava, or invite her to lunch with them as Kate thought she would. Dee simply changed the subject and quickly guided them away from the bookstore.

Together they walked the short distance to Frank's Diner. Away from Ava, Emma bounced back to her bubbly self with remarkable speed. She was back to being happy and chatty and seemed unaffected by the interaction.

Frank's was located three blocks from the bookstore on Spring Street. It was packed, as usual, but Jules and Lilly had nabbed them a table against the front window. Jules waved to them as they made their way inside.

"Hey, Jules. This is such a pleasant surprise," Kate said, smiling at the pretty woman and turning her attention to Lilly who was busy coloring. "Hi, baby. How are you today?"

Frowning, Lilly glared and corrected her. "I'm not a baby. I'm a lady."

Kate laughed and scooped Lilly up. "I'm terribly sorry, Lady Lilly. Of course, you're not a baby. My mistake. I have a surprise for you, though."

Lilly's eyes lit up. "Give me, pu-weese."

"Kisses first, madam. Then I will give you your surprise."

Lilly hugged Kate around the neck, nearly choking her, and placed a sloppy, wet kiss on her cheek. Kate laughed and put her down. She pulled the picture book she grabbed on her way out of the bookstore, out of her bag—*I Don't Want to Be a Frog.*

"Here you go."

"Mine?" Lilly asked, big blue eyes staring at Kate in wonder.

"Yes, it's all yours, cookie. Have a seat and you can read it."

"Thank-um," Lilly said, sitting down and opening her book.

Kate glanced up to find the women watching her with smiles on their faces.

"You're so good with her. You're going to be a wonderful mother one day," Jules said, smiling at Kate.

Kate felt a tug at her heart as she took the seat next to Dee. "Thanks, but I'm not sure motherhood is in the cards for me. I do enjoy other peoples' children, though."

"Why?" Jules asked. "You're still young. One day you'll find your prince charming, and maybe he'll want to make pretty babies with you."

Kate focused on her hands. How was she supposed to explain that her gene pool sucked? It was too long of an explanation and too heavy of a subject for this light lunch. Maybe one day these women would turn from acquaintances to friends she could trust. Wouldn't that be something?

By the way Dee was behaving, however, they'd lost ground, not gained it, in the friendship department. She allowed Ava's words to penetrate. Apparently, Dee didn't approve of her relationship with Noah, and that sucked. Kate didn't want to lose Noah or her friendship with Dee, and this was a small town. How would it work if Dee and Clare disapproved of her? The Reeds were a beautiful family, a tight family, and no way could she be the person who tore them apart.

"Hey, Kate. I'm sorry if I made you feel uncomfortable. It's none of our business, of course. I'm sorry," Jules said in a hesitant voice.

Kate raised her head and shoved her thoughts to the back of her brain. She smiled at both women.

"It's fine, don't worry about it. I'm overtired today. I was up late baking last night, and I'm a bit grumpy."

Jules accepted Kate's explanation with a smile and changed the subject. Once Kate allowed herself to relax, she enjoyed the time she spent with the women. But something was definitely off with Dee. She wasn't rude, just standoffish. If Dee disapproved of her relationship with Noah, why did she keep inviting her out? Was it a matter of 'keep your friends close and your enemies closer'?

Eventually, Dee and Kate said goodbye to Jules and a sleepy Lilly. They walked back to the bookstore together with Emma skipping in front of them. Kate had a stack of books for Emma at the bookstore that Noah ordered for her.

Smiling at Dee, Kate decided to take the bull by the horns. They had to stop tiptoeing around the topic of her and Noah sooner or later.

"Thanks for inviting me to lunner and lunch today. Both were lovely."

Dee turned her head and studied Kate with a small smile. "You're welcome. Emma loves spending time with you."

Well, that statement said a lot. This was for Emma? Kate didn't think so. Dee had an ulterior motive.

"Dee," Kate started. "You know Noah and I are seeing each other. It's new. We're new. But…" Kate's face heated with embarrassment. Why was this so hard? She was a single adult, as Noah was. They weren't doing anything wrong or hurting anyone. Why on earth was she so nervous?

Kate stopped walking, and Dee followed.

"Yes, I know," Dee said in a flat tone. "If you're looking for my blessing, don't. You don't need it. He's an adult."

Kate was taken aback. Dee wasn't hurtful or nasty in the past, but she was bordering on it now. Kate didn't know what she did to deserve this kind of treatment. Dee still let Emma come to the bookstore and left her with Kate for hours. How could Dee trust her with her daughter, but not with her brother? It made no sense.

Kate took a deep breath and tried again. "Dee, I'm not sure what's…"

"Kate," Dee interrupted, "You make Noah smile, and he's happier than he's been in a long time. I guess I have you to thank for that."

Kate frowned. "Isn't that a good thing? You don't sound happy about it."

Deidra studied Kate. Her lips thinned and she sighed.

"You know about Kristin, right?"

"Yes. Some."

Dee sighed again and focused on her feet. "Do you have time to sit down and chat for a few minutes?"

"Sure. My session at the dojo doesn't start for

another hour."

Kate and Dee walked toward the bookstore in silence. As they rounded the corner and the bookstore became visible, Kate gasped. Kyle and one of his friends were sitting on the front porch in two of the rocking chairs. Their eyes met, and he smirked.

Kate took a deep breath, willing herself to stay calm. After all, the boys weren't doing anything other than innocently sitting on the porch. Kate knew better. Kyle was a bully, and he was sending her a message. But she didn't want a scene, especially not in front of Dee and Emma.

As the women approached the stairs leading to the porch, the boys stood and made their way down the stairs, still smirking at Kate.

"See you soon, Miss Kate," Kyle said in nearly a whisper as he past Kate and brushed her shoulder with his.

Kate froze halfway up the stairs. She didn't want a scene, but she also didn't want Kyle to think he could get away with this behavior. She wouldn't allow him to bully her.

As Emma ran into the bookstore, and Dee made her way to one of the rockers, oblivious to what was happening, Kate turned and called out to the boys.

"Boys."

Both boys turned and smirked at her. She met Kyle's eyes and stared coldly at him.

"You're not welcome here, not now, not ever. If you come back, I'll call the sheriff. Consider yourselves warned. Do you understand?"

The boys looked at each other and burst out laughing. Then turned and walked away.

Shit. That was not effective. Kate's blood boiled. She wanted to throw something at them. Maybe she should get a German Shephard or a Doberman.

"Kate? Is everything okay?"

Shit. Dee. She'd forgotten about Dee. That was it, Kate wanted a redo! This day was quickly unraveling. Why did every rotten thing have to happen on the same day?

Kate turned to Dee with a reassuring smile. "Yes, all is well. Just some teenage antics."

Deidra nodded and focused on something in the distance as she rocked back and forth. Kate sat in a rocker next to Dee and waited for Dee to start. Dee appeared deep in thought and Kate took the time to get her breathing and heart rate under control. She couldn't deal with Kyle right now. She had to focus on Dee. Later she would allow herself to dissect what happened and come up with a plan to deal with him.

"Kate," Dee started.

Kate turned her head and studied Dee.

"I think you need to know more about our family and more about Noah to understand where I'm coming from."

Kate nodded.

"I'm the oldest of the Reed brood. Next comes Reed and then Luke. The three of us are about eighteen months apart. Baby Clare, however, was a surprise. She's twelve years younger than me. Growing up, our family was big, boisterous, and amazingly, we all got along. Each of us had our unique personalities, though. Clare, being the baby, was our free-spirited, wild child that we all worked hard to keep safe and to keep dad from putting her in a convent, which he threatened to do often."

Kate smiled and shook her head in disbelief. "Really? Sweet, quiet Clare? I don't believe it."

"Oh, believe it. Underneath this new, mature Clare lives a wild woman. Anyway, I'm the mother hen, always trying to take care of the brood. Luke is the prankster. And Reed…well…Reed was the kid, the man, that everyone was drawn to, and everyone loved. He had a soft, giving heart and always wore a huge smile. Nothing upset him. He laughed frequently and easily. But all that changed the day Kristin walked into his life. She almost destroyed my brother. To this day, part of him is missing."

Kate sat up straighter. She was ready to hear whatever Dee had to tell her. Maybe if she understood where Dee was coming from, she could address her concerns.

"Right from the start I could tell Kristin wasn't the right girl for Noah. She had a lot of problems— serious problems. But Noah didn't care. He was drawn to her like a moth to a flame and in the end, he was burned badly."

Dee turned to Kate and studied her before continuing.

"The thing is, Reed was born with a big, generous, loving heart. He can't stand to see someone in trouble and not help. Because of that, from a young age, he was attracted to only one kind of girl. With his charm, easy demeanor, and good looks, he could have any girl he wanted, but my brother has always been attracted to damsels in distress. Kristin was that and then some."

Dee stood and walked the length of the porch before turning and meeting Kate's eyes again.

"Reed lost a part of himself and almost lost his family trying to help her. She tore his heart out and ripped our family apart in the process. We are a tight family. We love each other and never give up on one another. It's how we were raised. Family first, family always. Reed forgot all of that. Kristin had no idea what family was and didn't want anything to do with us, no matter how hard we tried. She sunk her claws into him and tried to drag him into the gutter, where she came from."

Dee ran her hand through her hair and swiped at her wet eyes. She took a deep breath and shook her head.

"Reed lost his mind. He was torn between his dying mother, his grieving father, and his broken beyond repair, needy wife. He couldn't give up on Kristin. Drugs, alcohol, trouble with the law, even infidelity, you name it. Those were the gifts Kristin kept giving Reed in return for all the love he rained on her."

Dee stared at Kate and tightened her jaw. "Kristin was into anything and everything you can imagine, and a few things you probably can't. Reed wouldn't admit she needed more help than he could provide. Then her antics escalated, and our lives exploded. He didn't just lose her, he, he lost…"

Dee stopped speaking and shook her head. "Never mind," she said with a deep sigh. "To this day, I know he blames himself for her death, although there was nothing he could have done to prevent it."

Kate didn't know what to say. She was shattered. Somewhere during Dee's explanation, her heart began to ache and then bleed. Her stomach turned. She was sick—sick with pain, humiliation, and shame. Her heart raced, and she broke out into a fine sweat, although the day was cool.

A damsel in distress.

Is that what Noah thought of her? Is that what they all thought of her? Was he with her only because he thought she needed fixing?

Last night he allayed her fears and told her he didn't think she was weak. But what if he was saying what he thought she needed to hear? What if he thought of her as some project, something broken he needed to fix? Apparently, he couldn't help himself. He was drawn to damaged people and she sure as hell fit the bill. All of Kate's insecurities, every ugly thing she'd thought of herself, rose to the surface and screamed to be recognized. Kate began to tremble.

"Kate? Are you okay?" Dee's voice brought Kate out of her dark thoughts before she spiraled into what was sure to become a full panic attack.

Kate nodded. "Uh, yes, of course. I'm fine. I-I have to go, though. I'm sorry. I've got to run. Thanks for lunch."

Kate stood, unable to meet Dee's eyes. She couldn't listen anymore. Dee had made her point abundantly clear.

Message received.

She wasn't good enough for Noah, and she never would be.

Dee grabbed Kate's arm before she could flee. "Kate, wait. Don't go. Please."

Taking a deep, steadying breath, Kate pulled her arm free, tried to compose herself, and met Dee's eyes.

Dee's face was lined with worry. "I didn't tell you all that to hurt you. I swear."

"It's okay, Dee. I'm fine. I'll be fine. It's best that we let this go. I understand how you feel."

Kate focused on her hands and laced her fingers together to hide their trembling.

"Noah's your brother and you love him. You want the best for him, and I'm not it. I get it. I'm glad you told me how you feel."

Grabbing her arm again, Dee said in a firm voice, "No, no, Kate, that's not what I meant. Please hear me out. Honestly, I'm not trying to be a bitch. It's…I don't know what to do, how to stop the past from repeating itself. You're sweet, but I'm not sure…I…"

Sighing, Kate closed her eyes and rubbed her temples. She was exhausted. The lack of sleep mixed with the emotional conversation sapped all her energy. She didn't have it in her to argue with Dee. She listened to what Dee had to say. Now, she needed to go inside and collapse in private. Her heart was breaking. To hell with class, she had enough abuse for the day. Sparring didn't sound the least bit enticing when she'd already been pounded into a bloody pulp.

"Kate, please listen. Reed and I are close. Our mother was gone by the time Kristin passed, so I stepped in. I held that man when he fell apart after the accident, and my heart almost broke when I heard him crying. I told you about Kristin because I wanted you to know the kind of man Reed is, what he's been through."

Dee squeezed Kate's arm. "Kate, please look at me."

It took all of Kate's strength and will to stop the tears that were stinging the back of her eyelids from falling. She opened her eyes and met Dee's.

"I know my brother. He won't survive another loss. If you hurt him, if you tear him apart as she did, he won't survive."

Tears ran down Dee's face, and she swiped at them.

"This time, when he unravels, I won't be able to stitch him back together. He'll be in too many pieces. He's become more attached to you in the short time you've been together than he ever was to Kristin. When you hurt him, when you run away and reject him, there'll be no putting him back together."

Kate could no longer hold back the tears or the hurt. "And did you ever think about me, or don't I count? I love Noah, and he loves me." Kate swiped at the tears that leaked out of her traitorous eyes. "I know you don't know me well, but I don't get it. You trust me with your child, but you don't trust me with your brother's heart? What about my heart? What about me? There are two people in this relationship."

Dee studied Kate with wide, troubled eyes for a minute.

"I can't give you what you want," Dee whispered in a tortured voice. "I can't give you my blessing. I won't. Noah may be ready to take a chance and dive into yet another unhealthy relationship, but I can't go along with him. I won't sit by silently, again as he ruins his life and tears apart his family. I know you must think I'm a heartless bitch, but let me ask you a question. What would you do for someone you love? How far would you go? If you insist on traveling this path, you'll tear us apart. Noah will lose his family. We can't go through this with him again. It's too hard to watch, too hard to endure. Is that what you want?"

Dee pierced Kate with a hard stare. "Kate, I don't know where you came from or what you're hiding. You may not have much of a family, but he does. I'll tell you something, when this infatuation you two have falls apart, he'll be by himself. You will have pulled him away from everything and everyone he knows and loves. Is that what you want for the person you claim to love?"

Chapter Fifteen

Kate lay in bed, under a down comforter, hiding from the world. Her head hurt, and her heart ached. After Deidra left, she went to the dojo after all. She spent two hours working out on her own and an additional hour observing a children's class. She knew better than to get in a sparring match when she was this emotionally cooked.

Master Lim took one look at her and said, "This will not solve what troubles you, but do as you must to settle your mind. The heart is a different matter altogether."

Master Lim was right, and he was wrong. While Kate didn't solve all her problems, she did reach some conclusions. Over the three hours spent at the dojo, she replayed the day's events and the conversations with Noah, Ava, and Dee.

I couldn't stand it if anything happened to you. The last time I was given a chance at happiness with someone, I fucked it up.

Reed doesn't need another poor, needy, damsel in distress in his life.

What would you do for someone you love? How far would you go?

The last question was the hardest because the answer was simple. She'd do anything for him. Anything. But could she walk away? Was that truly the best thing for him? For her, it would be catastrophic. She couldn't imagine her life without him now. But what about Noah? What if Dee never came around? Would he lose his family because of her? Kate didn't want that for him.

Then there was the whole damsel in distress thing. Ava was a jealous bitch, no doubt. Normally, Kate wouldn't have been affected by her words, but along with Dee's message, it was difficult to ignore everything they said.

As much as Kate wanted to, she could not place Dee in the bitch category. Dee loved her brother, and every word that came out of her mouth was said with love and concern. How could Kate fault her for that kind of love? Just because Kate never experienced that adoration and loyalty didn't mean she didn't understand and value it.

At first, Kate was hurt. Every word Dee said was a well-placed surgical incision that left Kate bleeding, with no accompanying anesthesia to dull the agony. Dee filleted her open. Every doubt and insecurity Kate ever experienced came pouring out. Initially, Kate was lost for a time in a sea of pain, anger, and confusion.

The easy thing to do was to give in to the anger and humiliation that naturally rose to the surface. Her mind raced.

She could tell Dee off.

She could call Noah and tell him what his sister said and how deep her words cut.

She could take the predictable route—the easiest course of action, the one she was most skilled at. She could run.

Kate could leave this little town, close Dreamscape, and sell the place through a realtor. She could run from Noah and their budding relationship, change her number, and lose herself in another small town or big city. She could resurrect Meghan Summerville, or she could create a whole new identity.

Kate considered each option. When she was through feeling sorry for herself, she decided it was time to put her big girl panties on and get her life together. Home, friends, family, a sense of community, freedom from secrets and fears, and the love of a good man—Kate wanted it all and she was willing to fight for it. She wasn't fragile and needy, and in time, her actions would prove it. She may have come from nothing, but she wasn't Kristin. Nor was she a damsel in distress. She hoped that with time, Dee and the rest of the family would come around because she didn't want Noah to live without all that beauty.

Kate threw off the covers and got up, grabbing her cell on the way to the kitchen. There was no use in staying in bed. Sleep was elusive, as usual. She needed to hear Noah's voice, needed to be reassured of his presence in her life and needed to keep busy. The Lakes Crossing Nursing Home was always happy to give her treats a home, and she decided they'd get a new batch of lemon cookies in the morning.

"Kate? Hey, sweetness. What a pleasant surprise."

Kate sighed and closed her eyes, absorbing the sound of Noah's rich voice over the phone. She let the tenor and cadence of it soothe her frayed and wounded heart. God, it was good to hear his voice.

"Kate? What's wrong, sweetness? Are you okay?"

"Hi, baby," she said in a husky voice. "I'm good. I wanted to wish you a good day, that's all."

Kate wanted to say more. She wanted to say she missed and needed him, wanted his arms around her and his lips on her. But no way was she going to act needy. She had to keep reminding herself of Kristin. She wouldn't be like her. She would be so different from her that Noah, Dee, and the rest of his family wouldn't see any resemblance whatsoever.

"Katie, I love hearing from you, especially when you call me, baby, but it's 1:00 AM in Jersey. What are you doing up so late again? Bad dream?"

"Nothing's going on," she said in an exaggerated, extra bouncy voice. "I'm making lemon cookies for the nursing home and thought I'd check in before you start your day. Did I catch you at a bad time?"

"This is a good time. Any time is a good time to hear your voice. I'm dressing and then having breakfast before I meet Luke at the office. How was your day? What did you do?"

Kate hesitated. She didn't want to add any more secrets, any more lies to their relationship, but she didn't want to start a family feud either. She wouldn't ask him to choose between his family and her. Kristin did that. She wouldn't go there.

"Well, let's see. I worked my butt off, as usual, then went out to lunch with Dee, Emma, Jules, and Lilly. Then I went to the dojo. Oh, Ava stopped by to check out the place."

"Ava? That's strange." Noah's voice lost its cheerfulness. "What was she doing in Lakes Crossing? She rarely leaves Manhattan. I didn't think you two hit it off at lunner."

Kate pinched her cell between her ear and shoulder so she could pick up the bowl filled with cookie dough.

"We're not going to be BFFs anytime soon, but it was fine. She said she was in the area. Anyway, she didn't stay long. Emma and Dee showed up to whisk me away to lunch a few minutes after she arrived. Don't worry. I can handle her just fine. All is well here."

As the words left Kate's mouth, her cell slipped from in between her shoulder and ear and into the batter.

"Oh, no. No, no, no!"

Kate backed into the counter as she reached into the bowl for her phone, knocking over a metal mixing bowl filled with flour and dropping the mixing bowl filled with cookie batter onto the floor. Batter and flour splattered throughout the kitchen.

"Oh, for fuck's sake!"

Kate stood with her hands on her hips, surveying the mess on the kitchen floor, counters and all over her feet. This was the perfect ending to a fairly miserable day. She grabbed a kitchen towel and sank to the floor in a fit of giggles as she wiped her face. Whatever! No cookies for the old people.

"Kate? Kate? What's going on over there? Are you okay?"

Kate couldn't stop laughing. Tears ran down her face, and she didn't know if they were from the hilarity of the situation or the overwhelming emotion of the day. It didn't matter. She tried to control her peals of laughter as she fished the phone from the pile of batter and cleaned it off with the towel. Fortunately, her cell phone cover was of the big, ugly, waterproof variety that made the phone twice as big as it actually was. But, thank God for it, because not a glob of batter made its way near the actual device.

Kate took a deep breath and let it out slowly, attempting to get some measure of control. Poor Noah was losing it on the other end.

"Noah, baby. I'm fine. It's all good," Kate said giggling once more as she licked her fingers.

Fine was an important new word in her vocabulary around Noah. She was going to be, *fine* all the damn time. That too made her laugh.

"What happened? What exploded in Betty Crocker land?"

In between fits of laughter, Kate explained what happened, describing it with so many embellishments Noah began to laugh right along with her. Kate loved the sound of his laughter more than anything else. She vowed to find more ways to make him laugh so that she could hear it on a regular basis.

"For such a sweet little thing, you have quite a filthy mouth. I find that remarkably sexy. You're filled with surprises, aren't you?" Noah said, filling her ears with more of his rumbling laughter.

Kate sobered. "Yes, I guess I am full of surprises. Not all of them are as entertaining as my dirty mouth, though."

Noah's laughter quieted and after a minute, he asked the question she was waiting for. He was a perceptive man and could tell she was in the midst of a meltdown.

"Tell me why you called, Katie. If you don't, I'm only going to worry. It's okay, sweetness. Talk to me."

Kate closed her eyes and drew her knees up to her chest, so her feet were flat on the floor. She settled against the cabinet and tilted her head back. She hadn't planned what to say to Noah once she got him on the phone. Maybe she should have, but the urge to call him and to talk to him was overwhelming.

There was so much she wanted to say, so much she wanted to share with him. She wanted him to understand how much he, Dee, Dreamscape, everyone and everything in Lakes Crossing meant to her—a girl who at one time had nothing and no one to call her own. Where to begin?

"When I was eighteen, I ran away from home. I left school and disappeared into thin air. Kate Willowbrook took a Greyhound bus headed toward Kansas and never looked back. Somewhere between Chicago and Kansas, I cut my hair and became Meghan Summerville."

Kate waited for Noah to ask the question anyone hearing this would. *Why?* But instead, he stayed silent.

"I only had twenty dollars on me. I was terrified." Kate's voice faltered, but she continued. "I told you what happened in the motel. That continued for three months."

Kate trembled thinking of that life. Tears filled her eyes, but she held them back. She gripped the towel so tight, her knuckles were white.

"I'm here, Katie. I'm with you, sweetheart." Noah's voice floated over the phone line, warming her chilled body.

Kate didn't know why she was telling him this now, over the phone of all things. But something in her propelled her forward and made her continue sharing another part of her past with him. She wanted to show him that although she came from nothing, she rose from the ashes. She was strong and capable. She was not Kristin.

Noah had only seen her emotional and unglued, but there was more to her than that. There was strength. There was the person who traveled thousands of miles on her own, building a new life from nothing. If she weren't strong and resilient, she wouldn't have survived her childhood or what followed.

Kate took a breath and cleared her throat. "Eventually, I got a job at a local diner. The owner was a horrible man with wandering hands and an abusive temper. I put up with it until I had enough money to get back on the bus. One town blended into another, until Edith Lawson entered my world."

Standing, Kate started cleaning the mess she'd created.

"I met her on a bus heading to Canton, Texas. She was loud, outrageous, and downright nosey. Even though she was in her seventies, she couldn't be described as elderly, and she didn't take shit from anyone, including me. She saw something in me, probably desperation, and therefore I became her project. She took me in, fed, dressed, and educated me. I lived with her for ten years."

"She sounds like a remarkable person."

Kate smiled. "She certainly was. Edith had a business degree and used to own several women's boutiques before she retired. When she found out my dream was to open my own bookstore, she taught me how to put a business plan together and how to run a successful business. She even got me my first job in a bookstore."

Kate laughed when she remembered Edith dragging her into the local bookstore and bullying the owner into hiring her part-time. The poor man was terrified and relented even though he didn't need the help.

"She was also an award-winning baker. That woman could bake anything from scratch, without the guidance of a recipe. She taught me to bake. She said the antidote to feeling ugly on the inside was a little sweetness on the outside. Weird treatment for nightmares, but it worked then, and it still works now."

"She sounds like a wise woman. Do you keep in touch with her?"

Kate sighed. "No, she's gone now. She was the first person on this planet that ever gave a damn about me, and I miss her every single day. She saved my life."

"You're not alone any longer. You have my family and me. We are your family now."

Kate smiled. Sweet Noah, always trying to save the world. But she wasn't his project, his damsel in distress. If they were going to stay together and if she was going to prove to Dee she was good enough for him, for all of them, she needed to be his partner, not his fixer-upper.

As for having him and his family—she certainly didn't have Dee. Clare seemed pleasant enough. In fact, they'd hit it off at lunner, and Kate had even convinced her to take a Taekwondo class for beginners. Luke, she'd never spoken to. Perhaps she still had a chance to get on his good side. Dee, however, was the matriarch of the family and spoke for all of them.

"Thanks, baby. That's sweet. I know you're there for me, but I want to be there for you too. Now, tell me what you're up to today."

Noah ignored her request. "Kate, why did you tell me about Edith?"

Kate paused her cleaning and dried her hands. She took a deep breath and hoped the words she said next would come out right. She hadn't thought this through, hadn't prepared adequately.

"I want you to know me, all of me. That's going to take a while because there's so much to tell."

Kate shook her head and sat at the kitchen table. She rested her elbow on the table and cradled her head in her hand, closing her eyes. She took in a slow and steady breath.

"Noah, I hope when you hear it all, you'll see I'm not a victim. I had a shitty start in life, but it hasn't all been bad. I did more than survive. Before Edith passed, she made me promise to leave Canton and to widen my world. She told me to stop hiding and start living, and that's what I did. She gave me the skills and left me the funds to do so."

Standing, Kate walked to the kitchen window and peered into the night. She wanted Noah to see her, all of her. She wanted him to not only see the damaged part, but also the smart, savvy, well-traveled business owner who could be his partner, his equal.

"I traveled all around the country for two years before I came to Jersey. I met a lot of people, saw so much, and learned a lot. I worked hard and saved money,

207

and when I saw the For Sale sign in front of Lakes Crossing Used Books, I knew I was finally home. I walked in and staked my claim. A year later, I made Dreamscape a reality."

"Uh, okay," Noah said in a puzzled tone. "Where is all this coming from, Kate? Why today and this late at night? What's going on, sweetheart? Please, tell me."

Kate let out a frustrated sigh. He still didn't get it. She would have to spell it out for him.

"I don't want you to worry about me so much. I'm fixing me, so you don't have to. I'm strong and capable. I'm probably stronger than most people because of what I've lived through. Do you understand?"

"Kate, I'm struggling here. Do you think I think less of you because of what you've shared with me?"

"No, of course not." Kate swallowed hard and rubbed her head. This wasn't going well, not at all. "That's not what I meant. This is coming out all wrong. Noah, I don't want to burden you with my problems. I don't want you ever to be ashamed of me. Despite my past, I'm strong and capable of making good decisions, and I'm going to…"

"Kate, stop," Noah clipped. "Ashamed of you? Where the hell is all this coming from?" He took a deep breath and started again. "You and I, we're in love, in a relationship, right?"

"Yes, of course, we are."

"Okay. Good. Glad we agree on that. People who love each other and are in a relationship share their lives with one another—everything, the good and the bad. I'm glad you want to do that, thrilled even, but Kate, people in relationships worry about one another. It's not a burden. It's a privilege."

Kate stayed silent. Part of her knew what he was saying was true, but how did they find balance? Truth be told, she wanted him to love her enough to worry about her. She didn't know what it felt like to be the center of someone's world. If she let him in all the way, would he get lost in her, spending all his time and energy trying to fix her? Would he lose himself and his family? Would she be nothing more than another Kristin to him?

The words were out of her mouth before she could stop them. "I'm not a damsel in distress. I'm not a project. I'm not Kristin."

Silence.

"What did you say?" Noah asked in an eerily quiet voice that sent chills down her spine.

Kate walked back to the table and sank down on the chair. She dropped her forehead to the table, and then banged it repeatedly. Shit. What had she done? With those few words, she did, what she swore she wouldn't do. Noah would put the pieces together. He was a smart man.

"Kate, answer me. What did you just say?" Noah's terse voice filled her ears.

The damage was done. Because of her stupidity, she'd started a family feud. This was the last thing she wanted to happen.

"Noah, I know there might be some similarities between Kristin and me, but I'm not her. I don't want to be the person who tears your family apart."

"Did Dee fill your head with all this shit? Is that where all this is coming from?"

Kate stayed silent.

"Katie, you're nothing like Kristin. There are no similarities, none whatsoever. But even if there were, even if you were like Kristin, and we made the decision to be in a relationship, to marry, to have a family, your burdens wouldn't be too heavy because you would be mine, and I yours. And that would be no one's business.

How I live my life and who I choose to share it with are no one's business."

Kate's eyes filled with tears that threatened to spill over. In a husky voice, she said, "I wish it were that easy, but it's not."

"Yeah it is, Kate." Noah's voice softened. "All that matters is you and me, no one else. Do you understand?"

Kate shook her head and ran her fingers through her hair. She'd screwed up this whole conversation, and she had no idea how to steer them back to smooth water. She had to get Noah to see how important his family was. She understood the value of family. It was simple. She never had family who gave a shit about her, and he was lucky enough to have the exact opposite problem. People do not live in bubbles. They need family and friends to love and support them.

"What I understand, Noah Reed, is that you are surrounded by friends and family who love you, who want the best for you. They've seen you suffer and don't want that to happen to you again."

"Screw them! Screw Ava, and screw Dee and her interfering ways. This is ridiculous. Kate, either you believe in us, or you don't. Our relationship is ours and no one else's. I'm tired of fighting you and trying to convince you of this all the time."

Noah wasn't the only one who was tired. Kate had enough. She'd reached her limit. She stood, shut the lights in the kitchen, leaving the rest of the mess for the morning, and made her way upstairs. All of the sudden, she was exhausted. This was all too much. She loved Noah and a few hours ago, she vowed to herself that she'd fight for them, but now she wasn't so sure. She'd taken one too many punches today, and she couldn't argue with him any longer. She was cooked.

Every day Kate woke up, pushed up her sleeves, and readied to fight her demons so they wouldn't get the best of her and wouldn't tear her and Noah to pieces. She thought her past, and all the fears and insecurities that came with it, would be the biggest stumbling block in their relationship. In some ways that was true, but there was also Noah's past and his demons to reckon with. Right this minute, she was tired of dealing with it all. She was undone and had no fight left.

"Kate?"

"Noah," she said in a small, defeated voice. "I'm tired. Actually, I'm way beyond tired. If you want to know the truth, today has been a shit day, from beginning to end. I shouldn't have called you when I'm this tired and emotional."

Kate was shutting down, powering off. She knew herself. When she got this way, it was best for all involved she be left alone to rest and recharge. Then, she could deal with her life.

"Here's what's going to happen. I'm going to go back to bed, lick my wounds, and forget this day ever happened. God willing, I'll fall into a deep sleep on my own. If that doesn't work, I'll use pharmaceuticals. I'll be fine. I always am. I can't do this with you right now. I need some time."

"Kate, don't you dare hang up. Don't you dare run away from me."

Kate heard the fear, panic, desperation, and exasperation in Noah's voice. It reached her and pushed through the sludge that was coating her brain. She recalled Dee's words.

When you hurt him, when you run away and reject him, there'll be no putting him back together.

No matter how tired, how distressed Kate was, she couldn't leave him like this. She couldn't hurt the man she loved. She didn't have it in her to cause Noah a second of pain. His pain was hers, and she regretted ever calling him. He needed her to fight for them. He needed to see that not all women fell apart when the going got tough, and he needed to be comforted for a change.

"Noah, baby. I'm not going anywhere. I'm fried. I need sleep. I promise I'm not running away from you. Baby, today was hard, but at the end of the day, I couldn't stay away. I ran to you, not away from you."

The words hit Kate like a train. They came out of her mouth, but until they hit her ears, she didn't realize their impact.

I ran to you.

Kate collapsed on the bed and let the tears flow. She'd never run to anyone. She'd never wanted to. She'd never found anyone she wanted to fight for and never found anyone who wanted to fight for her. Now, she was home. At last, she'd found the beauty she'd been dreaming of since she was a child. Noah, her Noah, was that dream. He was everything she'd dreamed of. Instead of running away from him, she ran right to him, into his arms. It was good, and it was right. Here, she could stay forever.

Chapter Sixteen

It had been the longest ten days in history, and Noah was ready to get off the plane that was taking him back to New York and back to Kate. Normally he enjoyed London, but this trip seemed to drag. Reconnecting with his little brother was great, and the arduous business meetings and negotiations with three new, high-powered clients went well, despite some unexpected hitches. But now, he was done. According to Luke, he'd been pretty worthless for the last few days.

Luke was right. Noah hadn't been able to focus on much of anything. More times than not, he found his mind wandering to Kate's smile, her soft, full lips, expressive forest-green eyes, and the sound of her voice when she called him baby. He grinned like a fool in the middle of a meeting one day when he recalled the way she scolded and cajoled Shakes like he was her child or the way she devoured a burger meant for two men, and then asked for popcorn. But the thing that brought the biggest smile to his face, and filled his heart to capacity, were the words—*I ran to you.*

Luke sensed something was different about Noah the second he saw him and teased him about "the great transformation."

"You forget something at home?"

Noah frowned. "What the hell are you talking about?"

"Your scowl, man." Luke grinned. "The one you've been wearing for years. Where is it? Not that I miss it. Just wondering, why the transformation?"

After twenty-four hours of Luke's endless mocking, Noah broke and told him about Kate and his troubles with Dee.

"Give Dee time. You know how much she loves you. I'm happy for you, man. You're all smiles. It's good to see you exercising the happy muscles of your face for a change. I was pretty certain your face was stuck in a permanent scowl. If Kate makes you happy, I'm certain she's special, and I'll love her."

Unlike Dee, Luke was genuinely happy for Noah and asked all kinds of questions about Kate. He begged to speak to Kate every time Noah had her on the phone. But after the way Dee behaved, Noah was protective of Kate and refused to give Luke the telephone.

"Come on, Noah, I'll behave, I swear. Dee's being a nervous mum. I promise I don't want to be your mummy or change your nappies. Let me speak to Kate so I can thank her for your rebirth."

One day, acting like an annoying teenager, Luke took matters into his hands and snatched the phone out of Noah's hand and introduced himself to Kate.

"Hello, Kate the Cat Tamer. I'm Luke, the better brother. How are you, my darling?"

After twenty minutes of hearing his brother charm Kate, Noah pulled the phone out of Luke's hand declaring, "You've reached your allotted Kate limit. Now you're cutting into my time. Go find your own woman."

Luke smirked good-naturedly and yelled into the phone, "Kate, sweetheart, it's apparent that big brother is reverting to his pre-Kate surliness. I gotta live with him a few more days, have a heart and work your magic. See if you can sweeten his disposition again. Will you, darling?"

Kate laughed and yelled back, "I'll do my best."

Noah was thrilled Luke and Kate hit it off. It was important to him that Luke liked Kate, especially after the damage Kristin did to their relationship. Of all his family members, Luke had been the most openly opposed to

Noah and Kristin's relationship. From the second Luke met Kristin, there was palpable hostility between them. This brought out Noah's protective instincts, and his relationship with his brother took a hit.

Two pivotal events were particularly damaging. The first occurred about fifteen months after Noah married Kristin. He and Kristin finished journeying around the globe and had settled back in New York. It was shortly after his mother was diagnosed with cancer and everyone in the family was on edge. Noah worked long hours and took on as much of his father's workload as possible. Out of the blue one day, Luke flew in from London and insisted they meet for lunch.

Over lunch, Luke pulled out his smartphone, logged onto a social media site, and asked him a simple question that started a firestorm.

"Do you have any clue at all what your wife's been doing every night while you're at work?"

Luke proceeded to show Noah a series of pictures and videos of Kristin drinking and dancing suggestively, in very tiny dresses that left nothing to the imagination, at various Manhattan clubs with men and women. Instead of taking it as a sign his wife and his marriage were in trouble, Noah became enraged. He focused all his anger and frustration on Luke.

Thinking about it now, Noah was ashamed of his behavior, but nothing was as bad as the day he accused his brother of coming on to his wife. Dee was hosting one of her famous lunners and Noah coaxed Kristin into going. They hadn't been to a family event in almost a year, and his mother's health was declining. She called Noah and begged them to come. Clare was in town and all his mother wanted was for her family to be together. Despite his strained relationship with his family and Kristin's spiraling behavior, he agreed.

Kristin spent the afternoon drinking, making inappropriate comments, and generally misbehaving. She despised family gatherings and had no trouble making her displeasure known.

Late in the day, after the sun went down, Noah went in search of his errant wife and found her at the side of the house, hidden from view, with Luke. Noah didn't think. He acted. He saw his wife in his brother's arms, struggling to get free, and he reached some very wrong, very disturbing conclusions.

Noah lost his mind. What ensued was a lot of ugliness that led to the fracturing of his relationship with Luke for several years. It took Kristin's death to start the healing process and to reunite him with his family.

Luckily for Noah, Luke had a short memory and a forgiving heart. Noah realized how much he could have lost and how much he needed his family, especially his siblings, in his life. But Dee was another story. Her resistance to Kate and her recent behavior troubled him. One positive thing came out of Dee's hurtful conversation with Kate. It brought Kate and him even closer, but it further damaged his relationship with his sister.

After hearing about Kate and Dee's conversation, he made sure Kate was calm and settled for the night, and then Noah canceled his morning meetings in London and waited 'til the sun rose in Jersey. He called his big sister and by the tone of her voice, she knew why he was calling.

"So, she ran to you, like Kristin used to."

Noah took in a deep breath, trying to control his temper. This catty behavior was so unlike Dee. It threw him each and every time she acted out.

"Dee, I don't know what to say to you this morning. I love you, sis, I really do. I appreciate everything you've done for me, but I'm only going to say this to you once. Stop this behavior. I love Kate. She's not Kristin. She's a good person, and you're hurting her. I can't allow you to do that any longer. She's had too much hurt in her life."

"This thing you have with Kate isn't healthy. You're going to get hurt. You don't see it, Noah. You never do. You fall and expect the rest of us to tumble with you and then cushion your fall. I can't stand by and watch you hurt yourself again. I just can't." Dee's voice broke.

Noah sighed, rubbed his forehead, and raked his fingers through his hair. Nothing he said would make this better for Dee. Only time would heal them all. Kristin may be gone, but the damage she left in her wake was substantial.

"We all make mistakes, Dee. We learn and grow. I've made my share of mistakes, and I've learned. I'm sorry you and the rest of the family were hurt along the way. I can't change the past, and I can't change your mind about the future. I won't try. I only ask one thing. If you can't stand by me, then step aside. Not having your love and support will hurt, but that's your choice. Don't be the one that tears us apart this time."

In the days that followed Noah didn't speak to Dee again, but he also wasn't able to speak with Kate as much as he would have liked. Due to their busy schedules and the time difference, Kate and Noah's conversations mainly occurred through texts, a form of communication he despised.

A couple of times he called and found her baking in the middle of the night again. Using the same strategy as before, he talked her out of the kitchen and into bed where he described California's Glass Beach, the Glow Worm Cave in New Zealand, and the Neuschwanstein

Castle in Germany. Each and every time, Kate floated off to sleep, and he'd hang up and hope she had peaceful dreams.

When Kate wasn't sleep-deprived, or baking, and they were able to have more than a five-minute conversation, she seemed troubled. Something was wrong, and Noah couldn't put his finger on it. At first, he thought it was his imagination, but a few days ago, she admitted the search for her parents was partially successful.

"I found my father," she said in a sad voice. "It was easier than I thought. I tracked down a neighbor that used to live next door to us. He drank himself to death. He's dead, Noah."

Noah sat down and ran his hand through his hair. He had no idea how to react to the bastard's death. He was glad her father was dead. Whatever he'd done to Kate caused her to flee into the world at the tender age of eighteen, and she suffered because of it. Kate was yet to tell him why she ran from home and took on a new identity, but Noah assumed her father was at the center of that mess. Noah had to tread lightly, however. He had no idea how Kate was processing her father's loss.

"I'm sorry, sweetheart."

Kate sighed. "I'm not, and that's the problem. I'm confused. I don't know what I'm supposed to feel. Am I supposed to be sad? Am I supposed to mourn what we could have had as father and daughter? I thought I'd find closure, but that's not the case. All I feel is rage at both he and my mother. They cheated me out of a childhood, and I'm so angry."

"Sweetheart, I think everything you're feeling is normal. Don't be so hard on yourself. I don't think there is a right or wrong way to feel. You feel what you feel and process things as fast or as slow as you need to."

Kate was silent for a few minutes.

"I guess you're right. He died the way he lived, alone and miserable. He didn't love my mother or me. He didn't love anyone except for himself. In time, I'll lay him to rest in my mind and my heart. He's not worth it. I know that."

Noah hated to hear Kate so sad and exhausted. It was enough she had to deal with the past and the emotions this dredged up. He hoped she trusted him enough now and would let him help her.

"Kate, I know you didn't want my help before, but please reconsider. You're wearing yourself down—working, searching for your parents, and dealing with all the emotions that come with resurrecting the past. You're barely getting any rest. I understand why you want to find your parents, and I respect your decision. But please let me help. Let me put an investigator on finding your mother."

Kate let out a breath. "I've been thinking a lot about my mother, Noah. I've decided not to search for her—not now, anyway. She walked away. She left me. She chose herself, instead of me. Now, I'm choosing myself over her. I'm not ready to deal with her, and I'm not sure I'll ever be. But, baby, if and when I am ready, I'll tell you and yes, you can help me."

Noah smiled as he recalled that moment and how his girl shared her burdens with him. They'd come a long way in a short time. He closed his eyes and rested his head back against the cramped airplane seat, fidgeting, unable to quell his excitement at seeing her again. He couldn't wait to gather Kate's tiny body in his arms, to feel her soft curves against his body or her silky hair sliding between his fingers and feathering across his skin.

The problem was, tonight was Halloween, and she was going all out and hosting a huge costume party at the bookstore. Kate had laid down the law. If he wanted to see her, he would have to dress up and be happy about it. The last thing Noah wanted to do was get off a seven-hour flight and dress up. He tried every negotiation skill he learned over the years and still, Kate won this battle. So, he would dress up, and although that part did not excite him, the prospect of seeing Kate did.

Two hours after landing at LaGuardia Airport, Noah found himself in his car battling Friday night rush-hour traffic, with a grin he couldn't take off his face. After clearing customs, he hopped into a taxi, stopped by his house, showered, changed and packed a small overnight bag. He and Kate had been apart too long. If he had it his way, he wasn't leaving her side or her bed the entire weekend. He and Kate never had the opportunity to spend an entire night together and to wake up in each other's arms. The time had finally come, and he was beyond excited.

Noah parked in front of Dreamscape. As he walked toward the bookstore, he felt in his jacket pocket for the gift he bought Kate from London. He'd made good time and arrived an hour before the party started. He hoped he'd have time to give it to her before things became too crazy.

"Hello? Kate? Anyone here?" Noah called as he walked through the brightly lit, but empty bookstore.

"Hell-low." Shakes responded.

Noah followed the sound of Shakes' voice to the back room where Emma usually took the bird after Storytime. Every room of the bookstore was decorated. Some rooms were dark and scary with cobwebs and spooky music, while others were brightly lit with grinning jack-o-lanterns and fall leaves hanging from the ceiling. Cookies and cupcakes, decorated for the holiday, as well as massive bowls of candy, were on every table of the bookstore.

Noah approached Shake's cage. "Hi there, Jaws. Where's your mistress?"

"Hell-low? Mmh-mmh treats."

"Well, that's new. You want a treat?"

"Mmh-mmh."

Smiling, Noah scanned the room until his gaze landed on a bag of peanuts on a nearby shelf. Holding a peanut out to show Shakes, he approached the cage again, surprised that the cockatoo didn't lunge or hiss at him.

"You want this, buddy?"

"Mmh-mmh, treats."

Inserting the peanut between the cage rails, Noah watched as the bird studied him and then the peanut. Shakes grabbed the peanut with his beak and got busy eating it.

Noah shook his head and chuckled. "Thanks for not eating my hand, man. Now that you have your treat, I want mine. Where can I find your rather tasty mistress? Help a guy out, will you?"

Hearing what could only be Kate's sweet laughter from behind him, Noah turned and was struck speechless by the sight of Kate dressed in what could only be described as a princess ball gown. She was a vision in spun gold. The entire dress was made of a shimmering gold material that fell off her shoulders, hugged her breasts and torso, and then flared out in layers of glittery golden taffeta that cascaded to the ground in shimmers at her feet.

Her hair was partially swept up on the sides with gold combs. It fell in loose curls down her back. Her hair had bits of gold glitter that floated on top and throughout, so it too sparkled and caught the light each time she moved her head. She wore a hint of gold glitter on her cheeks and around her eyes, and her lips were outlined in a deep, rose color that made him want to run his tongue over them.

He was spellbound. When she smiled a flirtatious smile, curtsied, while seductively flashing him with her green eyes, he felt himself harden. Lust raced through him. He wanted her right that second and had to remind himself to go slow and not launch himself at her and devour her whole.

"Hello sweetness," he said in a husky voice. "I'm not sure who you're supposed to be, but God, Katie, you look good enough to eat." He stalked toward her and watched as she retreated, eyes wide and a seductive smile on her face.

"Noah," she said, shaking her head in warning as she held her hands out in front of her and continued to take one step back for each of his steps forward. "Baby, I'm happy to see you too, really I am, but it took forever to get into this getup. You must promise not to crush me. In fact," she said as her tongue darted out and ran across her pink lower lip, "it might be better if we don't touch at all, not yet anyway."

Noah stopped a few feet from her. His eyes devoured and scorched her until her face was as rosy as her lips.

"No can do, gorgeous," he whispered. "I've missed you, Katie. I need you. Come to me, sweetheart." Noah opened his arms.

Kate didn't hesitate, not even for a second. She launched herself at him, and he caught her in his outstretched arms, crushing her and her dress to him. She buried her face in his neck and peppered his neck and face with kisses. Her body melted into his, and she moaned.

Noah inhaled her sweet scent as her hair feathered over his face. Kissing the side of her neck, he made his way up to the underside of her jaw and then to her lips, dropping light kisses along the way.

He took her mouth in a long searching kiss, rediscovering the taste and feel of her. Kate didn't hold back. She gave a soft sigh, then wrapped her arms around his neck. Her tongue danced with his, and she moaned in pleasure when he deepened the kiss and gathered her tightly to him. She tasted so damn good and felt even better in his arms. When he felt her fingers slide into his hair and tug, he knew that if he didn't stop this now, he wouldn't be able to, and he'd be carrying her upstairs, not giving a damn about the party.

Pulling his lips away from hers, he kissed her nose and her forehead, then laid his forehead against hers as they both tried to catch their breaths.

"Sweetheart, if we don't stop now, that dress is not only going to be crushed, it's going to be off you and on the floor. Now, I'm perfectly happy with that plan, but something tells me you're not going to be."

Kate's eyelids fluttered as she attempted to focus her dazed eyes on him. She licked her lips. His eyes focused on her tiny, delicious tongue and followed its path across her lips. Noah couldn't help it. His mouth was on hers again as he scooped her up and started walking toward the stairs that led to her rooms.

Kate pulled away with effort. "Noah, baby, stop. We can't." She giggled. "Put me down."

Noah buried his face in the V of her dress that showed a significant amount of cleavage. He kissed the side of her exposed breast and licked it.

"Sure I can't persuade you to go with my plan? I'll even help you put the dress on afterward. Come on, we'll be fast," he cajoled.

Kate smiled but shook her head. "Uh, no. This dress has to stay on cause in about thirty minutes this place is going to be crawling with tiny humans."

Noah put Kate down but continued to hold her in the circle of his arms. He hated to let her go and to show his displeasure and the sacrifice he was making, he pulled her close and ground his erection into her.

Kate glanced down and grinned. "Maybe we could pick this up later? Say, in three hours or so? That is, of course, if you're going to cooperate and be a beast."

Noah furrowed his brows and kissed her nose. "Okay, you have my attention and my cooperation, but what in the world is a beast?"

"Well," Kate said, as she stepped away from him and twirled around, her dress flaring out around her like a golden halo. "I'm beauty, and you're my beast. I've got your costume ready."

"Ahh, beauty and the beast. Well, I hope I don't fit the part. You, sweetness, on the other hand, are perfectly cast. You're stunning."

Noah pulled her back into his arms and kissed her softly on the lips.

"Thank you, baby," she said as she fisted his shirt in her hands and snuggled closer to his chest. "I wish we could stay like this, but I've got to get a few things ready, and you've got to get into character."

Noah sighed. "Got it. Before I let you go, though, I've got something for you."

"Oh, what?"

Reluctantly, Noah let her go and reached into his pocket, pulling out a small, pale-pink velvet pouch with a matching satin drawstring. Embossed in gold letters on the pouch was the name Alexander Edwards. Noah reached for her hand and turning it palm up, he placed the pouch in it.

"What's this?" she asked, quirking her head to the side.

"It's a little surprise from London. Open it."

Kate stood frozen with the small pouch in her hand.

"Kate? Open it. It's not a big deal. Just something I thought you'd like."

"You bought me a present?" she asked in a small, incredulous voice as she continued to stare at the gift in her hand.

"Yeah, sweetheart, I bought you a small gift. Open it." Noah was puzzled at Kate's reaction. She appeared happy, but also tearful. He wasn't sure what to make of her reaction.

Kate stroked the pouch with her fingers. "It's beautiful."

Noah held his breath as she unknotted the satin tie, opened the pouch, and peeked inside. A soft, wistful smile made an appearance on her sweet lips.

He let out the breath he'd been holding and perched on the edge of a small wooden table watching as Kate turned the pouch upside down and the delicate, gold daisy chain bracelet fell in the palm of her hand.

Kate gasped. "Oh, Noah. It's magnificent." She traced the tiny daisies with her finger.

Kate's big green, tear-filled eyes met his. Then she quickly glanced down. He held his hand out to her. "Come here, Katie."

Kate took his hand and he pulled her toward him until she stood between his legs. He put two fingers underneath her chin and pushed up, forcing her to meet his eyes again.

"Sweetheart, clue me in. What's happening here? Why the tears?" With his thumb, he wiped away the tears that escaped and were making their way down her face.

Kate wiped at her eyes and sniffled. "I'm silly, that's all. I'm not used to receiving presents. I love it. It's beautiful. Thank you for thinking of me." She reached up and brushed his lips with hers.

"Don't you know by now I never stop thinking of you? You've been on my mind so much that Luke said I was pretty useless to him."

"Really?" she asked in a hopeful voice that was so filled with longing it tugged at his heart.

He stroked her cheek with the back of his hand, enjoying the softness of it. "Yeah, Kate, really. I love you, sweetheart. Now, no more tears. Okay?"

Nodding, she held the bracelet out to him. "I love you too, Noah. Will you help me put it on?"

Noah fastened the bracelet around her tiny wrist. "I'm glad you like it. It's handcrafted by a friend of mine who owns a shop in Cambridge. This design is one of a kind." Meeting her eyes, he continued. "According to the artist, it's delicate, yet remarkably strong and unwaveringly resilient. The design is deceivingly simple but unerringly complex. If you take a closer look at the daisies, you'll notice each one is distinct and different than the other."

Kissing her wrist right above where the bracelet lay, Noah's eyes locked with hers.

"Like the woman who now wears it, it's a rare, precious treasure, meant to be cherished."

Chapter Seventeen

Sunlight warmed Kate's face as her body and mind drifted back to consciousness after a deep sleep. For the first time in months, she felt rested, but something wasn't right. What day was it? Why was she still in bed?

Then it hit her. Sunlight. She always woke up way before the sun. Oh, dear Lord! She overslept on a Storytime Saturday. Kate tensed, readying to sprint out of bed, but when she tried to move, something heavy and warm pinned her down. Her heart raced, and her eyes flew open, scanning down her body and around her bed as her brain fully engaged.

Noah.

Kate let out a shaky breath as her brain sent a message to her muscles to relax and her nerves to untangle. Noah was in her bed with a possessive arm thrown over her body and a hand cupping her breast. One of his legs covered her lower abdomen and legs, and his face was buried in the side of her neck. Kate took in a deep breath and let it out, snuggling deeper into his embrace.

The morning fog left her brain, and she remembered it was Saturday, but the bookstore was closed after the big party last night. Kate sighed in relief, and a smile spread across her face.

No nightmares. She'd slept the entire night without a single nightmare plaguing her. Despite the emotional overload that came from finding out about her father's death and the ongoing harassment from Kyle and his friends over the last few weeks, she'd slept through the entire night. It was a miracle.

It was Noah.

Her miracle worker was curing her of all her woes

and lifting the heavy weight she carried. She'd come to a decision while he was away. She was ready to tell him everything. It was time to share her past, in its entirety, with her man. Kate vowed to find the right time and share the last piece of her story with Noah. She'd resurrect Jesse one last time and then bury him forever. Then, she would go on with her life and never look back again.

Kate smiled and admired the bracelet Noah brought her from London. It was beautiful. She never had anything like it, and coming from Noah made it even more special. Throughout the party, she found herself glancing at it, and it never failed to bring a smile to her face. But then she'd see him in that crazy costume and burst out laughing.

"Something isn't right here. Why do you get to wear a gorgeous dress, while I resemble a hideous creature in a tux?" Noah grumbled, good-naturedly as he modeled the dreadful costume she rented for him.

Noah resembled an overgrown, hairy beast dressed for a wedding. It was rather mean of her to insist he wear the heavy costume, but the kids loved him. While some of them were initially terrified of him, they came around and cuddled up to him like he was a lovable teddy bear. The poor man didn't get a moment of rest the entire evening. But he was fantastic with the kids and gave an Oscar-winning performance.

Deidra, Aimee, Clare, and Julia all attended in various costumes, ready to help. Although Dee was civil, she kept her distance and was cool to Kate. But Kate was too happy and too busy to care. She assigned anyone who wanted to help a room to man and then ran around keeping the show going all night.

Everyone seemed to have fun except Emma. Lilly, dressed as an angel, ran around with the other children with Ethan on her tail. But poor Emma, a vision dressed as Tinkerbell, spent most of the night playing with Shakespeare in the back. One of the mean girls cornered Emma at the start of the party and taunted her.

"You don't need a mask. Your face is already scary."

The Beast overheard the conversation and came to life. It took Beauty, Snow White, and several superheroes to calm him down. Eventually, the mean girl was disciplined by her mother and left, but the damage was done.

Overall, the Halloween party was a success. When the last cupcake was eaten, and the door was locked, Kate and Noah indulged in their own celebration that lasted deep into the night.

Now her beast lay in an exhausted sleep, appearing quite docile. Kate maneuvered herself so she was lying on her side, facing him. Using her index finger, she traced over his full eyebrows, down his cheek, to his square, stubbly jaw. She outlined his slightly crooked nose and then his full lips, first the upper and then the lower. She hadn't finished the lower lip when he opened his mouth and caught her finger between his teeth in a sudden move.

Kate screeched, trying to pull away, but her beast pulled her close to his warm, naked body. He cocooned her between his solid arms and body and flipped her so she was underneath him. They were skin to skin as neither one of them bothered with clothing the night before. Kate decided this was the only way to sleep with Noah and the best way to wake up with him.

"Noah." Kate giggled. "Let me up, you beast, before you crush me. I swear you weigh three hundred pounds."

"Sweetness," Noah said in a gravelly voice as he raised his head and smiled a sexy, sleepy smile. "That's no way to speak to a hungry beast. Give me a kiss and tell me you love me, then I may consider your request."

Kate was trapped, and although she complained, she loved his weight on her. It grounded her and made her feel safe and protected like nothing ever had. She pulled one hand out from the sandwich their bodies made and ran her fingers through his hair, pushing it away from his eyes. She cupped his cheek and rubbed her hand up and down it, loving the feel of his morning stubble.

"Good morning, baby," she said, kissing his cheek. "I love you," she said dutifully.

"Hmm," Noah said, pushing his growing erection into her belly. She spread her legs and wrapped them around him, rubbing her core against him.

"Well, that was hardly acceptable. Let me show you how it's done."

Noah outlined the seam of her lips with his tongue and took her lower lip between his teeth, tugging at it. He devoured her mouth, leaving no inch of it unexplored.

"Now that's a kiss," he said huskily. "Problem is, I'm still hungry, and I want to eat right now."

Noah growled as he kissed her neck and down to her breasts. He traced around her nipple with the tip of his tongue and then took it in his mouth, sucking it in greedily. Kate arched into him and rubbed herself against him, searching for relief. His mouth was wicked. She loved the way he touched, licked, and sucked her. She couldn't imagine a more skilled lover.

Kate whimpered and held his head to her breast as he switched breasts and began the same routine. She ran her hand up and down his back and grabbed handfuls of his tight, muscular ass as her legs tightened around him. She was soaking wet and needy. She tried to urge him to take her, but he had other plans.

"Noah." Kate took in a ragged breath and nipped

his earlobe. "Baby, I need you," she moaned. She pulled at his hair, and he let go of her nipple with a loud pop.

Noah peeked up at her with a sensual smile, his eyes meeting her fevered ones.

"Noah, baby, please," she whimpered, as her body shook with need. She was already so close and needed just a little more. Then she'd fly.

Noah took her mouth in a scorching kiss, and she didn't hold back. She opened her mouth and let their tongues duel as her nails scored him, and she all but fused herself to him. One of Noah's hands pushed between them. His fingers found their way to her clit and caressed her tiny bundle of nerves then pulled back.

Kate was far gone. She closed her lips and teeth over his shoulder and bit down as her body tensed, readying for release.

Noah groaned, but he wasn't thwarted from his task. He circled her entrance with his fingers, never quite giving her what she wanted. She thrust herself toward the fingers that were making her lose her mind.

"Sweetness, you're soaked," he said as he continued his torture, rubbing her clit in circles with his thumb, enough to make her crazy, but not enough to push her over the edge.

Kate whimpered.

"Shh, Katie. I've got you."

Noah kissed and licked his way down her body—between her breasts, her flat belly, and right above her mound.

Kate froze, she tried to close her legs, and pushed up on her elbows, ready to scoot back.

"No, Noah," she said in a panicked voice, with her face burning.

She hadn't done this before. She couldn't. Jeff never even tried. She felt too exposed, and although she'd cleaned up after their lovemaking last night, she was all sweaty. He would find her gross.

Noah raised his head, and his hands stopped their roaming. He held her waist firmly and kissed her navel. "Kate, look at me."

Kate peered up at him when all she wanted to do was bury herself under the covers.

Noah reached up and caressed her hot cheek with the back of his hand. "You haven't done this before?" he asked, quirking an eyebrow.

Kate shook her head, blushing even more. She couldn't hold his eyes and dropped her gaze once more.

"Eyes, sweetheart. Let me see them."

When Kate met his gaze, he asked, "Do you trust me?"

Kate didn't have to think. She nodded and chewed on her lower lip. She knew the answer. It came to her without hesitation. Of course, she trusted him. She loved him. He said she was his, and he was hers, and she believed him, but at this moment, she was dying of embarrassment. Kate took a shuddering breath and let her knees open. She lay back, pinched her eyes closed, and waited, fisting the covers on either side of her.

Noah kissed his way up her body. "Open your eyes, Katie. Come on, sweetheart. Look at me," he persuaded as he kissed her eyes, chin, nose, and cheek.

Kate was once again under Noah's comforting weight, and she opened her eyes as he brushed her hair off her face and ran his fingers through it.

"Whatever we do together, and we're going to do a lot, none of it is shameful. I'm going to love you and you, me. If I do something you don't like, just say so. I have a feeling, though, you're going to like this," he said with a cocky smile.

The love and tenderness Kate saw in Noah's eyes

gave her the courage she needed. She kissed him and wrapped her arms and legs around him once more. He took over and within seconds had her whimpering for him again. He kissed and licked his way down the valley between her breast to her belly and then her mound once again.

Noah spread her thighs and kissed the inside of each, then up one thigh. When his tongue licked through her folds, Kate gasped and arched into his mouth, unable to stop herself. With every lick, Kate lost her inhibitions and swore she was losing her mind. Her legs shook as she arched closer to him.

The second his tongue touched her clit, licked, and then he gently bit down, Kate exploded. Her back arched, her hands weaved into his hair, and she held him to her and screamed his name. Kate was certain that every cell in her body burst from the arc of electricity that raced through her, but Noah wasn't done. His clever mouth and tongue explored every inch of her until she came down.

Noah kissed his way up her body. She wrapped her arms and legs around him and held on as he plunged deep into her over and over again. She was a quivering mess, but her body reawakened and she felt that familiar ache begin. Soon she was frantic with need once again.

Kate guided Noah's mouth to her. She kissed him, sucking on his lower lip and tongue, tasting herself on him. It was one of the sexiest things she'd ever experienced. She wanted more and wanted to give him more. She urged Noah to let her on top. She rode him with everything she had. This time, she knew what she was doing and rode him hard and deep, with him holding on to her hips guiding her.

Finally, when she didn't think she could take any more, he pressed his thumb to her clit and said, "Get there, Kate, let go."

Kate let go. Her orgasm took over once again, and she fell forward on top of him as he plunged into her a couple more times, seated himself deep, and then exploded within her. Blissed out, she gave in and let her body drift.

Kate woke up, nestled once more in Noah's arms. This time, she was sprawled all over him.

"Morning, sweetheart," Noah said, kissing the top of her head and squeezing her to him.

Kate stretched and kissed the underside of his chin and jaw.

"Hi," she murmured. She kissed her way up his neck to underneath his ear. "Love you," she whispered as she inhaled his spicy scent, mixed with the scent of their lovemaking.

Noah wrapped her in his arms and crushed her to him. "Love you too, sweetness. Love you always," he said in a husky voice, filled with emotion. "You ready to get up?"

"Mmh-hmm," Kate said, peering up to meet his eyes. "What're we doing after you feed me? After all, I fed you."

Kate turned beet red thinking about all they had done to and with one another. She couldn't believe she'd just said that.

Noah burst out laughing. "That you did, sweetheart. Come on. I've got a plan."

An hour later, after they'd shared a shower, they sat next to each other at Frank's having brunch. They were talking, laughing and enjoying each other's company when Dee walked in with Ava and Emma. Emma spotted them and raced to their table. She climbed into her uncle's lap.

"Hi, Uncle Reed. Hi, Miss Kate."

"Hi, beautiful. How are you, today?" Noah asked the child as he gave her a hug and kiss. He'd spent a lot of time with her the night before making sure she recovered from her trauma.

"Good," she said, stealing a French fry off his dish and smiling.

Dee and Ava approached slowly. Dee handed Emma a few quarters and said, "Here you go, Imp. Good luck with the toy machines."

Emma squealed and ran off. She was obsessed with bubble gum toy machines.

"Well, don't you two look cozy," Ava said with a sneer.

"Ava, Dee," Noah acknowledged the two women with little warmth in his voice.

As usual, Ava was dressed head to toe in designer wear—skinny jeans, an oversize cream sweater, and a massive designer purse. Kate felt dowdy in her wholesale jeans, boots, and turtleneck, but she had Noah. She smiled at the women and laid a possessive hand on his forearm and squeezed it. Noah's arm came around her, and he kissed the top of her head.

"Good morning, Dee, Ava," Kate said. "It's a beautiful day out today, isn't it?"

"Yes, it's warmer than usual," Dee answered. "You did a nice job with the party yesterday, Kate."

"Thank you and thanks for coming."

Dee turned to Noah. "Why don't you come to the house for dinner today? Ava is staying in town for the day, and Clare will be joining us. Jackson is making his famous ribs. It'll be a nice family get-together."

Kate didn't miss the fact she was left out of Dee's invitation and neither had Noah. His body stiffened. Kate squeezed his forearm again and focused on her empty coffee mug, unable to hide the hurt from showing. She hated making him choose between her and his family.

Kate didn't understand how she and Dee would ever get past this if Dee insisted on keeping her at arm's length. If Dee never gave her a chance, how could Kate show her she wasn't anything like Kristin, that she and Noah were good together and for each other? The entire situation was frustrating and painful. Kate felt like she was breaking up his family and worried one day he would resent her for it.

"That's not going to happen, Dee," Noah said as he pulled Kate further into his embrace. "Anyway, Kate and I have plans. We're going to see my new house and then we're going to the City."

Noah emphasized the word *new,* and Dee picked up on it. She gasped, and Kate turned back in time to see the surprise and pain cross her features.

"New house? You bought a house? Without telling me? Where? I didn't know."

"No, you wouldn't know. You've been preoccupied with other matters, haven't you? If you continue to wage the campaign you're hell-bent on winning, you're going to be missing a lot more in the future." Noah glared at his sister.

Dee's eyes filled with tears and she hung her head. "Where's your new place?"

"I bought it a few weeks ago. It's the Easton Estate at the highest point of Forest Mountain. I close a few days after Thanksgiving."

Dee's head came up, and she gave a tremulous smile. "We're going to be neighbors. That's wonderful."

"Is it, Dee?" Noah asked, still staring his sister down as he continued to ignore Ava.

"Oh, Reed. Of course, it is. I've missed you. Don't be like that." Color crept up Dee's cheeks, and her eyes filled again.

Noah slid out of the booth, stood, and pulled Kate behind him. He tucked her into his side the instant she was standing.

"Have a good day, Dee. Say hi to Jackson and Clare for me. Kate and I would have liked to attend." Noah's voice softened. "Maybe that will happen in the future if *we* get the appropriate invitation."

Noah gave Dee a peck on the cheek. It was evident he was affected by their distance, but he was making a point, and Kate loved him for it.

Traffic into the City was a nightmare and by the time they arrived at the penthouse, Kate and Noah decided a walk in Central Park was what they needed. The penthouse was located at 10 Central Park West, a magnificent tower with a twenty-four-hour doorman, a private dining room, library, a screening room, health club, and pool. It was a fantastic location, right near the restaurants and shops of Columbus Circle and the Lincoln Center for the Performing Arts.

Noah left the car with the valet, and they crossed the street hand-in-hand as they entered the park. The park was packed with people of all ages enjoying the beautiful foliage of the fall and the unseasonably warm day. Noah held Kate's hand as they walked in silence, people watching, absorbed in their thoughts.

Kate let Noah guide her through the crowded park and soon, she was lost. She watched a little girl with pigtails pushing a doll stroller in front of her parents. Mom was heavy with pregnancy and dad held the leash of a golden retriever. They were a beautiful, perfect family.

Kate sighed. This was the type of family she'd dreamed of having when she was a child. She wondered if she would ever have a child of her own. Without thinking, she put her palm on her flat belly and smiled.

How would it feel to carry Noah's child, holding it safe in her body, under her heart, and then one day in her arms? Two months ago, that thought would have never crossed her mind. Now the image of a chubby-cheeked baby boy with blond ringlets and warm brown eyes danced in her mind.

Noah's hand covered Kate's palm, and she startled. Kate stopped walking and peeked up at him.

Noah smiled and in a soft voice said, "One day, sweetheart. Maybe one day."

Heat flooded Kate's cheeks. How the hell did he know what she was thinking? Was she that transparent?

He took her hand from her belly and held it up to his mouth, kissing her palm, never taking his eyes off her. There was something in his eyes, something far away and sad. Kate saw it on occasion when he held Emma, and she couldn't figure out where that sadness came from. He would make a terrific dad. Had he wanted a child with Kristin and it never happened? Before she could ask him, Noah pulled her into his arms and gave her a long, passionate kiss that had a group of teenagers passing them clapping, whistling, and calling out, "Dude, you may be old, but you've still got it. She's hot!"

Kate pulled away and buried her face in his shirt.

Noah threw his head back and laughed. "Come on, sweetness. Let's get out of here before you draw a bigger crowd of admirers."

On their way back to the penthouse, Kate and Noah stopped at a local Chinese restaurant and picked up a ridiculous amount of takeout. Considering the size of their appetites, the majority, if not all of it, would soon be gone.

As Noah plated their food, Kate wandered through the penthouse. Everything was modern, sleek, and white. It lacked warmth, and it lacked any sign that

Noah lived here. In fact, *her Noah* wasn't here. Everything Kate knew and loved about Noah was missing. This had to have been Kristin's design and décor choices. The place was beautifully decorated, but it was too stark, too cold. It felt more like a showroom than a home. No throw pillows, no Afghans, no warm lighting—only glass, steel, and sharp edges. It was the exact opposite of her home.

Kate and Noah sat at a glass and steel dinette in the kitchen to eat. Kate couldn't hold back the question any longer. She wanted to see if her intuition was right, and she wanted to know more about Kristin. Noah knew a lot about her already, and she knew little of him.

"Can I ask you a question?"

"Sure. Anything." Noah smiled.

Kate quirked her head to the side. "This place, it's nice, but it's not you. You didn't design or decorate this, did you?"

Noah stopped eating and gave her his full attention.

"No, this was Kristin. All of it. I love the City, but I don't love this place. Kristin fell in love with it the second she laid eyes on it. It was everything she always wanted. I wanted to settle in Lakes Crossing and raise a family there, like my parents did. But, country living wasn't her thing. It didn't matter to me where we lived, though. I wanted her to be happy. So, I bought this and let her do whatever she wanted with it."

Kate scanned the room and reached for Noah's hand, entwining her fingers with his. "There are no pictures, none of her or your family."

Noah shrugged. "People usually have pictures when they want to be reminded of something good or someone who's special to them. She only had her mother, and they weren't close. She didn't want me to put pictures up of my family. She said it made her sad. When she was alive, there were a few pictures of us. But after, I couldn't stand looking at them."

Noah stood, refilled his wine glass, and walked to the window overlooking the park. Kate picked up her glass and went to sit on the white loveseat facing the windows.

"Do you want to tell me about her?" Kate asked. She wouldn't push him. She would open the door, and if he chose to walk in, she would be right beside him, helping him through the memories.

After a couple of minutes of silence, Noah sighed and started speaking in a haunted voice.

"Kristin had a self-destructive streak that worsened over time. I think marrying me destroyed her. I blame myself every day for her death. People say there was nothing I could have done, but I'll never know that."

Kate heard the agony in Noah's voice and ached to go to him, but she didn't move. He rarely spoke about himself and Kristin, and she wanted to give him that opportunity now, uninterrupted by her grief for him.

"Kristin had nothing growing up. I'm certain she found plenty of trouble to get herself into when she was poor and barely made ends meet. But when she married me, she had unlimited resources and time available for her to run her life into the ground. I tried everything to help her, but after her death, I learned I didn't know my wife at all."

Noah raked his hands through his hair and sighed.

"She was addicted to pain medications, alcohol, and was even dealing cocaine. No matter what I did, it wasn't enough. I couldn't protect her from herself."

Noah walked toward Kate and sat down next to her. "But that's not the worst of it."

Kate reached for his hands. She wanted him to

know she was with him, that he wasn't alone in his grief. His pain was hers, and she longed to wipe the expression of sheer agony off his face.

"Kristin was drunk and high when she lost control of her car on I-95. She slammed into a car head-on. Two teenagers were coming home from prom. They were all killed on impact. The medical examiner said she probably lost consciousness and overdosed while driving and…"

Noah's voice broke. He turned his head and focused on something across the room. "And, she was twelve weeks pregnant. She killed herself. She killed two kids. And she killed our baby, and I couldn't do a damn thing to stop it."

Kate's eyes widened and filled with tears. Noah had lost his wife, and he'd lost his child. She pulled him into her arms and held him as he cried. Noah blamed himself for the death of Kristin and two innocent teenagers. But as if that wasn't enough, he blamed himself for the death of his child.

Her man cried for all that he lost, and Kate's heart broke for him. There was no way to change the past or to erase it for him. If she could, she would. But for the rest of her life, as long as he'd let her, she'd hold Noah Reed. She'd stand beside him, comfort him, and carry his burdens with him. She'd make damn sure he knew when he awoke in the morning and when he laid his head down at night, he wasn't alone, and he was loved.

Kate Willowbrook held her man and cried right along with him.

Chapter Eighteen

To say Kate was a holiday fanatic was an understatement. As soon as Halloween was celebrated, she decorated for Thanksgiving while sneaking in a bit of Christmas here and there so no one would think she was a complete nut. But the real fun would start in ten short days, the day after Thanksgiving. Then she would allow herself to go crazy and decorate every inch of the bookstore for her favorite holiday, Christmas. The theme this year was a winter wonderland. Not very original, but each room of the bookstore would have a unique twist, Kate style.

"Baby, you're busy. I know you'll hate shopping for decorations with me," she soothed Noah. "You'll try to rush me, and I won't be rushed, not even the tiniest bit. Stay home, get on your conference calls, catch up with Luke, and we'll do dinner tomorrow."

And that was how Kate ended up walking around The Reindeer Ranch, one of the state's largest decoration outlets, alone for two and a half hours. She loaded up on everything she ever dreamed of for the perfect winter wonderland. Kate was blissed out! With only ten days until Thanksgiving, she had to get what she needed before all the good decorations were taken by other holiday fanatics.

It was nearly 10:00 PM when Kate pulled up in front of Dreamscape. Her feet and back ached, but her face was decorated with a huge smile. She couldn't help herself. This was going to be the best holiday of her life. She had bags filled with decorations, and her hunt for the perfect holiday stocking for Noah was a success. Life couldn't get any better.

Kate dragged bag after bag into the bookstore,

leaving them in the front hall. She locked her car and the front door then went upstairs. She was wiped out and needed her bed. Tomorrow she would deal with the loot. She washed her face, brushed her teeth, and changed into flannel PJ bottoms covered with skiing Santas and a white tank. She sank into her bed and cozied under the comforter.

The last thing Kate did before falling into a deep sleep was text Noah.

Shopping successful. I'm home. Going to bed. Love you. XOXO.

Kate startled awake, sitting straight up, in a cold sweat with her heart beating in her throat. She had no idea how long she'd been asleep, but something woke her, and this time it wasn't a nightmare. She scanned the dark room, her ears hypersensitive to any sound in the apartment and bookstore below. Nothing seemed amiss.

Kate pushed her hair out of her face and took several deep breaths in and out, trying to control her racing heart and her overactive imagination. She lay back down, closed her eyes, and forced her muscles to relax, but something wasn't right. She had a sick, uneasy feeling she couldn't shake. She sat up again and strained to hear any sounds beyond the pounding of her heart and her choppy breathing.

At first, she heard nothing. Then a faint sound hit her ears. Scraping? No, shuffling—shoes? Was someone downstairs?

Bang. Thud.

Shit, she wasn't alone. Someone was in the bookstore!

Kate's blood ran cold and every inch of her body covered in goosebumps. This time, she clearly heard someone or something hitting the floor and the crunching of the plastic shopping bags she'd left in the front room.

Kate trembled. She quickly surveyed the room as her brain launched into overdrive. What should she do? Did he know she was up here? What did he want? Why the hell hadn't she replaced the locks? Why hadn't she let Noah fix the alarm system?

Jesus! God!

Kate shook her head. She had to get a grip. There would be plenty of time for self-recriminations, but now she had to survive the night. She scrambled out of bed, searching for her cell on her nightstand. She had to call for help. She dialed 911, but before the call connected, she heard the creak of the old wood steps that led from the bookstore to her apartment. Was someone coming up the stairs?

Kate panicked. Her hands shook, and she dropped the cell on the bed. She didn't know what to do. For a second, she froze. Then she heard Shakespeare's screech, followed by a loud squawk. Oh, God, he had him. He was going to hurt her baby. He was going to hurt her.

"9-1-1, what is your emergency? " A woman's voice came over the cell and echoed throughout the quiet room.

Kate jumped and ran to the door. God, she was stupid. If the intruder didn't know she was tucked away in this old attic apartment, he sure did now. With shaking hands, she locked the door using the old skeleton metal key that was always in the keyhole. The door had self-locked twice without that key, and now she always kept the key in it. Truthfully, the door was old and the locking mechanism rusty. It wouldn't keep anyone out who wanted to get in. But it was better than nothing.

"Is anyone there? Do you need help?" the emergency dispatcher said.

Kate ran to her bed, grabbed the cell, and whispered, "Help me. Someone's in the house, in the bookstore. Help me."

She dropped the phone back on the bed, not caring what else the dispatcher asked. Kate couldn't focus on two things at once, not now. She was a trembling mess and had to think. Any second now the intruder would be at her door.

All kinds of sounds were coming from downstairs. The crashing of furniture, the breaking of glass, and another high-pitched screech from Shakespeare filled Kate's ears. There was more than one intruder, and they didn't care who heard. They were wrecking her place and tearing apart her world. Tears filled her eyes and spilled down her cheeks. She closed her eyes for a millisecond and re-focused, forcing herself to slow her breathing.

Kate recalled what Master Lim taught her to do in a crisis.

"You don't have to be a victim if you use your brain. Breathe, clear your mind, set your goal, and push everything else, including your fear, to the side. Your fear will cement you in your place. Your fear will paralyze you and get you killed."

Opening her eyes, Kate ran and grabbed one of the dinette chairs and jammed it under the doorknob. People did that on television. Maybe she'd get lucky and it would work for her. She needed a place to hide, and she needed a weapon. She scanned the room. Her only choices were the closet or the bathroom.

The walk-in closet was her best choice. The closet was massive and was used to store decades of old furniture, books, and shelves. Kate knew it well since she was the one who cleaned it and kept it organized. She would have the advantage in the closet.

Kate darted around the apartment searching for a weapon. Again, not many choices. She ran to the kitchen and pulled out one drawer after the next until she found a large serrated knife. It would have to do.

Someone jiggled the doorknob.

"Open the fucking door, you fucking bitch. You think this is going to save you?"

Kate froze. She knew that voice. The man's voice was slurred, but she recognized it.

"You've been asking for it, and now you're going to get it," he said with a nasty laugh.

Kate's body shook, and the knife fell from her hands and landed on the ground.

Jesse?

No. No. Of course not. That wasn't possible.

Kate's head hurt and her mind raced as she tried to assimilate and categorize the bits and pieces of information from the present and the past that were bombarding her brain.

This wasn't Chicago.

She wasn't eighteen and in high school.

This wasn't a dream.

She was wide awake and at Dreamscape...alone.

"You think this fucking door or the fucking police are going to keep you safe? Fuck that and fuck you. You're mine."

Jesse?

Kate shook her head. She had to keep a grip on reality. She couldn't let her mind wander to the past. She couldn't let the fear take over.

"Open the door, Miss Kate," he taunted in a sing-song voice. "I have a special present to give you since you love Christmas so fucking much."

Kyle Granger. The voice belonged to Kyle Granger. Kate shivered. God, she was an idiot. Why, why hadn't she told Noah or Sheriff Jordan about Kyle and his friend's continued harassment? Why did she think she could handle them on her own?

Thud.

Kate jumped out of her thoughts as Kyle slammed his body against the door. The door shook, and the lock began to splinter.

Kate scrubbed her hands over her face, gathered her hair from around her shoulders, and tugged. She needed the pain of that tug to bring her back to her senses. Kate didn't want to admit it, didn't want to give in, but she was terrified. She wanted to make Master Lim proud, but sparring at the dojo was so different. There, her partners weren't out to deliberately hurt or kill her. But she couldn't and wouldn't freeze, and she wouldn't let the fear take over. She'd put up one hell of a fight if she had to. The police would be here soon, but until then, she would fight with everything she learned and every bit of energy she had.

Kate's gaze shifted to her trembling hands, then to the knife on the floor. She shook her head. She had a better chance of fighting him off using her self-defense and martial arts training than with a knife she could barely hold steady. Leaving the knife on the floor, she ran to the closet. She closed the door as quietly as possible and cocooned herself in its darkness. It was stupid to hide like a coward in the closet. She knew that. But it would give her time to get her breathing and shaking body under control, and when he came for her, she'd take him out, the way she was taught.

As the body slams continued with more and more of the locking mechanism and door splintering, Kate picked her way to the back of the closet and hid behind a massive bookshelf.

She heard the bedroom door slam open and hit the wall, and Kyle crashed in. Within seconds she heard the closet door ripped open.

"Come out, you fucking bitch. No use hiding from me. It's you and me now."

Kate closed her eyes and took a deep breath in, letting it out slowly. She focused on her breathing and her heart rate. Her world narrowed to just the closet, just her breathing, and just the sound of Kyle's mocking voice as it drew nearer. She was ready. She knew she only had one chance at disabling him, and she was going to take it.

Kate wasn't a cowering little girl anymore, hoping to avoid her father's blows. She wasn't a teenager, trying to survive the daily challenge of staying alive in a gang-ridden high school, and she wasn't the girl who cowered in the bathroom stall, watching her teacher being raped and murdered, feeling powerless to stop it.

Kate drew on all her years of feeling helpless and powerless. She let the rage in and let it take over, and when Kyle came at her, she went after him. Using her body weight and the element of surprise, she dealt a quick, powerful blow to his throat with her forearm, followed by an elbow to his solar plexus. He doubled over, cursing and gasping for breath, giving her the opening she needed to knee him in the groin. Kyle went down. She leaped over his crumpled body and ran for the closet door only to be met with one of Kyle's friends.

"Where do you think you're going?" He sneered as he grasped a handful of her hair and dragged her toward Kyle's writhing body on the floor.

"I told him to go gentle on you, but now I'm gonna let him do whatever he wants with you, bitch. I'll even warm you up for him," the boy said as he backhanded Kate across the face and threw her to the corner of the closet.

Kate landed with a thump against the wall, her head crashing against a piece of furniture on the way down. The pain in her head was agonizing and her cheek was on fire. Her vision blurred and for a moment she thought she was going to be sick. She blinked repeatedly and focused on the teenage boy helping Kyle up. Their lips were moving as they advanced toward her, but she couldn't hear them.

Kate began to shake and her teeth chattered. She started hyperventilating. She couldn't hold on. She couldn't fight. The fear was winning. She didn't have a chance of surviving, not with two of them. She stopped fighting the fear and gave in. She let it wash over her. Soon she was drowning in it.

Kate scrunched her eyes shut. She drew her knees up to her chest, lowered her head, and wound her arms around her knees. If God had any kindness left for her, he'd let the darkness overwhelm her, and she'd pass out. A heart attack would be better than this. She couldn't survive being raped, being violated and torn apart from the inside out. She'd watched Mrs. Ashley go through it, and she knew for a fact, she was nowhere near as strong.

In her mind, Kate screamed and cried for Noah. The world she so carefully built in Lakes Crossing was being dismantled piece by piece. Shakespeare was most likely dead, as he was silent now. Dreamscape was destroyed. Noah was nowhere near to help her. She was on her own once again, dealing with violence, rage, and God-awful, heart-stopping fear. This time, there was no place to run and no place to hide. It was over.

Kate heard nothing more. She did what she used to do when her father went into one of his rages. If she shrunk herself into a tiny ball, then no one could see or hear her. In this position, she was insignificant.

She allowed her mind to drift as she rocked back and forth. She wasn't huddled in the corner of the attic closet. She wasn't alone and terrified. She wasn't about to be beaten, raped and possibly killed. She was with

Noah, in his arms. He was holding her tight, rocking her, and telling her how much he loved her.

Seconds, minutes, hours, even days, passed. Kate had no recollection of time passing.

Kate heard her name called, but the voice was far away. She slowly emerged from her cocoon, her mind trying to reconnect with her body. Loud, angry voices filled her ears. She didn't want to come back to her body. All she wanted was to be left alone. She was fine where she was. She curled further into a ball and moaned.

"N-no. G-go a-away. P-please," she stuttered, shrinking against the corner.

"Kate, it's Dee. Open your eyes. You're safe now. You're going to be okay."

Dee reached out to smooth the hair off Kate's face. Kate flinched at her touch and whimpered. She started rocking again.

"Dee, we're not getting through to her. Why don't you let the paramedics take care of her? They know what they're doing," Sheriff Jordan said as he stepped toward Deidra.

Dee whirled to face Jordan. "If the paramedics could help, they would have by now and Jordan, you damn well know I know what I'm doing. You've called me to help you in much worse situations."

Dee put her hands on her hips and glared at the sheriff. "I have the experience and credentials to take care of her. Now, back off. All of you get out. You're terrifying her. I don't want her traumatized any further."

Jordan threw up his hands and nodded to his men. He turned to Dee once more. "You have five minutes. Then, I'll have the paramedics sedate both of you if I have to."

Dee's jaw hardened and her lips thinned. "Touch me, Billy Jordan, and you'll be sorry." Dee pierced him with her laser eyes. "Touch her, and you'll be signing your life away. He's on his way here, and if you've hurt or touched his woman forcibly, only God can help you."

Jordan let out a frustrated sigh, held his hands up, and walked out of the closet.

Dee sat on the floor cross-legged. For a few minutes, she let the silence fill the room as the men's voices faded.

"Kate," Dee began in a low, soothing voice. "You're safe now. You're okay. The boys are in custody. You're safe."

Kate whimpered.

"Noah's on his way. He'll be here soon. Jordan called him a while ago and let him know he was responding to an emergency call out here. Any second now, he'll be here."

At the sound of Noah's name, Kate stopped rocking. She raised her head and attempted to focus on Dee. She remained in the corner, huddled, on alert, waiting for the next blow.

Dee sighed and smiled at Kate.

"Hi there. It's okay. You're safe. Everything's going to be okay. The police are here. The boys are gone, and Noah's on his way."

Kate was confused. What was Dee doing here? Where was here? Boys? Police? She surveyed her surroundings with her eyes, never uncoiling from the corner. She was in the attic closet. The place was a wreck, and Dee was sitting on the floor. Why was Dee…?

"Kate," Dee's soft voice interrupted Kate's confused thoughts. "It's Saturday evening. You're at the bookstore, in your apartment, in the closet. Do you remember what happened?"

Kate studied Dee. What happened?

Images and sounds flowed through her mind.

Shakespeare squawking, screeching.

Crashes, thuds, breaking glass.

Kyle.

Pain.

Overwhelming, paralyzing, mind-numbing fear returned.

Kate screamed. "*No!*"

The door to the closet flung open with such force, it crashed against the wall shattering the plaster. Kate jumped, slammed her eyes shut, and sunk into the corner while Dee whipped around as a frantic Noah rushed in. His eyes were wild and his gaze bounced around the room until it landed on a sobbing, shaking Kate.

Noah rushed toward Kate, and Dee tried to hold him back.

"No, Noah. She's terrified. Go slow. She doesn't know who…"

Noah threw his sister's hands off him and rushed toward Kate's huddled body. He dropped to the floor in front of her, as she rocked and sobbed.

"Katie, sweetheart," he begged in an agonized voice. "I'm here, baby. I'm here. I'm sorry, baby." Noah tore his hands through his hair. "I'm sorry, sweetness. I'm here now, and I swear you're safe. Please, sweetheart. Please, stop now and come to me. Let me hold you."

Kate heard Noah's voice. She tried to stop crying, but couldn't. She tried to unglue and uncurl her body from the tight ball she was in, but couldn't move. She wanted Noah. She needed Noah. But she was trapped in her mind. The crushing fear that first introduced itself to her in the girl's bathroom at Elmore High School thirteen years ago was back with a vengeance, adding today's horror to its repertoire.

A new wave of terror threatened to take her under. But Noah was here. She heard his voice. She needed to swim long enough against the riptide to somehow connect with him. If she could make it to him, to his arms, he'd hold her. He'd hold back everything and everyone that threatened her. Kate knew she'd be safe in Noah's arms.

Kate harnessed the little energy she had left and raised her face to the sound of his voice, as tears continued to stream down her cheeks.

"N-Noah," she sobbed.

Noah moved with the speed of light. He reached out and pulled Kate onto his lap. Instantly, she repositioned herself. She straddled him, wrapping her legs around him and her arms around his neck. She fused her small body to his large one and buried her face in his neck.

Kate breathed in Noah. She felt his racing heart connect with hers. His heart captured hers and coordinated their rhythm. Their chests rose and fell as they breathed heavily and within seconds, tandemly. Kate's arms and legs tightened around Noah.

"D-don't g-go. N-need you," she managed to stutter as her entire body quaked and her teeth chattered.

One of Noah's arms went around her body in a vise grip, plastering her even further to him, and his other hand cradled the back of her head. He kissed her hair, forehead, cheeks, face, eyes, nose, and finally, her mouth. She continued to weep as he rubbed her back and rocked her.

"I'm here, Katie. I'm here. I'm so sorry, baby. I should've been here. I should've been here."

Noah buried his face in her hair and held her to him. "I love you. You're safe now, sweetheart, and I swear I will never let anyone hurt you again." Noah repeated this mantra over and over again until Kate's sobs faded, and she lay limp against his body.

Noah continued to sit on the floor holding her as the paramedics examined her, and although they wanted to take her to the hospital, she staunchly refused. All she wanted to do was sleep in Noah's arms and forget the night's events.

"Let's get out of here, okay sweetheart?" Noah whispered in Kate's ear.

Kate nodded against his chest. She was exhausted, utterly shattered. She couldn't move, even if she wanted to. Her head throbbed, her face ached, and every bone in her body hurt. She used all her energy to keep her heart beating and her lungs absorbing oxygen.

Noah went to his knees with Kate now cradled in his arms. With Dee's help, he stood. Kate's head was down. She nestled against his body. One of her hands fisted his sweatshirt on his chest, while the other did the same on his back.

Kate raised her head. "Wait. The bookstore, Shakes, I … I have to…" she said, as her eyes filled with tears once again.

"Shh, baby. I'll take care of everything."

"Shakespeare, is he?" Kate asked in a broken voice. She already knew the answer. She felt the pain deep in her heart, but she couldn't stop the question from leaving her lips.

Noah regarded Kate, regret and sadness written all over his face. "Yeah, sweetheart. He's gone. I'm sorry."

Kate's eyes welled with tears that once again slipped down her cheeks and her breath hitched as she tried to control her breathing. Her baby, her best friend, was gone. They killed him. Kate dropped her head once again against Noah's chest. Her brain could no longer process the world she lived in. Nothing made sense. She couldn't deal with any of it.

"Sweetheart, close your eyes. Let's get out of here. We're going to spend the night at Dee's. Tomorrow, we'll figure all this out together."

Noah raised his head and turned toward Dee, quirking his head to the side in question.

"Yes, of course, you're coming home with me," Dee insisted. "You're welcome to stay as long as you want. Jackson and I came together. He can take care of things here and then drive your car back to our place. I've got the Jeep, and I'll drive us home."

Noah nodded. "Okay, Kate?"

Kate searched his face. There was so much to do. She had to deal with the damage to the bookstore and the police. But she couldn't, not now, not tonight. All she wanted to do tonight was to sink into oblivion and sink into Noah. She nodded, too tired to find her voice.

"Good, sweetheart. Now close your eyes. I'm going to walk us out of here. I've got you."

Kate closed her eyes. She didn't want to see anything. She only wanted to sleep. Maybe if she closed her eyes and fell into a deep sleep, when she woke up she would find that all this was only a nightmare. She burrowed into Noah's chest, turning her face into him, and inhaled his spicy scent.

Dee walked in front of Noah and soon Kate felt and smelled her bed comforter wrap around her. She sighed and sunk deeper into Noah's hold. As Noah carried her down the stairs, through the bookstore, and out the front door, Kate heard the chatter of people and bits and pieces of sentences and conversations.

"Targeted, well-thought-out attack."

"His daddy isn't getting him out of this."

"They were drunk and reckless, didn't care about anything. Trashed the place."

"Poor animal."

"God knows what would have happened to her."

The words bounced around in Kate's head. She tried to block them out, but it was useless. She shivered. She didn't want to hear anymore, didn't want to see any of it. She let out a low, agonized whimper.

"Hold on, sweetheart. We're almost out of here. I swear."

Kate felt the cold November air hit her skin, and she shivered, despite the heavy comforter wrapped around her. She smelled snow in the air. She loved snow, and this would have been the first snow of the season. A snowy Thanksgiving weekend would have been perfect. She could have spent it decorating and by Monday Dreamscape would have been a winter wonderland.

Noah slid into the car, keeping her in his arms. When the car door slammed shut, she jumped in his arms and reality hit once again. There would be no winter wonderland this Christmas. There would be no Storytime—*Shakespeare Goes Skiing*, *Shakespeare at Rockefeller Center*, and *Shakespeare Sits on Santa's Knee.* There would never be another Shakespeare anything. All her dreams were shattered. Kate sobbed, and her body shook in Noah's arms.

Maybe it was all an illusion. Maybe she dreamed everything—the bookstore, the bird, the friends, Lakes Crossing, and Noah. Then it hit her. If Noah had gone shopping with her, she could have lost him tonight. Of all the things to lose, losing Noah would be her undoing. She thanked God she'd convinced him to stay in the City.

Kate took in a deep, shuddering breath and sighed. If she had to, she could survive just about anything. She'd proven that. But losing Noah? Dear God in heaven—no! If she had to live without Shakespeare, without Dreamscape, without all the little things that made her life full and beautiful, she could. But she never wanted to experience a life without Noah. She wouldn't survive it.

Chapter Nineteen

Noah held Kate throughout the night and well into the next day. His arms ached, and he was stiff. Still, he didn't let go. By the time they arrived at Dee's, Dr. Neilson, the Reed family doctor, was there. Noah wanted Kate to have a thorough exam, and once the doctor finished his exam, and agreed Kate didn't need hospitalization, Noah gathered her in his arms. Kate fell asleep seconds later.

Halfway through the night, Noah laid Kate down on the bed and went to the adjoining bathroom to clean up. He kept extra clothes at Dee's for nights he chose to stay over or in case he got stuck there due to a storm. He changed into sweats and got back in bed with Kate. She rolled into him and glued herself to his body. His arms went around her, and he held her all night, swearing to himself and her he'd never let her go or compromise her safety again.

Plain and simple, he'd fucked up—again. He wasn't watching close enough and somehow evil found its way to another woman he loved. Was he cursed? Did God hate him so much that he'd take away every woman he loved?

Kate was safe in his arms, but if the police hadn't arrived when they did, she might not have been. Noah was beside himself, imagining all the ways Kate could have been injured or worse, killed. He hadn't prayed in years, not since he was a child. But during the night, he broke down and screamed at his maker.

"Anything you want, anything. Just don't take her from me. Not again. I'm not strong enough to live without her. You'll tear my heart out. If you take her, take me with her. Better yet, take me instead."

Kate woke up several times during the night, in

the midst of one nightmare after another, screaming for people he didn't know—Mrs. A, Jesse, Jaz. At first, Noah tried to make sense of what she was saying, but it was no use. These were ghosts from the past and last night's horror show brought them to life.

Kate had warned Noah from the very beginning she was damaged. He'd come into their relationship with eyes wide open, and he didn't regret it. But he'd been patient with her long enough. It was time Kate told him everything about her past because it was slowly eating away at her. Her reaction to what happened last night was exaggerated by the events of the past. It was a wonder she didn't completely shatter.

Kate was sprawled on his chest, her cinnamon-colored hair fanned all around them, her head tucked underneath his chin. Her breathing was slow and even, and her heart beat in rhythm with his. He tightened his arms around her as he remembered the mind-numbing panic that gripped him when Jordan called and told him he was responding to an emergency call from Dreamscape. He'd thrown clothes on and called Dee from the road. Dee lived a few minutes from Dreamscape, and she was family. He was confident, regardless of how she felt about Kate, she would help him, and he wasn't wrong.

Noah didn't think he would ever forget the sound of Kate's piercing scream when he entered the attic. It, along with the memory of her curled-up, shaking body, tore his guts out. Noah pushed the hair off his face and rubbed his face with his free hand. He was wiped out, and there was no rest to come anytime soon.

Dreamscape was trashed. In the short time Kyle and his friends were at the bookstore, they did thousands of dollars' worth of damage. Furniture was broken, books were torn apart, and walls were spray-painted. Then, there was poor Shakes. It was evident the creature put up a good fight, biting all three boys. In the end, one of them went after him with a heavy object until his little body was destroyed.

Noah sighed. Kate was the only thing that mattered to him, and she was relatively unharmed. As if sensing his thoughts, Kate shifted and stretched. Her eyes fluttered open, and she raised her head. She rested one elbow on his chest and peered down at him with her luminous green eyes. Her skin was pale and there was a bruise on her left cheek. There were shadows under her eyes. Her gorgeous hair was a wild mess. Still, she was the most beautiful woman he'd ever laid eyes on.

"Hi."

Noah smiled and tucked her hair behind her ear.

"Hi, sweetheart," he said, kissing her nose. "How do you feel? You were up much of the night with one nightmare after another."

Kate shrugged. "I don't know. Numb. Exhausted. My life's a wreck. Shakespeare's dead and Dreamscape is destroyed, isn't it?"

Noah thought about sparing her the details, but she wouldn't want that.

"There's a lot of damage. Your insurance should cover it, but I'm not going to lie to you. It's a mess."

Kate sighed.

"Why? Why did they come after me? I didn't do anything to them. I knew they were escalating, but I didn't think they'd go this far."

Noah stiffened. Escalating? What the hell was she talking about? She hadn't mentioned the boys in a long time. He assumed Jordan put the fear of God in them, and that they decided to move on to their next victim. Why the hell didn't she tell him they were still messing with her?

Noah rolled them, so she was trapped underneath him and pierced her with his gaze. He did his damnedest to control the sudden anger that hit him, but he knew it was evident in his voice.

"What do you mean escalating? Had Kyle and his friends been bothering you? Why didn't you mention it?"

Kate squirmed and tried to move from underneath him, but he was immovable. She turned her head to the side and focused on the wall. "I thought I could handle them."

"You thought you could handle them? How long has this been going on?"

Kate met his eyes. "A few weeks. Noah, I'm sorry I didn't tell you, but I didn't want you to do anything rash, and I was managing them. I think…"

Noah's temper simmered. He clenched his jaw and breathed deep, attempting to calm down. She'd needlessly put herself in jeopardy. He could've protected her if only she wasn't so stubborn.

"Kate, stop. Bottom line, you should have told me they were still harassing you. At the very least, you should have told Jordan. Did you at least tell Jordan?"

Kate closed her eyes and shook her head.

Noah sighed and dropped his forehead to rest against hers. Last night could have been avoided if she trusted him enough to help her. She could have been raped or killed. He tried to be understanding, to respect her boundaries and her need for control over her life, but enough was enough. He couldn't go through this again with another woman. If she wouldn't allow him to help her and be fully in her life, then they didn't have a future. He too had boundaries.

Lies, secrets, deception—these were the elements that destroyed relationships. A lie by omission was still a lie. Although Kate had shared a lot of her past with him, he knew there was still a lot she hadn't told him. She was used to being a one-woman show. He'd lived through this once before and he sure as shit wasn't doing it again. Kristin had jerked him around in a similar manner, and he'd let her. No matter how much he loved Kate, either she started trusting him and sharing her life with him fully, or he was done.

Noah rolled off Kate and the bed. He stood and regarded her as he ran a hand through his disheveled hair.

"I know you've been through a lot in the last twenty-four hours, and maybe this isn't the best time for this conversation, but it's going to happen. It's time you let me in, Kate. I know I said I wouldn't rush you, and I've been more than patient. I've backed off and let you do things your way, but I can't do this anymore, not when your life is in jeopardy. I can't live knowing only half of you, and I can't live questioning whether you've told me everything or spoon fed me only what you think I need to know. I'm not that kind of man."

Noah saw panic cross Kate's features, but he wasn't giving in. He raked a hand through his hair. "Either I'm fully in, or I'm not, Kate. Your choice. I can't do this again. I can't sit back and watch another person I love put herself in harm's way and self-combust."

Noah looked away and then back to Kate. His voice cracked as he said, "It'll kill me, Kate."

Kate studied him from the bed without moving. Her big green eyes were going to be the death of him. They were wide and filled with fear and tears.

Damn it! Why was everything so damn hard with this woman? He hated giving her ultimatums and felt like an ass for doing so, especially after last night, but she wasn't giving him many choices. He had to be firm with her, even if it ripped out both their hearts. Perhaps, if he had been firmer with Kristin, she, their baby, and the teenagers whose lives she recklessly took would still be alive.

Noah sat on the edge of the bed and stroked Kate's cheek with the back of his hand. He let out a slow breath. "I need a few minutes, but we're going to talk. I'm going to grab us some food and coffee. I'll be back. You think about what I said. This is no longer only about you. When you love someone, Kate, you think beyond your needs and wants."

He bent, touched his lips to hers, and pressed his forehead against hers. "I need you to trust me," he whispered. "I need you to let me protect you. I can't have the past sandwiched between us, holding you away, keeping you from being mine fully. I can't live like that. Please don't make me live without you."

Kate closed her eyes as tears escaped down her cheeks. She wrapped her arms around his neck and kissed his lips.

"Okay," she whispered. "Okay."

Noah made his way to the kitchen. Dee, God bless her, was up and had been to Kate's house earlier. Although the police were there taking photos, they allowed her to pack a bag for Kate. She had that, along with bagels, fruit, and coffee, ready for Noah.

The minute Dee saw Noah in the kitchen, she walked to him and hugged him.

"How is she?"

Noah shook his head. "She's okay, given the circumstances. I think there is a long road ahead, though, since she hasn't seen the wreckage yet."

He gave Dee a grateful smile. "Thanks for letting us stay here. I know you have reservations about Kate, but…"

Dee took his hands in hers and squeezed. "Stop, Reed. Please. I'm sorry, brother. I'm sorry. You were right. I've been an overprotective bitch. I've behaved badly. I get it now."

Dee peered down and shook her head. "I don't know what got into me. I was so afraid for you. I didn't want you hurt again. I thought I was protecting you. Instead, I was the one hurting you. Please forgive me. She adores you and trusts you with her life. Just hearing your name yesterday calmed her. She was undone, wouldn't let anyone near her, until she heard your name. She's nothing like Kristin. She's given you her whole heart. You're everything to that woman. I see how you love her, and I see how she loves you back. You and Kate can stay here for as long as you want. My home is your home and her home."

Noah's smile grew, and he hugged Dee to him. Thank God one good thing came out of this mess.

"Love ya, Dee."

"Love you too, baby brother, always," Dee said, stepping back and wiping a tear from her cheek.

Noah kissed Dee's cheek and gave her another hug. Then he lugged Kate's bag, along with their breakfast, to the guest room. Dee's guest room resembled a five-star hotel suite with a private bathroom and a sitting area with a loveseat, overstuffed recliner, and coffee table.

As Noah closed the bedroom door, he turned to find Kate coming out of the bathroom. She was wrapped in a towel and was pink and warm from the shower. He showed her the bag Dee packed and as she dressed, he showered and dressed.

They sat side-by-side on the loveseat, drinking coffee and picking at the food.

"Yesterday was bad, Kate," he started. "But yesterday's events weren't the only trauma you were living. You were also reliving the past, weren't you?"

Standing, Kate walked to the window. She drew the curtains to the side and stared out into the falling snow. "I grew up in one of the worst gang-ridden neighborhoods of Chicago, made up of African-American and Mexican gang members who were constantly at war with one another," she said in a haunted voice.

"My life at home was hell, but my life at school was the wild west, anything and everything happened—drugs, alcohol, weapons, gang shootings. The police, school administrators, and parents gave up. We were the throwaway kids that no one gave a shit about."

"It's a miracle you survived."

Kate shook her head and gave a harsh laugh. "It's no miracle, Noah. At home, I learned to cower, to disappear to stay alive. At school, I did the same. But, I only had my father to deal with at home. At school, there were hundreds of kids ready to end my life for no good reason. I wasn't a wallflower; that would have been a luxury. I was a weed someone was always trying to pull up from the roots and kill."

Resting against the windowsill, Kate regarded him. "Are you sure you want to hear this? Jeff couldn't handle it."

Noah stood and walked to her. He took her hands in his and raised them to his lips. "I'm not Jeff. Have I ever let you down or walked away from you?

Straightening, she reached for him. She kissed him and cupped his cheek. "No, Noah Reed, you've never let me down. Not ever."

Kate walked them back to the loveseat and sat down, pulling Noah next to her. She took a big gulp of air and met his eyes.

"I was a senior in high school. I could see the light at the end of the tunnel. I was going to be free soon. I had one good friend, Jaz, and I had Mrs. Ashley. Mrs. A was my math teacher, my confidante, and friend. She was young and beautiful—wavy blonde hair and big blue eyes." Kate smiled. "She was idealistic. She thought she was a one-woman army and could change the world. Well, our little piece of it, anyway."

Shaking her head, she focused on their joined hands. "She never had a chance. From the very beginning, she was a target for both gangs, a tasty treat to devour."

She licked her lips. "One day, I stayed after school to help her tutor struggling students. When we finished, I went to the bathroom before walking home. The school was empty. No one was around but some janitors. I was in a stall about to walk out when I heard them."

Pulling her hands from Noah's, Kate, brought her knees up to her chest and wrapped her arms around them. "At first, I didn't understand what was happening. I couldn't see them. I could only hear them. He told her to stay silent, or he'd kill her. I could hear him hit, punch, and taunt her."

Noah gathered her against him but kept silent.

"I huddled on top of the toilet so he couldn't see me. I was so scared. I didn't help her. I couldn't. I was paralyzed with fear." Kate swallowed and took a deep breath. With a tremulous voice, she continued. "He dragged her into my line of vision and threw her to the ground. After that, I saw everything through the seam of the stall door. I-I heard it, I saw it, and I didn't help her. I watched as he did unspeakable things to her, brutalized her in the worst ways a woman could be, but I did nothing. If only I'd moved, done something."

Noah couldn't stay silent. He pulled Kate on to his lap and wiped the tears from her cheeks with his fingers. "Sweetheart, you were so young and in an impossible situation."

"No, you don't understand," Kate interrupted, her eyes filled with self-recrimination. "She saw me. She knew I was there. She knew I could help her, and I didn't. I'd been taught to cower, to hide, and that's what I did. I protected myself, but not her. She didn't struggle once she knew I was there. She sacrificed herself for me and let it happen."

Kate rose from his lap and started pacing, again.

"I escaped, but she didn't. I was frozen, as I hovered over that toilet, hiding, trying to disappear, praying I would go deaf and blind, so I could no longer hear and see what was happening a few feet from me. I didn't move—not until the gun went off."

Noah collapsed back into the loveseat. His heart raced. Jesus. A gun?

"I don't know the sequence of events. My eyes were squeezed shut. I heard two gun shots. One of the janitors walked into the bathroom. Jesse shot them both."

Walking to the window once more, Kate closed her eyes, and laid her forehead against the cold glass. She continued in a flat, dead voice. "When the gun went off, I jumped, lost my balance, and fell off the toilet. Jesse heard me, busted open the stall door, and pointed the gun at me. If another janitor hadn't walked in, I would have been his next victim. Jesse stepped out of the stall to face the janitor, and I bolted out of the stall, and then out of the girl's bathroom."

Kate opened her eyes and turned toward Noah. "But, Noah, before I ran, I—I saw Mrs. Ashley's naked, abused body, lifeless on the floor and Mr. Kenkin, slumped next to the bathroom door with blood pouring out of his chest. I didn't wait, though. I didn't call for help. I turned my back on them and I ran. I heard another gunshot, but that didn't stop me, it propelled me. I ran and ran and ran."

Returning to the loveseat, she collapsed next to Noah. He reached for her hands and held them. They were ice-cold.

"Jesse?" he asked.

"Jesse Alvarez. He was a member of the Mexican gang that ruled one-half of the school."

Noah rubbed Kate's hands with his, trying to warm them up. He was stunned and had no idea what to say. This was way beyond anything he could have imagined.

"Where did you go?"

"I couldn't go home. I ran to Jaz, my best friend. She and her boyfriend, Tyrell, saw the state I was in. Tyrell was in the rival gang at school, and the minute I said Jesse's name, he stuck me on a Greyhound bus."

Noah let out a long breath.

Kate raised her head and her bleak eyes met his.

"Jesse knew who I was, and that Jaz and I were tight. He knew I would go to Jaz for help. I shouldn't have gone, shouldn't have pulled anyone else into my sordid mess. I should have gone to the police, but they never helped me in the past. They didn't give a shit about kids like me. I was terrified and stupid. I ran to Jaz and due to my stupidity, I started a gang war. I got her killed."

"I don't understand, sweetheart. What happened to Jaz?"

"A week after the incident, I called Jaz. I didn't know whether Jesse was caught or if he was searching for me. I wanted to come home. Even though I lived in hell, it was still better than the streets. Jaz didn't answer, so I called Tyrell."

Tears slipped down Kate's face and she swiped them away. She cleared her throat. "Jaz was dead. She'd been raped and killed, like Mrs. Ashley. Jesse's gang was on the warpath and took her out along the way. They were searching for me. Jesse was still on the run."

Noah pulled her trembling body against his so her back was to his front and he had his arms around her, once again. He tried to assimilate her story. So many things made sense now. But where was her father in all of this? Where was Jesse? Was she still in danger?

"Was Jesse ever found? Is he still looking for you? What about your father in all of this?"

Kate shook her head. "No, no one is looking for me. The only danger I'm in is all in my head." She nestled closer to him, drawing up her legs to the side and resting her weight against him. "A few weeks after I moved in with Edith, the nightmares were so bad, neither of us was sleeping. I broke down and told her everything. A simple Internet search revealed Mrs. Ashley and both janitors died at the high school that evening. Jesse and most of his gang were killed a month after, in a standoff with the police."

"And your dad?"

Sighing, Kate shrugged. "He wouldn't miss me one way or another. By that time, he barely acknowledged my existence. He was probably happy he had one less mouth to feed. I don't know."

Noah shook his head. Kate's story, hell, her life, was convoluted. If he hadn't witnessed her reaction to the sound of gunfire at the theater, the nightmares, and heard her cry out Jaz, Jesse, and Mrs. Ashley's name, he would have a hard time believing it all. But he believed every word, and his heart ached with pain and sorrow. She survived a hellish childhood and was almost free, only to witness a brutal crime and was then thrown out into the world without any coping skills whatsoever. But she survived and rebuilt her life from scratch.

Kate had disappeared, dropped out from existence, and no one in her life missed her. How could that be? What was wrong with society today? How could a young girl cease to exist and no one give a damn?

Noah brought her hand to his lips. "No one ever looked for you? How did you disappear?"

Kate tilted her head up and gave him a sad smile. "No, Noah. No one of any consequence missed me. In the beginning, I was terrified. I changed my name, the color of my hair, everything about me. I never went back, never contacted anyone. I hid my driver's license, and I didn't have credit cards. I worked for cash, and I changed locations often. I didn't settle until I met Edith. I went by the name of Meghan Summerville for years, with only a library card as a form of identification. It took years and a lot of Edith therapy before I liked myself enough to become Kate once more."

"That's extraordinary."

Kate shook her head. "No, Noah. That's where you are wrong. There are thousands of runaways on the street, each with their own story. I was no different. Before Edith came along, people passed me every day on the street, and no one took a second look. No one cared whether I was hungry, cold, scared, safe, or sick. I wasn't important to anyone."

Noah turned Kate around, forcing her to straddle him. He gripped her chin, and when her gaze connected with his, he kissed her and said, "Kate, that may have been the case then. You need to know that now, today, you are the most important person to me. In my world, you are my everything."

Chapter Twenty

Kate was losing her mind. She was going to kill her man if he didn't back off. Since the night of the attack, Noah had become an overprotective, intrusive beast who was getting harder and harder to rein in. When he wasn't with her, he insisted on knowing where she was at all times. She loved hearing from him, but she was flooded with so many texts and phone calls from him, she didn't have a moment to herself and felt stifled. Something had to give.

More worrisome than his hypervigilance was the disturbing change in Noah's personality. There was a hardness, an edge to Noah that wasn't there before the attack. He didn't smile as much, was jittery, and lost his temper easily. He seemed to be on alert at every moment, waiting for something to happen, even in his sleep.

Kate tried to draw him out of his dark mood, but nothing helped. He refused to admit anything was bothering him. One night, as they lay in bed, she joked and said she was going to change her cell number and not give it to him. He lost his mind.

"What's going on with you, baby?"

"Nothing's wrong. I'm sorry," he grumbled, kissing her forehead. "I'm tired." He turned and gave her his back. "Let's get some sleep."

Sleep was all they did lately. They didn't make love with the regularity or urgency they once did. This too, troubled Kate. She missed the intimacy they once shared and tried everything she could to entice Noah into a better mood, and back into her arms. But Noah was preoccupied and distant.

After the attack, Kate bounced back at a much faster speed than Noah. She mourned Shakes and burying her beautiful boy was hard. Kate had a resilient spirit, though, and was quickly absorbed in remodeling and repairing the damage done to the bookstore. In Shakes' honor, she dedicated the Dreaming Room to him and called it The Shake Shack. She hired a local artist to fill the walls with images of Shakespeare going on all the adventures she'd written about and read to the kids during Storytime.

For Kate, telling Noah everything about her past was freeing. For the first time in her life, she had no secrets and no burdens. Every night she slept peacefully in Noah's arms, nightmare free. But while she felt light and free, Noah seemed to be drowning, deeply troubled. If she had to guess, Kyle's attack, her past, and his past were combining forces and torturing Noah.

Kate understood, she really did. She lived with the past and the fear for thirteen years. She had woken up and fell asleep with it for so long. It had become her daily companion. She was used to its tight hold, yet managed to escape it every now and then to build a life. But this was all new to Noah. Although he said he was fine, she knew otherwise. Kate wondered how she could help Noah break free from his fears if he wouldn't allow her in.

Kyle's attack added to Noah's fear for Kate's safety and his ability to protect her. She was not the only one affected by the attack. It scared the hell out of Noah. The boys were no longer in jail. All had posted bail and were out awaiting trial. Noah was enraged at the justice system and Jordan. Jordan assured them he was keeping a close eye on the boys and Kate. It would be months before the justice system dealt with the boys.

Noah wasn't satisfied with anything Jordan said and took matters into his hands. At first, Noah followed Kate everywhere, but he had work to do, and she had to deal with insurance adjusters and contractors. That was when he lost his mind and hired Axel, her new bodyguard. Everywhere she went, Axel followed. He was her shadow—a huge, brick wall of a man who dominated every space she was in. He was impossible to miss with his bald head, dark shades, and big, beefy arms folded over his chest. The man had a permanent scowl etched on his face and he scared the crap out of her the first time she met him.

Noah assured Kate Axel was a temporary addition to their household, but when Axel was invited to Thanksgiving dinner at Dee's, Kate knew she was in trouble. Kate sat sandwiched between him and Noah the entire night. What did Noah think was going to happen to her at Dee's? Did he think the turkey was going to rise and lead an attack with the sweet potatoes, corn, and gravy in tow? For the love of God!

When Kate complained to Dee, she got nowhere.

"Give him time, Kate. He'll loosen up. I've never seen him so scared in my life. Noah feels he didn't protect you from Kyle, and he's terrified something will happen to you when he's not around."

Kate sighed. "He can't protect me from everything. It doesn't make any sense. We have to put the past behind us and live. I want to forget about it all and enjoy being with Noah and my new family. Axel is not family."

Kate and Dee had rekindled their friendship, and Kate couldn't be happier. Dee, Clare, and their friends, Aimee and Julia, circled Kate in the days after her attack. Having Noah was a beautiful thing, but having girlfriends to share her life with was a joy she'd always longed for.

With only a week until Christmas, everyone chipped in to help her ready Dreamscape for a grand re-opening in the new year. Axel, the wall, however, was constantly in her way and managed to piss her off more than usual. Kate was exhausted. She wanted to finish the display cases so she could rest and enjoy the holiday with Noah and her family, but Axel was making the task harder than it needed to be. He followed her from one room to another, like a lost puppy. At one point, she stopped him from walking into the restroom with her. That was when she lost it.

Kate closed the bookstore and directed Axel to drop her at the penthouse where she was meeting Noah for dinner. Since the attack, they either spent the night at Noah's place or hers, neither wanting to be apart from the other. Lugging things back and forth was tiring, and they spent too many hours in the day commuting to and from Manhattan and Lakes Crossing. They decided to move into the Easton Estate together after the holidays, and were looking forward to the stability.

Once at Noah's, Kate showered and dressed in comfortable, kick-Noah's-ass-in-gear clothing. She was putting a stop to this nonsense tonight. Whether Noah was ready to talk or not, they were going to deal with the elephant in the room; or the brick wall, in their case. She'd been patient, but enough was enough. She couldn't have Axel in the bookstore once it reopened. He would scare her tiny customers away.

"Call him off, Noah," Kate said in a firm, no-nonsense tone over dinner.

"No," Noah said, glancing up from his dinner.

"No? That's it? No discussion? Just no? Are you kidding me?"

"Kate, we've talked about this. I need to know you're safe. I need to protect you. The boys are still out there."

Kate sighed, trying to control her frustration. She put her hand over his.

"Noah, I've let you install a security system in the bookstore and my apartment. The sheriff keeps a close eye on me. I don't go anywhere without either you or one of the girls with me, and I sleep and wake up in your arms every day. We can't live like this forever. He must be costing a fortune. Please, baby. Please, we need to try to find a degree of normalcy."

Noah put his fork down and drained his glass of wine. He studied her for a minute, and she thought she saw his eyes soften.

He shook his head. "No."

"Noah Reed. I swear on all that's holy, if you don't call him off, I'll use him as a sparring partner. I may be small, but I've learned a new trick this week. I swear I'll bring your man to his knees and then I'll do it to you."

Noah pushed away from the table and stood. "I'm going to work out. Don't wait up," he said in a brusque voice and walked to their bedroom.

Kate sat, frozen at the dining table. What just happened? Since when did they speak to each other that way? Since when did they walk away from one another? She had two options. She could continue giving Noah space and hope, in time, he'd find his way beyond his fears and back to her, or she could follow him and do what she needed to, to get through to him.

Sighing, Kate shook her head. He wasn't giving her a choice. If they continued like this, fear would turn into anger, and anger would turn into resentment. The love they built would get trampled on by all the other unhealthy emotions that were bound to take root and grow.

Kate rose and followed Noah to the bedroom. She hated this room with its white walls, white comforter, white everything. She hoped the decorator Kristin used for this place was cheap because they had done a crappy job. The only thing Kate liked was the massive, king-size mahogany bed with a padded headboard and built-in storage drawers at the base. It sat in the middle of the room and didn't match any of the décor. Noah admitted he purchased it after Kristin's death.

Noah was in the bathroom pulling on a t-shirt. Their gazes met in the bathroom mirror as Kate walked up behind him, sliding her hands over his back and broad shoulders, and then around his waist. Noah froze and continued to glare at her with a closed-off, stoic expression.

"The subject is closed, Kate. I'm not going through this with you again. I don't need this. I don't need you fighting me every step of the damn way. Haven't you learned your lesson? We agreed you would let me take care of your security and that's what I'm doing. Now"—he said, grasping her hands around his waist and beginning to pull them away—"let go. I need a run."

Kate's eyes filled with tears. In all the time she and Noah had been together, he'd never spoken to her so coldly. He'd never pushed her away and touched her with such indifference. She was hurt by his words and actions. Her first instinct was to give up, walk away, lick her wounds in private, and give into the tears. But Kate loved Noah and loved what they shared too much to give up so easily.

Wrapping her arms tighter around his waist, she laid her head against his back.

"Enough, baby," she said in a hoarse voice, unable to hold back a few tears from escaping and wetting his back. "Enough. I'm here, and nothing is going to happen to me. Nothing. You're mine, and I'm yours. Don't do this. Don't push me away. I can take anything else, but I can't take that."

She kissed his back over and over again, as more tears fell from her face and cascaded down his back.

Noah groaned, dropped his shirt, and turned in her arms. He gathered her in his arms and roughly pulled her to him, crushing her against his hard frame.

"Jesus. Jesus," he said, his voice overflowing with emotion. "I'm sorry, sweetness. I'm sorry. Stop now. Stop crying."

Noah dropped his head into her hair and inhaled. As one of his hands tangled in her hair and held her head to his chest, the other molded her small frame to him.

In time, Kate's tears dried and Noah's grip loosened. Kate ran her hands the length of his back, tiptoeing her fingers up and down his spine. She turned her head and kissed her way up his chest and neck, and stood on her toes to get at his chin and mouth. She ran her tongue over the seam of his lips and bit at his lower lip until he opened his mouth and let her in. Once she ran her tongue over his, he surrendered.

Noah took over the kiss, devouring her mouth as he crushed her to him. His large hands spanned her bottom, and he hoisted her up so she straddled him. She wrapped her legs around his waist and her arms around his neck, kissing him with ferocity. This wasn't going to be slow and sweet. She needed him, and he'd denied her for too long. Now, this would be fast and furious.

They both needed this. They needed to reconnect and to be reminded of who they were together, without the past shoving its way between them. They'd been dancing around each other since the attack. Enough was enough.

Kate raked her fingers through Noah's blond strands and pulled. In seconds, her back was against the wall. He pulled her tank off, and when he found she wasn't wearing a bra, he growled. He took one breast in his hand, squeezing and pulling at her nipple, while his mouth sucked at her other breast.

Kate arched her back and let out a low whimper. "God, yes," she said as she held his head to her breast. Her nails dug into his back, and she dropped her head to his shoulder. She sucked at the skin where his neck and shoulder met and then bit down.

Noah let go. He went wild. He dropped her legs long enough to pull off her yoga pants, as she pulled at his shorts, and within seconds she was pinned against the wall.

"Noah, please. I need you. Take me," she panted in his ear as she ground into him.

Noah's hand shifted in between them, and he found her hot, wet core. He thrust two fingers into her tight sheath as his thumb found and rubbed her clit. That was all it took. Kate threw her head back and screamed his name as she detonated. Her internal muscles squeezed his fingers as her arms and legs held him to her.

Noah took her mouth as his fingers continued to work her and she rode his hand without shame. Noah withdrew his fingers, dropped her legs, and turned her so she was facing the bathroom vanity.

He took her hands and placed them on the vanity and whispered, "Hold on," in her ear.

Kate held on and saw their reflection in the mirror. She caught Noah's gaze and mouthed, "I love you."

Noah kissed her shoulders, neck, and back. He spread her legs and drove himself into her waiting body. He held Kate tightly around the waist as he drove himself deeper and harder into her.

Kate's legs weakened, and she would have fallen if his muscular arms weren't holding her up. She pushed back against him, wanting him as deep as she could get him. She tightened every muscle around his hard erection and heard his muttered, "Fuck, Kate," right before he let go, taking her with him once again.

When they came down from their exquisite high, Noah picked her up and carried her to the bed. He pushed pillows together and lay back with her sprawled on top of him. Noah kissed the top of her head and ran his hand up and down her back as she drew circles on his chest. They stayed cocooned in their own world, holding and kissing each other for a long time until Kate broke the silence.

"Talk to me, baby," she said, kissing his chest, and then raising her head to kiss his chin.

Noah sighed and ran a hand over his face and then through his hair. He pulled away and sat up against the headboard, but Kate wasn't going to let him do this by himself. She straddled him. He smiled absently, and his arms went around her.

Noah dropped his head to her shoulder, and she held him to her.

"I don't know how to do this with you, Kate," he said in a ragged voice. "I am so in love with you. I can't think straight. The thought of losing you is more than I can handle. I can't lose you. I feel like if I look away for too long, when I look back, you'll be gone. I can't go through that again."

Kate understood fear more than anyone else. She understood where it came from and how it felt when it dug in underneath her skin and spread, coating every inch of her until she was too paralyzed to breathe, let alone move. She didn't want that for Noah. She had to get him past this so they could live guilt-free, fear-free, secret-free.

"Noah, look at me," she said, tugging at his hair.
He raised his head and met her eyes with his

tortured ones.

"I could tell you all day that you're not responsible for what happened to Kristin or me, but until you're ready to believe it, it won't sink in. I can try to assure you that nothing will happen to me, but no one can guarantee the future. What I can tell you is that fear is a destructive force. It's the gift that keeps on giving after a tragedy. I should know."

Kate gave a half-smile.

"If we live in fear, we may keep out some of the bad, but we'll also keep out the good and the beautiful—friends, family, community, and eventually, we'll lose love. I did that. I ran in fear. I isolated myself from the world, and if it wasn't for your persistent ways and sexy body, of course"—she wiggled her eyebrows at him, and he laughed—"I'd still be locked up in a very lonely world."

She touched her lips to his. "Baby, please don't lock me in that world again. I've never felt this free. It'll take a while, I know. But try to let go a little at a time. Don't get sucked into the illusion that living a happy and fulfilling life means controlling every aspect of it."

"Katie, I'm sorry." Noah brushed her lips with his. "I don't want to lose you, to lose us. I want you to have everything you've ever dreamed of. I never want you to feel trapped. I only wanted you to be safe and to feel safe."

Kate cupped Noah's cheeks in her hands and kissed his lips tenderly. "I am safe. With you, *not* Axel, I feel safe, cherished and loved. All I need is you. Call off your pit bull, okay?"

Noah held her gaze for a minute, then sighed and nodded.

From that moment on, Axel disappeared out of their lives, and over the next week, Kate watched as *her*

Noah relaxed and came back to her. He was still vigilant, but he smiled and joked more. He didn't text-stalk her anymore, and each morning before he left for work and every evening before he closed his eyes, he held her, made passionate love to her, and told her he loved her. Then, they both fell into a peaceful sleep.

On Christmas Eve, Kate woke up satiated and at peace. Her gaze roamed over the man sleeping next to her and she studied his every feature. From his wavy blond hair to his strong jaw, and crooked nose, to the stubble on his cheeks. She loved every inch of him. There was no doubt in her mind that she wanted to wake up next to him every day for the rest of her life. Without him, her life would have no meaning.

Kate had lived through enough to know, if she wanted something, she had to reach out and grab it herself. She eased out of bed, careful not to disturb Prince Charming, and padded to the kitchen. As she waited for the coffee to brew, she chewed on her lower lip, mulling over the decision she'd come to.

Kate poured herself a cup of coffee and went to her favorite place in the penthouse. She leaned against the floor-to-ceiling windows in the living room that overlooked Central Park. The view was magnificent. There was a lot she disliked about the penthouse, but this view wasn't one of them. Even in the snow and bitter cold, people jogged, moms and nannies pushed strollers, and dog-walkers were dragged along by their rambunctious herd. Everyone had a busy life, someplace important to be, and something important to do.

Smiling, Kate sighed. This morning, she too had something important to do. She had a surprise for her man.

"Kate, did you hear me?"

Kate startled and turned to find Noah standing

behind her, holding a mug of coffee. She brushed his lips with hers. "Good morning, handsome. Sorry, I was people watching. I didn't hear you."

Noah kissed the side of her neck. "Handsome?"

"Mmh-hmm. Want some breakfast?" Kate asked, pulling away, suddenly overcome with a serious case of performance anxiety.

"Ahh, okay," Noah said in a quizzical voice as she turned and walked to the kitchen.

Maybe keeping busy for a few minutes while she did some deep-breathing exercises would give her the courage she needed to execute her plan. Four small words. That was all she needed to say to him. Why was this so damn hard?

Kate opened the refrigerator and pulled out random items, placing them on the middle island. The eggs rattled in their container as she dropped them on the counter, followed by milk, juice, cheese, leftover Chinese, butter, and ketchup.

Kate was so lost in her thoughts, she didn't hear Noah approach. She jumped when his hands covered her shaking ones. He pried the salad dressing out of her grip and closed the refrigerator.

"What's going on, Kate?" he asked, frowning, as he led her to the couch and pulled her onto his lap.

Meeting his gaze, she opened her mouth, but the words caught in her throat. She cleared her throat and tried again. This was important. She had to get it right. She'd never done this before, and she hadn't prepared well enough for it.

"Noah," she said in a trembling voice. "I've dreamed of you my whole life. I thought I'd never find you. I didn't think I deserved you, but somehow you found me. You pulled me out of the darkness and into the sun with you."

Kate cupped his cheek in her hand. "You're it for me. You're everything I've dreamed of. Nothing good existed before you, and my life would be meaningless without you. I want you to know, my heart will always be yours if you want it."

Capturing Noah's hand, she held it tightly in hers and smiled. "Here goes. I love you, Noah Reed. Will you marry me? Will you make me yours, forever?"

Noah's eyes widened, and a huge smile broke over his face.

"Woman, did you just ask me to marry you?" he asked, unable to keep the laughter from bubbling up.

Kate's body was on fire and her cheeks burned with heat. She was going to die of mortification if he turned her down. She dropped her head against his chest and nodded. Why was the man laughing at her? Women proposed to men these days, didn't they?

"Sweetheart, look at me. Come on," he cajoled.

Kate shook her head and buried her hot face in his neck. She wasn't ever going to look at him again, especially if he said no.

Noah's chest rumbled with laughter. He stood, carrying her the way she was. She wrapped her legs around him and continued to hide her face. Where the hell was he taking her and why hadn't he answered the question?

Kate peeked to the side to see they were in the bedroom. She heard a drawer open and close. Still, she hid.

"Kate, sweetheart," Noah coaxed in a gentle, loving voice as he sat down at the edge of the bed.

"Give me your eyes, Katie."

Kate raised her eyes to Noah and the love she saw there took her breath away. Her man was opening up, pulling out all the stops. He was laid bare. Every emotion he was feeling was there for her to see. Kate couldn't tear her eyes from his.

"Katie, you are my whole world. I was lost without you. Without you, I merely existed. I woke up, breathed, ate, drank, worked, and slept. I didn't live, and I didn't feel. I didn't want to. Life held no meaning for me. The word love doesn't begin to describe what I feel for you. You have captured my heart, and I don't ever want it back."

Tears streamed down Kate's face, and Noah wiped them away with his thumbs and took her mouth in a deep. drugging kiss.

"If you'll have me, I will marry you, Kate," he whispered against her lips.

Did he say yes? Did she hear him right?

"Say it again," she whispered.

"Yeah, baby. Yes, I will marry you."

Kate smiled and raised her head. She let out a long, relieved sigh. Noah kissed her nose and lips.

"I have something for you, though." Noah reached next to him and produced a small blue jewelry box.

Kate's mouth hung open as her heart raced. Noah opened the box and pulled out a breath-taking engagement ring—a pear-shaped, yellow diamond encircled by a double row of bead-set white diamonds.

"Sweetness, I intended to propose to you tonight, in front of all our family and friends. Dee's been planning every detail with me. You beat me to it, and that's fine with me. But we're going to have to redo this little scene, with me taking the lead, for Dee, or she'll be crushed."

Kate's eyes filled with tears as he took her left hand, slid the ring into place, and kissed it.

He was going to propose!

The words rang loudly in Kate's head. Even

though she proposed to him, she was thrilled. Every girl wanted to be proposed to, and she was no exception.

Kate's eyes met Noah's as their mouths connected in a soft, sensual kiss.

"Will you marry me, Kate? Will you be mine forever?" Noah asked against her lips.

"Baby, I'm already yours and forever isn't nearly long enough."

The End

www.norahbennett.com

NORAH BENNETT

EVERNIGHT PUBLISHING ®

www.evernightpublishing.com